Monster Child
a novel by L. Lee Shaw

*To K·A·T·Y and Jose,
who was the real Katie and Jose grew
rages 1.   L. Lee Shaw*

This is a work of fiction. All of the characters, organizations and events portrayed in this novel are either products of the author's imagination or used fictionally.

Monster Child

Copyright © 2009 by L. Lee Shaw

All rights reserved. No part of this book may be used or reproduced in any manner whatsoever without written permission except in the case of brief quotations embodied in critical articles or reviews. For information address Boho Books, POB 824, Molalla, OR 97038

Library of Congress Control Number: 2008910932

ISBN: 978-0-9814709-2-4

Printed in the United States of America

Boho Books paperback edition / April 2009

To the young members of my family whose names I swiped for this book...Brandy, Katie, Lacey, Nate, Jesse, Scott, Alix, Johnathan, Taylor, and Dylan

Prologue

She curled into a tight little ball to quiet the hurt of her empty stomach. Her bruised back protested and she stretched out slowly trying to find the place where both would be eased.

Once again the monster dwelling within her had called down violent fury. She had no memory of its coming; she only knew it had shown itself by the pain left in its departure.

A tear escaped, rolling obliquely across her cheekbone and dropping onto the bare mattress. She clenched her eyes to stop any more. She must keep her horrible secret and tears were tattle tales.

Gingerly, she turned towards the wall. She slipped her hand under the thin mattress to touch her hidden companion. She dare not draw the tiny orca whale out. He survived because no one knew of his existence.

When her fingertips rested against his cool vinyl skin, she closed her eyes. She tried to travel to the safe world she had created in a corner of her mind but there was no strength to make the journey. As desolation consumed her, she begged to ride with her friend into a vast ocean of oblivion and sink to a place where she could never feel and never be found.

Her silent cry of hopelessness echoed through the rain swept January night, summoning those who mind the darkest hours. Invisible, they came to watch with her and intercede for her.

Chapter 1

He sensed a child in great distress in his sleep. He struggled toward consciousness seeking to respond but was sucked back into the womb of dreams. There he floated down nearly forgotten passages to the place where whales breached.

It had been so long. Even when he was drowning in grief's riptide and had implored them, they resolutely kept their distance, swimming away beneath the surface of his memory.

But now they were there, their haunting song calling him back to the Sound. He was running…running over the rocky shore, pleading with them to stay.

The hollowness under his feet told him he was once more on the dock. "Wait, oh, please wait," his heart beseeched. "Forgive me and wait."

Her great black and white head rose above the water, majestically riding the waves, as her wise eye searched for him. Minowah, beloved matriarch, opened her mouth in pleased recognition. She clicked her greeting and dipped from sight.

He dropped to his knees, his upturned hands reaching after her in supplication.

With a roar of rending water, she rose, arcing her tremendous body against the sky. She left her message in the spume of her return to the sea. A face…a young face formed in the cascade of sunlit droplets; the spray falling like pale hair.

Drifting deeper than dreams, he clung to the image. Minowah had called for him. He would not betray her a second time.

The face was waiting for him as he edged into wakefulness. He lay still, gathering the remnants of his dream. It had the feel of a mandate. He breathed slowly seeking clarity. None was forthcoming.

Noises from downstairs began to seep into his awareness. He heard water running, youthful voices in escalating volume and the rattle of pans in the kitchen. Spirit Wind Ranch was waking.

As he opened his eyes to the early morning darkness, Boomer felt the itch of irritation rising in him. He wondered why if the Universe wanted him to act on something, it couldn't just come out and say so in plain terms instead of sending him on some blamed abstruse scavenger hunt. It seemed a damned inefficient way to get things done. He thrust the covers back and grumbled off to the bathroom.

Showered and shaved, he came downstairs, automatically tracking the smell of freshly brewed coffee. He sidestepped young bodies shambling toward the dining area in various degrees of wakefulness.

Harley was at the stove flipping French toast on the large griddle while shaking a huge cast iron skillet filled with sizzling sausage when he entered the kitchen.

Boomer filled the mug waiting by the coffeemaker. Sipping, he stared unseeingly out the window. Who, where, when, why? The questions circled the image remaining stubbornly at the center of his thoughts.

He was only peripherally aware of Carlita thrusting her pottery teapot under the instant hot water tap and turning it on. When the pot filled to overflowing he noticed she, too, was staring out the window, her lips pressed into a thin line. He reached out and shut the water off. The action startled her back into the present. She stared at the forgotten teapot.

"Something on your mind?" Boomer asked.

Carlita sat the pot on the counter. "Mal sueños. Bad dreams. I hear a niño crying in them. My heart hurts at the sadness in the tears."

It felt as though a celestial finger flicked him on the head. "Did you catch that?"

"Yeah, I caught it," he mentally answered. "We're on a mission here. We're going to do some unknown thing for someone we haven't met who is someplace we haven't found for reasons we don't know at a time we haven't a clue about. Sum it up?"

The thought flashed into his mind he would be farther along the path of intuiting guidance if he wasn't quite such a smart ass.

Escalating giggles from the dining area snagged his attention and he moved to the doorway of the kitchen. The kids were watching two chrome topped syrup pitchers moving fitfully down the long table apparently of their own accord.

"Come on, Katy, don't let Ralph beat you," Brandy squealed as one of the pitchers moved slightly ahead.

"Are we playing with our food again, people?" he asked.

Instantly, the pitchers stopped moving. Then one of them began to nudge forward until it was a spout past the other.

"Yea!! Katy wins," Brandy said.

"Hey, that's not fair. Boomer said stop," Ralph whined.

Boomer shook his head. "No. I asked if you were playing with your food again. Katy listened correctly and used the fact that I didn't specifically say stop to win."

Ralph reached across the table and speared a sausage link on Brandy's plate, eliciting a sharp "Jerk!"

"I listened," he said around the sausage he stuffed in his mouth.

"Maybe, but you didn't process it. Remember, it takes total integration of all your senses to support your abilities," Boomer answered.

"Ralph's still operating on a 286 chip while everyone else is up to a Pentium," Jesse said as he maneuvered off the bench with his used plate and utensils.

"Eat my shorts," Ralph shot back.

"I think we're going to get some more kids, Boomer," Dylan said as he followed Jesse to drop his dishes in the tub. "I saw them last night in my sleep."

"It's too late in the year for anybody new to come," Alix said.

The boy shrugged as he rolled up the sleeves on the man-sized Oregon Ducks sweatshirt he adored. They bunched like manacles around his young wrists. "I know but I saw 'em. I think one's a boy. I couldn't really see the other too well. It was kinda like they were in a shadow or something but I know someone's coming so you better get Jesse to clear his junk off the empty bed in our room."

"Like I'm the only one with stuff on it," Jesse said.

Boomer stared at Dylan. It was quite obvious someone or something had been very busy during Spirit Wind's nocturnal hours. Three tollings in, he glanced at his watch, less than an hour. The significance of whatever they were being called into was very clear.

He refilled his coffee cup and headed to his office. It was time to tune in to Channel Universe.

Aimee was already seated in front of the ranch's business computer inputting numbers from a pile of bills stacked beside the keyboard.

Boomer went around his desk and shoved debris aside to set his cup down as she finished and clicked off the program. She stacked the papers together, slipped them into a manila folder and, standing, placed them in the file drawer.

"Done your card yet?" Boomer asked.

Aimee shook her head. "Just getting to it."

Boomer watched Aimee pull the binder she used to record her tarot readings out of the small bookcase next to the desk. With her notebook open and pen at ready, she opened the left hand drawer of her desk to retrieve the small silk bag she kept her cards in.

"Oh, that's weird," she said as she stared into the drawer. "That's totally weird."

The tone of her voice brought Boomer out of his chair to look. All he saw was a single card lying face down on top of the bag. He looked at her questioningly.

"A card has been pulled from the deck," she said.

He shrugged. "So?"

"So I didn't pull it. In fact, I decided it was time to clean my cards last night. I put them in order and put a crystal in the bag to clear them. I haven't touched them since."

"Maybe one of the kids was fooling around."

"If so, I'm ripping their arm out and beating them with it. They know the rule of nobody touching anyone's personal tools."

Aimee reached in and carefully slipped the bag out from under the card. The top was still tied shut. "That's my knot," she said as she studied the bag. She untied it and turning it down, she shook out a small crystal. She held it up for Boomer to see then set it aside. She pulled out the deck, fanning them out. "In order just like I left them." Setting them next to the crystal, she picked up the single card.

She placed it on the desk; then turned it over. The Justice card stared up at them. She retrieved her deck and quickly flipped through the major arcana. "It's mine. But how?"

Boomer straightened up. "Maybe the question isn't just how but why."

"Okay, why?"

"Don't know."

"Want to hazard a guess?"

"Nope."

"Yet another enlightening conversation," she said as she picked up the deck to replace the card.

"Mind leaving that out?"

She glanced at him then carefully centered it on her desk before slipping the rest back into the bag and returning them to the drawer.

"Do not touch it," she said sternly. "I do not need your disorganized vibrations messing up my cards." She shot a meaningful glance towards his desk as she left.

Boomer stood staring at the card letting all the concepts and ideations of the term justice play through his mind. They triggered nothing. Sighing, he went back to his chair and picked up his coffee.

When his hip tickled, he realized he hadn't turned his cell phone ringer on yet. He hitched it off his belt.

"Boomer. It's Meredith."

"Easy Rider, how's it going?"

"I got new wheelchair. Zero to three miles in a heartbeat."

"Oh, oh. There's a speeding ticket in your future now, girl."

"Speaking of futures, how about me seeing another kid in yours?"

His senses pushed up a notch. "What you got?"

"A kid who talks to animals."

"Lots of kids talk to animals. Since when is that a juvenile offense?"

"It is when you steal the animals."

"You know our stand on delinquency issues, Meredith."

"The kid's not a delinquent. He's a good kid, top student, bright as all get out, and, except for the incident before me now, he's never been in trouble of any kind…not even getting sent to the principal's office."

"So give him a scolding and ground him for a couple of weeks."

"Let me give you some of the background. One of the teachers at his school had a couple of iguanas and a turtle in the classroom. She assigns students to care for the animals. Unfortunately, she injured her back and has been out. The substitutes weren't monitoring the situation. Our boy claims he heard the iguanas crying because they were hungry and thirsty from two classrooms away. The turtle also had a cough from dehydration which he hears. He tries to tell the sub but she blows him off. So after a week or so of listening to the animals suffer, he stays behind one day, sneaks into the room and grabs them."

"And gets caught."

"Not exactly. He takes them to a pet store specializing in reptiles. They confirm their neglected state, turn it over to the Humane Society which, then cites the school."

"And all hell breaks loose."

"You're good at this psychic stuff, you know."

"So what do you want from me?"

"I want you to be at Juvenile Court three weeks from tomorrow to talk with the kid's parents about him coming to Spirit Wind. If they agree, we send him home with you and expunge his record."

The silence stretched as Boomer thought about Dylan's words. Meredith broke it.

"Boomer, I know it isn't your customary method of accepting students, but I'll vouch for this kid. He's got some pretty special abilities but right now the school thinks they've been harboring a covert delinquent who's bogusing up the animal talk thing to get out of trouble. They have told me an incident like this will not happen again…heavy on the not. It is their plan to require counseling and so on to convince him he really can't talk to animals, ergo crush his abilities. The alternative is we pitch him to you and give him a safe haven to develop his unusual communication skills. So what do you say?"

"Three weeks is just about enough time for the boys to uncover the extra bed. I'll be there."

"Thanks, Boomer. See you February 8, 8:30 a.m."

He flipped his phone shut and hooked it back on his belt. As he rose from his desk to refill his coffee cup, he caught sight of the Justice card on Aimee's desk. "Okay, now who's being a smart ass?" he asked it.

A whisper came back. "He's not the one."

Chapter 2

Boomer pushed back into the waiting area of the Clackamas County Juvenile Court. The meeting had gone quickly and well. Meredith had done an excellent job of explaining the recommendation for Domingo's placement at Spirit Wind. The Chivaras had not only immediately agreed but beamed with pride that their son had earned this special honor. While Meredith was getting the judge's signature on the court order, Domingo and his parents left to pack his things. They were to meet back at the juvenile court at 11:00 o'clock.

Boomer glanced at the clock over the reception counter. That gave them about two hours to kill. Maybe Carlita would like to go to that fabric shop she loved. It was her tradition to make a special quilt for each student and she would want to do the same for Domingo.

Maneuvering across the room, he dropped into the vacant chair next to her. "It's a done deal but we need to meet the Chivaras back here at 11 to collect Domingo. So want to hit Starbucks and go to that sewing shop of yours for a while?"

She shook her head vigorously. "No, we are to wait."

"Why?"

"Because it is here, now, we find that we have been looking for."

Boomer glanced at Carlita's round face. She was determinedly watching the comings and goings in the area. He leaned back and stretched out his legs. "Been hanging out at Heaven's gate again, huh?"

Raised in a tiny Mexican village, she had grown up where life centered on the Church. The priest had been a man who escaped seminary with his simple, direct faith intact. He had passed it along to his parishioners, including a young Carlita.

Ask, seek and knock weren't just words in the Good Book to her. They were actions for which results were expected. She was relentless when there was a need and it was, with gentle amusement, the rest of the staff observed her stalwartly at the Gates of the Universe, pounding away until she got what she sought. Harley claimed it was the only way Heaven could get some peace.

But the staff also knew that if Carlita had a message from on High or through one of her revered 'Santos', they best listen up. Boomer resigned himself to wait.

He was just thinking about going back to beg a cup of coffee from Meredith when the outside door opened and a woman came through guiding a young girl with waist-length light blonde hair.

The shock of recognition brought Boomer to his feet.

"Sí, es ella," Carlita said softly beside him.

The child was pulled in on herself as far as she could and still remain upright. Her face was a study in terror as the woman guided her to a chair. She said something to the girl and then vanished through the doors leading back to the courtrooms.

The girl sat frozen with her head ducked down, clenching white-knuckled hands. She reminded Boomer of a small animal feeling the hot breath of annihilation.

"Watch her," he said to Carlita and chased after the woman who had brought her. He caught up with her as she entered Meredith's office.

"What's the story on the girl you just brought?" he asked the woman who was pulling a folder out of her briefcase. She looked at him in alarm and stepped back.

"It's okay, Sonia. This socially graceless person is one of our resources. Boomer is the director of Spirit Wind Ranch in Molalla."

The alarm was replaced with the amused skepticism he had become accustomed to seeing whenever the ranch's name came up.

Meredith stretched across the desk and held out her hand for the folder Sonia was holding. "I assume you are referring to Alyson," she said as she opened the file and began to glance through papers. "We took her into custody a week ago."

"She passed out at school. When the school tried to get a hold of her mother, they discovered she's in New York. Poor kid's been left alone…no food, no money. She fainted because she hadn't eaten in over two days. That's when we caught the call," Sonia said. "At the hospital, we find out the mother not only is starving her but has also been physically abusing her. So here we are."

"What's going to happen to her?"

Meredith leaned back. "I don't know. Momma's got clout."

Boomer raised a questioning eyebrow.

"Alyson is a Maguire, as in own half the state of Oregon Maguires."

"Then what is she doing being starved? It sure isn't the standard case of mom selling the food stamps to pay for a drug habit while the kid goes hungry."

"That is just one of about two thousand questions we'd like answers to but we're getting stonewalled by the lawyers who seem to have the only pipeline to the woman," Meredith said.

"What does the girl say?" Boomer asked.

"I don't suppose it would surprise anyone that she hasn't said much," Sonia responded. "And what she has said hasn't made much sense, at least not to me."

"Tell us anyway," Meredith instructed.

"Well, you know how these situations are, the kids frequently try to justify the parent's actions. She said her mother hits her because she says things. When we pressed to find out what she said, she told us she didn't know. Her statement was," Sonia retrieved the folder and riffled through the pages before pulling one out. " 'It's like it gets all white in my head and I don't know what I say.' The doctor thinks she's blocking out the memories, hence the white."

Boomer began to nod his head slowly. "Or she really doesn't know what she said because she's slipped into another place."

Meredith and Sonia looked at him blankly.

He continued. "Alyson's grandmother was Meri Maguire, right?"

"So?" Meredith asked.

"So Meri Maguire was well known for being clairvoyant. Maybe, just maybe, Alyson has inherited some of her grandmother's ability and she doesn't remember because she's speaking while in a trance."

Meredith's expression sharpened. "You're not here because you wanted to know the story behind a sad, scared kid, are you? You already knew about Alyson."

"Let's just say we had some information we followed and it led here."

Meredith stared silently into space for a long moment, then began to ask rapid-fire questions. "Although you have state certification, Spirit Wind is private, right?"

"Right," Boomer answered.

"Any reliance on the Maguire money or power in any way?"

"Nope."

"Any plans of needing it in the future?"

"No."

"Scared of Rhonda Maguire?"

"Hell, no."

"Wanna make it two for two today? Then go watch over her while Sonia and I talk to the judge."

Boomer pushed back into the waiting area. The girl was still sitting exactly as she had been when he had left. He took up position next to her.

***

Alyson sensed someone looming beside her and chanced a quick peek. It was a tall man, wearing a shirt, tie and jacket like a lot of the men in the room. But instead of slacks, he had on jeans, worn white at the seams, and cowboy boots. She quickly looked back down to avoid his notice and missed seeing another man advancing on her.

"Well, Alyson, you have made a fine little mess for your mother, haven't you?" It was the lawyer who had been at the house when they had gone to get her things.

Alyson hunched over even further, trying to become invisible.

"Your actions are totally unconscionable; something I intend to rectify today," the man continued, snapping his words at her like little projectiles. "Now your mother told me you know exactly what you are supposed to say and you better say it, is that understood?"

Someone stepped in front of Alyson, blocking her from the lawyer. She recognized the jeans. He folded his arms over his chest and tilted his head back slightly. Alyson couldn't see the look on his face but she saw the muscles in his jaw bunching.

The lawyer looked him over slowly and distaste swept his face. "Excuse me but you are interfering with my client's instructions to her daughter."

"Since the circumstances place your client in an adversarial role with her daughter, it could be construed that you are attempting to intimidate a minor who is at present under the protection of the court."

A scarlet flush spread up the lawyer's face. The girl was intrigued to see it even rise beyond his forehead to meet his receding hairline. "I don't know who you are...."

"No, you don't." Menace rumbled in the words.

The lawyer caught it and, after opening his mouth, closed it into a tight little line and headed towards the doors leading to the inner area. Boomer turned slowly keeping a fixed look on the lawyer until he had pushed through, knocking into the girl's caseworker.

Rubbing her arm, the woman crouched down beside the chair. "In a few minutes, Alyson, we will be going before the judge. She is going to remove you from your mother's care."

Alyson's eyes widened. Conflicting emotions roiled through her. She knew the price she would pay if sent back to her mother but would they now send her to someplace worse? "I'll be good. I promise. I'll be..."

"Alyson, you are not bad. You don't deserve what you're mother does to you. It is wrong...very, very wrong. No one should be beaten like you've been or abandoned to starve."

The wheeze in Alyson's breathing was becoming more audible with each exhalation. She twisted her hands together in her lap. The woman put her hand over Alyson's. "It's going to be alright, sweetie. Trust me."

A man stepped through the door and called out "In the matter of Alyson Christine Maguire. The Court is ready."

Boomer followed the caseworker and girl to the tiny courtroom.

Within minutes, it became clear the judge was not impressed with either the Maguire name or the wealth inherent in it. The lawyer had begun by apologizing for Mrs. Maguire's inability to attend the hearing, citing the extreme need for her presence in New York City. He then launched into an itemization of all the charitable projects funded by the Maguire Foundation, providing statistics on the number of children helped by the donations.

The judge cut him off. "We are here for no other purpose than to determine if Rhonda Maguire is fit to retain custody of her daughter. You will keep your remarks directed exclusively to that end."

He was less sure of himself as he rendered an explanation for the circumstances that had brought them to the courtroom.

The black-robed woman looked over the top of her half-moon glasses and fixed hard blue eyes on the man. "So your explanation to this court is that a 13-year-old 7th grader was deemed old enough to care for herself without any adult supervision or protection while her mother traipses off to New York."

"You have to understand, Alyson is a very capable, mature young woman," he said.

The woman held up a sheaf of photos. "This is the Maguire kitchen. I do not see one scrap of available food in any of these pictures. There is nothing in the refrigerator. The pantry and freezer are padlocked. What exactly was the child to eat in her mother's absence?"

"Well, I'm sure she was left money to eat on. You know how kids are; they take off to the mall and blow it on clothes, CDs, makeup with no thought about tomorrow."

The judge shuffled through the pictures in the file in front of her and held up another group. "I don't see anything in these pictures of her room to indicate Alyson has ever been in possession of any money to blow."

There was a heavy silence as the judge studied the photos and then laid them down.

"What I do see here, Mr. Lithauer, is extreme child neglect." She picked up other papers. "Extreme child neglect combined with evidence of prolonged physical abuse according to the medical examination. And since they go hand in glove, I can only assume mental abuse as well."

"But, Your Honor, don't you think you ought to let Alyson tell her story?" the lawyer protested.

"What story? The one drilled into her? The one she told the doctor at the hospital? The one you were coercing her to tell in the waiting room where my bailiff heard your exchange with Boomer?"

The lawyer went white.

She leaned back in her chair. "Boomer, approach the bench, please."

The tall man came from the back of the room. He spoke quietly to the judge. No one could hear what was being said, but in a few minutes, they were both nodding their heads in agreement.

He stepped back. The woman pounded her gavel loudly. "In the matter of Alyson Christine Maguire, it is the decision of this court she should be entered into the custody and protection of Spirit Wind Ranch."

"But, your Honor, please...." the lawyer pleaded. "I'm sure we can work out whatever arrangements are necessary for Alyson without removing her from her mother's care. There are ramifications to that decision the Court is unaware of."

"Mr. Lithauer, I don't believe the woman is fit to care for a rabid wolverine, let alone this child. The only way I can safeguard Alyson is to put her far beyond the reach of her mother. Whatever ramifications Rhonda Maguire may face because of my decision are not my concern."

The judge nodded to Boomer and the caseworker. "You are free to take Alyson with you now. And, Boomer, you will have the full support of this Court to do whatever you need to protect her. That woman is not to be seen within 10 miles of this child without a court order, understand?" She looked back to the lawyer. "I believe it is only fair to tell you, I plan to turn the case over to the District Attorney's office with the recommendation they proceed with criminal charges. Have a good day, Mr. Lithauer."

When they were back in the waiting area, the woman led Alyson back to a chair. Squatting down once more, she brushed Alyson's pale hair back behind her ear. "This is where I leave you. You are going to go to Spirit Wind. It is a very special place for very special people, Alyson. You don't know it yet but in time I hope you learn just how special you are. Good luck and Godspeed, dear." Alyson was startled when the woman kissed her on the cheek before getting up and moving toward Boomer.

Just then the doors opened and the attorney came out busily talking on his cell phone. He stopped in front of Alyson and thrust his phone at her. "I believe Virginia has some words for you."

Alyson stared at the phone.

"Take it, girl," the lawyer said shaking the phone.

Wordlessly, Boomer crossed and grabbed the phone out of the lawyer's hand. He put it to his ear for a moment. He could hear a woman's shrieks mixed in the static. He pulled it away from his ear, clicked it off and handed it back to the lawyer. He then jerked his thumb over his shoulder toward the outside doors. The lawyer scuttled in their direction.

He practically ran over a short heavy-set woman bustling in from the outside. She looked like a plump parrot with her gathered skirt in a jungle of brilliant colors and green shawl wrapped around her shoulders. Her grey-streaked hair was braided and coiled around her head while silver ear hoops swung brightly with every move. She stopped to talk to Boomer, her arms wrapped around a huge woven straw purse. He nodded in Alyson's direction. She came over to sit down beside the girl, and reaching for her hand, let loose a cascade of accented words. "Ahh, I am so excited that you are at last coming to us, Alyson. I am Carlita. I am la mamacita to las chicas at Spirit Wind."

Carlita felt the child brace herself. She maintained her hold on Alyson's hand as she studied the scared girl's pallid energy field. The child's aura was like a limp grey shroud surrounding her. Oddly, it was not as damaged as she would have anticipated. Somewhere inside the thin body was a fierce will to survive.

Carlita caught a faint shimmer in the air to Alyson's left. Someone was making their presence known to her. Alyson had an unseen guardian. She nodded slightly to the air and mentally acknowledged it.

"Come, mi Alyson, we should go to the baño, sí?"

She tugged Alyson from her chair and prodded her toward the ladies' room.

As Carlita and the girl disappeared down the hall, Boomer followed the caseworker out to the parking lot. Sonia opened the trunk of her car. "Her things are here."

There was only one cardboard box and it wasn't full. He looked at the woman in surprise.

"Unbelievable, isn't it? Look at this." She moved aside a small pile of clothing. Underneath were old spiral notebooks and sheets of paper. "She retrieved these from the school wastebaskets so she would have something to draw on at home." Silently, she held up a small bundle of stubby pencils. Then she lifted up what looked like the sleeve of a man's dress shirt, once white but now yellow with age and grimy from much handling. "It was her father's. It's the only thing of his she has."

Boomer nodded grimly as he lifted the box out.

* * *

Inside the bathroom, Carlita locked the door and, balancing her bag on the edge of the sink, she began to pull things from it. She handed Alyson new underwear, a new long sleeved pink tee-shirt, jeans, socks and shoes.

Alyson shyly took the items and went into the larger handicapped stall to change. As her old clothes dropped to the floor and she replaced them, she felt strange, like this was happening to someone else.

When she emerged, Carlita took the discarded clothes and pushed them through the top of the garbage can. "It is a vida nuevo," she said as they disappeared from sight. She touched Alyson's cheek. "Today prayers are being answered."

Carlita dug in her bag once more; this time pulling out a soft blue coat lined with snowy pile. "You are to be warm now."

Boomer was not in the waiting area when they returned. They pushed out of the building with Carlita leading the way to the parking lot. The worn jeans, along with a shorter pair of jeaned legs, were visible below the open back door of a van. Several suitcases and a couple of boxes, including her own, were stacked on the asphalt.

When everything was stored in the back and the door was shut, Alyson saw a boy with Boomer. "Domingo, this is Alyson. She's also starting with us today. Alyson, this is Domingo." He pulled open the side door. "In you go. Next stop Spirit Wind."

As the two youngsters climbed in, he opened the front door for Carlita and gave her a hand as she hefted her weight into the van.

Alyson fastened the seatbelt and cast a side glance at Domingo who was fussing with his sweatshirt.

Boomer hoisted himself in and turned to look at the kids.

"Now?" Domingo asked excitedly.

Boomer nodded, "Now."

Domingo carefully slipped his hand under his sweatshirt and pulled out a small kitten. "Do you like him? We got him over there," he said, pointing to the Animal Control building located across the road from the Juvenile Court.

Tears sprang to Alyson's eyes. Black and white with large yellow eyes, he looked like the kitten she had drawn over and over to keep her company during the long hours in her room. She reached out a hand to touch him and then withdrew it.

Suddenly she couldn't get her breath. She had just received more in the last few minutes than she had in her remembered life. She was overwhelmed and afraid. "You want, you pay," her mother's voice hissed in her ear and the cost was always pain.

Boomer and Carlita exchanged glances as they sensed the degree of Alyson's trauma. Domingo looked at both of them in bewilderment.

Boomer took the kitten from Domingo and placed it in Alyson's lap. She opened her eyes and for a moment they were blank. But the kitten's weight was real as were the tiny claws catching in her shirt. He looked up at her and mewled.

Boomer lifted her hands and placed them over the kitten; then he tilted her chin up so he could look into her eyes. "You are safe, Alyson. I give you my word."

Chapter 3

Alyson didn't remember the drive to the ranch. The events of the morning caught up with her and she fell asleep. The kitten spent only a moment washing his face before he crawled up under her chin and, giving off a purr bigger than his body, slept as well. When the van stopped, Alyson awoke with a start.

Gates hanging from two tall totem poles were slowly swinging open. Once they passed through, Boomer leaned out his window and aimed the control at them. They began to close and the van continued up a long, narrow gravel road.

"You promise me I will get to see the ghosts, won't you?" Domingo said.

"Actually, they're not ghosts. They're spirits. There's a difference," Boomer answered. "But, yeah, sooner or later you'll get to meet Helga and Canute."

The road curved around an area dense with old growth Douglas firs, bare vine maples, and sprawling sword ferns. It widened into a graveled parking area. A huge ramshackle house sat against the rising rim of foothills. It was surrounded by a number of outbuildings, some which looked ready to fall down.

As the van stopped and Boomer turned off the engine, Domingo elbowed Alyson and pointed up a small rise. Coming out of another building half-buried in the earth was a man in a buckskin jacket, his long graying hair blowing back in the wind.

"Is he a real Indian?" Domingo asked as he stretched between the front seats to see.

"Sí, he is of the Molallas. This once was their land."

"Too cool. What does he do here?"

"Chayote is the Keeper of Ancient Traditions at Spirit Wind. He also teaches history and shamanic customs so you will have him for classes soon," Boomer said as swung his door open. "Welcome to Spirit Wind Ranch."

Domingo nearly tumbled out of the van in his excitement. Alyson was slower in joining him. Gazing around, everything she saw was starkly alien to her frightened eyes.

A gangling youth with bleached hair standing up in spikes was carrying on an animated discussion with what appeared to be a scarecrow beside a raised garden bed. His arms flailed about in the falling rain as he gestured to the house, the trees, and the rise of the land behind them.

Another boy was hanging by his knees from a rope strung between two of the posts supporting the wide porch roof, the hood of his red sweatshirt dangling like a second head. A girl was seated on the railing. She had a large set of cards in her hand and was holding one up, staring at it intently. The boy swung gently and, just as Alyson and Domingo stepped up on the porch, shouted "Wavy lines." Alyson jumped and clutched her kitten so tight it cried out.

Carlita herded them across the porch as though she saw nothing unusual.

They stopped inside the front door. Immediately to the right was a room lit by computer monitors. Shelves held small televisions and other electronic paraphernalia. A second doorway opened off the foot of a worn staircase climbing the wall to the upstairs. A massive living room stretched around a great stone fireplace on the left. It was filled with shabby furniture, stacks of books and a scattering of coats and shoes. Straight ahead, through an archway, were long wooden tables and benches.

Somewhere out of sight, a man's voice began to chant in a long, low sing-song when there was an explosive noise like a giant farting. Wild giggles erupted from under the staircase. When it was again silent, the voice began to chant again; only this time there were words. "I will hunt you down and I will kill you."

Two older teenagers came into the dining room. The boy had a spoon stuck to his nose and one on each ear. The girl held several spoons which she waved at the boy as she talked. "If we concentrated on the molecular structure, we might actually be able to effect a transmutation."

Carlita grabbed the red-haired boy by the collar as he sauntered by. She hung on as she snatched the spoons from his ears and nose. She held out her hand for the spoons the girl was carrying, waggling her fingers impatiently. "I tole you before. You want to bend things, you get junk. No usa las cucharas."

She stomped off as they slunk away muttering to each other.

Boomer came in with an armload of suitcases and a box from the van, stacking them by the door. "Well, what do you think?"

Domingo's eyes were shining as he looked around. "This place is just wizard."

"That's a good thing, right? What about you, Alyson?"

Alyson had backed up until she was stopped by the stairs. Her mother's voice was snarling in her ear. "You're going to be locked up one of these days. That's where they put freaks like you." And it had happened. She had been brought to a loony bin. Her chest was getting tight and she started fighting for her breath.

Boomer squatted in front of her. "Whoa, whoa, baby. What's wrong?" The lines and creases of his lived-in face softened. His brown eyes were warm with concern. He gently pushed a wisp of her hair back. "You don't understand, do you? It's just feels like more of an ugly dream that won't end, doesn't it?"

Domingo touched Alyson's shoulder. "This is not a bad place. This is a good place. It is for people like us. They don't understand us in the other places," he said jerking his thumb toward the door. "Here they do and they help us grow better at what we are."

Confusion now swirled in the fear. Boomer and Domingo exchanged looks. Alyson was as lost as the kitten she held.

Boomer stood up. "Harley! Yo, Harley!"

A framed painting flew away from the wall in the living room wall and a man's head poked out of the opening behind it. "You bellowed?"

"Need a coffee and one of your special cocoas."

"And his lordship wants his ass served where?"

"Any reason I shouldn't use my office?"

"How should I know? I'm only let out during the full moon when it's time to grow fur and fangs."

"You go look around, Domingo. We'll get you set up in your room in a while."

Boomer guided Alyson through the dining room. A second arched entrance opened into another area of the house with what looked like classrooms.

Boomer turned left toward a door where a flip of the light switch revealed an office. He motioned her in and pointed to a dilapidated overstuffed chair sitting beside an overflowing desk. "Sit there, Alyson."

As Alyson sat down, she saw two glossy black eyes peeking out of a wooden file box. A wet little black nose followed and sniffed the air. It looked like a skunk.

Boomer was leafing through a stack of mail when he, too, spotted the face. "Ah, geez, Ruby, what are you doing in here again? You're supposed to be out eating grubs and earning your keep, not lazing around and getting hair in my files."

He scooped her out just as a man came through the door with a tray holding two cups and a small bowl.

Harley looked like he had just walked in from some distant time. His long red hair was pulled back in a ponytail tied with a cord. A dark green shirt with full sleeves and a wide collar was leather thong-laced at the neck and pulled over heavy canvas pants with fringe running down each side. He wore stained and shabby moccasins. The wide bead-worked belt buckled around his lean middle supported a flapped leather pouch on one side and a huge knife in a buckskin sheath on the other. His bearded face was scowling.

Boomer held out his empty hand to take the tray as he thrust the skunk at the cook.

"Do I look like a pet carrier?" Harley snarled looking at the creature straining out of Boomer's hand, her nose pointed eagerly in the direction of the pouch.

He took the skunk. "You are one disgusting beast. And bone-lazy to boot," he said. But there was gentleness in his tone and his hand dipped into the pouch to pull out a small piece of food which the skunk immediately grabbed.

"Alyson, this is Harley, our resident grouch. He is head of the kitchen and between meals, he teaches geology and a class in the special properties of stones and gems."

Harley reached out to give Alyson's hair a light tug. His eyes narrowed when the girl shrank back. Scratching the skunk's head, he covertly studied her. She had the pinched look of someone seldom fed adequately and the automatic protective responses of the abused.

Dropping to one knee, he leaned in conspiratorially. "I'm going to let you in on a secret," he said. "I am also in charge of the secret goodie stash. You want anything, you just come see old Har, understand?"

Although her eyes were fearful, she managed a small nod.

"Now I'm taking that as a promise," Harley said as he stood up. "See you keep it."

She nodded again solemnly and risked a quick look at him. He winked at her as he left.

Boomer handed Alyson a cup, then placed the kitten on his desk to lap at the small saucer of milk. Pulling a chair over, he dropped onto it and swung his feet up on the desk. He reached for the coffee and was just taking a sip when the scarecrow appeared in the door.

"Boomer, it happened again," she said.

Alyson saw the scarecrow was actually a very pretty young woman dressed in bib overalls over a thermal undershirt. The raggedy brown barn coat topping her ensemble hung over her hands while a shapeless felt hat shadowed her face.

The scarecrow pulled off the hat and blonde hair fell over her shoulders. She jammed a hand in the jacket pocket and began pacing the room. "I tell you someone is stealing herbs, and some pretty potent ones at that, out of the medicinal bed."

"Are you sure it isn't just some of the critters sneaking in at night for a nibble?"

"No way. The motion sensor lights would come on and scare them away for one. For two, they would leave signs; footprints, crushed plants, plants that were chewed or torn up. No, it's definitely not an animal."

"Maybe you need to get Jesse to put out a couple of his spy cameras."

"He has and...." She hesitated.

Boomer gave her a questioning look.

"And all he has been able to catch is a dark shadow that seems to float over the medicinal bed and then disappears."

"Are you telling me you think we have a discarnate raiding the herb beds? What would a spook want with herbs?"

"I'm not saying it is a spirit but if it's not then there's someone out there with some very powerful abilities."

"Someone that has no business being on the ranch," Boomer responded softly.

Alyson shifted uncomfortably in the chair. An unpleasant sensation crept up her spine.

Boomer caught the movement and mentally smacked himself upside the head. This conversation wasn't going to help calm the girl's fears. He abruptly changed topics.

"Alyson, this is Aimee Justice. She's our herbalist. She also teaches botany and is in charge of the gardens among other things."

Aimee swung around and noticed Alyson for the first time. She held out a grubby hand. "Are you into plants?" she asked brightly.

Alyson hesitated before touching the hand proffered her but said nothing, only shot a scared look towards Boomer.

Aimee's eyes widened as she grasped the thin hand. It was like holding a wraith. The girl barely made an impression on the air surrounding her.

Boomer cleared his throat meaningfully.

"So how about we finish this discussion at the staff meeting tonight?" she said giving a reassuring smile to Alyson.

"Good plan."

Aimee left, closing the door behind her. Boomer took another swallow of his coffee, then brought his feet to the floor and leaned forward to rest his forearms on his knees so he could look directly into Alyson's eyes.

"How much do you remember about your grandmother?"

Alyson looked up at him in surprise. Somewhere she felt a very dim recollection of sheltering arms, warm laughter and feeling safe. It had been so long ago she didn't know if it had really happened or if she pretended it. But that was not the litany instilled in her with each swing of the belt; each strike of the hand. "Grandma was an evil person who did awful things. That's why she gets so mad at me. She says I'm just like her," she whispered.

"Your grandmother was not an evil person. Nor did she do bad things. She and your grandfather did many wonderful things to help people. Your grandmother was, also, what we call a clairvoyant. Do you know what that is?"

Alyson faintly shook her head.

"A clairvoyant is someone who sees through time. Sometimes they can look into the past; see things from a time which once was. Sometimes they can look ahead and see things that haven't happened yet. It is an exceptional talent and your grandmother was extremely gifted. She had an unusually high percentage of accuracy in her readings and was respected even by people who don't exactly believe in that sort of thing."

Alyson's eyes widened. She couldn't remember ever hearing anyone talk about her grandmother like this. She unconsciously leaned toward him seeking affirmation in his words.

"From what you told the caseworker, it sounds like you have inherited a similar ability, Alyson. It could be the reason why it feels like 'your head gets white' and you don't remember saying things."

"Can you make it go away …?" A silent plea underlined her question.

He shook his head. "You weren't sent to be with us so we could make it go away. That's not what we do here at Spirit Wind Ranch. Our purpose is to provide a supportive environment for young people, like yourself, to explore and learn to handle your unique abilities. Every kid on the ranch is here for that reason. Each can do something most other people can't."

"Brandy and Dylan can read thoughts. Taylor can hear way beyond the normal range. Scott sees places far away while Katy and Ralph can move things and even change an object's shape," he held up a bent letter opener, "just by thinking it. Domingo's come because he is an animal intuitive. He can hear and talk to animals with his mind."

He gave her a moment to absorb the information before continuing. "Your gift is part of you, Alyson. If we made it go away, we would be interfering with a Higher Power who gave it to you. And, although it is probably hard for you to understand after what you have had to endure, that Power knows more than we do and we must trust Its wisdom."

As her mind grappled with his words, she unconsciously drew a small orca whale hanging on a shoestring leash from under her shirt. She stroked it with her thumb as it lay in her curled fingers.

The sight of the little black and white figure jolted Boomer. The memory of his dream collided with the immediate moment, again sparking awareness of the forces at work beyond his comprehension. He stared at Alyson for a moment.

Alyson drew back as she felt the intensity of his gaze. He shifted his eyes to the whale. He slowly reached out and cradled her hand holding it.

"I once knew an orca like this. Her name was Minowah. I'll tell you about her sometime."

He looked back at her with quiet gravity. "Before we go find Domingo and look around, I want you to remember you are under our protection now. Spirit Wind will not let the nightmares find you or touch you again." As he spoke, something loomed at the back of his neck and he felt its shadow fall over his words.

Chapter 4

It had taken Attorney Virginia Thornley most of the afternoon to reach her client so she wasted no pleasantries when the woman's voice finally answered.

"Rhonda, the Court has removed Alyson from your custody. It's temporary now but there is every indication they are going to try to make it permanent."

"That wasn't supposed to happen. You were supposed to keep that from happening. What do I pay you the big bucks for...bad news phone calls?"

"You pay us to give you sound legal advice which we did when we told you to hightail it back the day she was made a ward of the State. It did not look good you not being at the hearing today."

"And since when do I care how I look to some kiddie court?"

"You better give a care. The judge has turned the file over to the District Attorney with the recommendation of pursuing criminal charges against you."

"And just what do they think they are going to charge me with?"

"How about aggravated child neglect and abuse for starters?"

"With all the publicity about my work with the Foundation, who's going to believe that?"

"That was Lithauer's thought, too. He led the hearing with that information. The judge wasn't remotely interested in the Maguire Foundation or your connection with it. In fact, she chopped him off at the knees mid-presentation."

"Well, Lithauer obviously bungled the whole thing. He's fired."

"Rhonda, this isn't about one of your frivolous lawsuits. This is very serious shit. They are going to try to indict you."

The sound of perfect white teeth grinding came over the phone line.

"My advice is that you pack up your Wangs, Herreras, and whoever else you bought and get back here. I shouldn't think I would have to remind you what's at stake here."

Rhonda's voice became frosty. "I cannot return before the end of the month. I have fittings scheduled; I have tickets for Broadway shows; and I have engagements I couldn't possibly break. That should give you plenty of time to get this situation in hand."

"And just how are we supposed to accomplish that without you?"

"Surely your firm knows somebody at the DA's office. Call them up and offer them whatever they want in terms of cash to lose the file."

"Oh, there's a brilliant idea. Let's just add bribery of a public official, tampering with evidence and interference with an investigation to the charges. With good behavior you could be out in 80 or 100 years. Listen, Rhonda, you're not going to be able to put this one on your American Express."

"Then write a check. I don't care how you do it. Just remember, it would not please me to come home to problems. If you aren't able to handle my affairs, then I will find a law firm that can." The phone went dead.

Virginia set the receiver in the cradle and looked out her 14th floor office window at the darkening Portland skyline. She didn't need any of the famed Maguire psychic ability to see disaster gathering.

Chapter 5

After dinner, Boomer carried a fresh cup of coffee to his office. Brandy and Katy were helping Alyson to settle in the girls' wing. When he had looked in the room, they were taking turns holding the kitten while the two older girls chattered away. Alyson appeared less apprehensive in their company.

He gathered up the mail and flopped down into the overstuffed chair. Hooking the toe of his boot in the rungs of a straight back chair, he dragged it over to rest his feet on. He had only opened a small amount of the mail when his eyes drooped and his head fell back against the chair.

Boomer jerked awake when his feet hit the floor. He sat up and rubbed his hands over his face. Reaching for the coffee, he grimaced when he swallowed its cold bitterness. Abruptly, he became aware of someone sitting on the chair staring at him. The woman was tall and attractive. Her ash blonde hair was stylishly cut in waves around her face. She wore a slim red skirt with a flowing top covered with bright red and orange poppies.

"Carlita would love that top," Boomer said. The woman smiled in amusement when he realized he could see through to the bulletin board behind her. "You're not Helga."

The woman's voice came into his head. "No, Helga has gone for a visit to her family. She has a new great-great-great-great-great-great granddaughter. And she needed a rest. The Kirilian photography project was making her very nervous."

"Canute go with her?"

"No. He says her family makes him very nervous. He's hanging out with Harley."

"So who are you?" Boomer studied the woman. There was something familiar in the shape of the woman's eyes; the tilt of her head. "Wait. You're Alyson's grandmother. You're Meri Maguire."

"Yes. And it is about Alyson that I have come to talk, Russell."

He started at hearing his given name. "I don't use that name much. It belongs to another time. Another life."

"Yes, it does. And I am sorry for the pain you endured."

The pain was old now. It had become a part of his being, never gone but rarely rising to consciousness anymore.

"Alyson's protected now. The Court will keep her mother from ever getting to her again."

Meri shook her head. "The Court holds no terror for Rhonda Maguire. She considers herself beyond the law."

"She's probably going to be indicted for aggravated child neglect and abuse. With the evidence gathered so far, she'll be cooling her expensive heels in jail for a while."

"She, no doubt, will hire a battalion of lawyers to avoid such unpleasantness." She leaned forward. "You must understand my daughter-in-law is a dark entity…a very dark entity. I didn't realize how dark until it cost me my son."

"I gave my word to Alyson that she would be protected here. I intend to keep it."

"It is more than just Alyson now. You and Spirit Wind itself will find yourselves ensnared in whatever evil web she chooses to spin. Cross Rhonda Maguire and she can only be satiated by the utter ruin of those who dare. She will do it anyway she can…and she does have means beyond money."

There was noise as the staff began to gather across the hall for the meeting "What are you saying? That Alyson's mother has some kind of psychic skill?"

"She has some. And its use makes her powerful at turning the will of others to do her bidding."

Someone knocked on his door. He glanced over his shoulder. "In a minute." He looked back. The chair was empty.

The evening melded into a long and restless night for Boomer. Uneasiness skulked along the edges of his dreams. He woke with a start. Videotaped images of the ranch's medicinal herb bed were running in his memory. He thought of the faint shadow appearing on the periphery of the gardens. Then the growing darkness covering the area as the shadow approached. The blackness spread over the herb bed hiding the thief before sliding back towards the cover of the trees and vanishing. He and the staff had sat dumbfounded. Even with their knowledge and experience of the unexplainable, they could not come up with a probable accounting of what they saw. Something or someone was able to override their security. Not a good feeling when you had a baker's dozen of kids to safeguard.

Baker's dozen! Boomer sat up. There were now thirteen kids at the ranch and Alyson was the 13th. Irritably, he shoved his covers back and swung his feet out of bed. What was the matter with him? Spirit Wind Ranch wasn't about ridiculous old superstitions. Here the paranormal was something as ordinary as brushing teeth or taking out the garbage.

He quietly padded barefoot downstairs. In the girls' room, he checked Alyson. She was asleep with her kitten curled on the pillow. The kitten opened its eyes and the outside halogen light filtering through the window caught in them, giving them an eerie opaque sheen.

He went to the boys' side to check on Domingo as well. He was asleep but a suspicious lump stirred under the covers. In a moment, a small black nose poked out, took a couple of sniffs and drew back under the bedclothes.

"Ruby," Boomer hissed but he left her rather than disturb the boy.

He crossed through the dining room and into the library/meditation room. He stubbed his toe on a book someone had left on the floor. Muttering imprecations under his breath, he hobbled to the windows overlooking the gardens and scanned the area closely. Nothing. He made his way back to bed and lay for a long time staring into the dark. Like a subtle change in the atmosphere when a storm is moving in, Spirit Wind Ranch felt different and worry sat heavily in his chest.

* * *

The kids were lined up the next morning helping themselves to breakfast when Alyson came into the room with Katy and Brandy. Katy was carrying the kitten. "You're going to have to think of a really cool name for him. Maybe something magical."

"There's Morgana," Brandy said.

Katy snorted. "For a boy cat? I don't think so."

Boomer ambled from the kitchen sipping his coffee followed by Carlita carrying her brightly painted earthenware tea pot.

As Alyson passed Carlita, the dusky scent of tea blended with bread browning in the toaster and she stopped. Listening to a far away whisper, her eyes glazed over and a distant look settled on her face. She moved unseeingly to Carlita's side. A warm feeling drifted through the aromas, wrapping itself around her like loving arms. "Grandma?" she whispered.

Alyson was unaware the entire room had quieted down to watch her. Gradually the sensation slipped away and Alyson was back in the present. She looked around disoriented.

"Sweet," said one of the boys.

"I wish I could do that," said Brandy. "All I can do is hear what people think and it is sooooo boring most of the time."

"What did you see?" asked Domingo, balancing a plate piled high with food.

Alyson looked at him in confusion.

He put his plate on the table. "You just went someplace. I wondered what you saw."

Alyson wrapped her arms tightly around herself. Had she really done it here in front of everybody? She braced herself for a violent response.

Instead someone placed their fingers under her chin and lifted it. She looked up into Boomer's face. His look was comforting. "You okay?" She nodded and dared to look around the room. Most of the kids were busily eating and paying no attention to her at all.

Harley stood in the kitchen doorway holding a platter piled high with scrambled eggs. "So our little Alyson is a trance clairvoyant." He nodded his head approvingly. "So was my grandmother." He pushed through the kids to tip the eggs into the warming pan. "Out of my way you useless mooches and leave something for Alyson." The kids just laughed at his snarl.

A slender black man appeared in the archway. He was dressed in something like black pajamas. He put his hands together and made a deep bow to the group. "Good morning most honorable staff and students."

"Good morning, Dr. Dao," voices echoed back.

He served himself and sat down at the table. He carefully placed the utensils beside his plate before unfolding and spreading the napkin on his lap. Sitting next to Alyson, Katy stretched her hand across the table, holding it about four inches above the surface. The boy with the red hair seated across from her did the same. They stared fixedly down the table at the man's plate. Just as he reached for his fork, it began to twitch. Suddenly it skittered down the table and stopped under their hands. The long suffering look on the man's face sent the rest of the kids into giggles.

Harley reached over the heads of Katy and Alyson to set a plate of toast on the table. He sent the fork sliding back down the table. "What have I told you guys about picking on dumb animals?"

The man placed his hands together in entreaty. "Most honorable ancestors, please award his most gracious kindness with chiggers in his long johns."

Amidst the laughter, a buzzer sounded. The kids swarmed into their day.

Chapter 6

The well-structured life at Spirit Wind encompassed Alyson; easing her fears and providing sustenance to her spirit. Under the daily routines of school, chores, and study Alyson began to breathe more easily and flinch less often. Although still not a vocal participant, she enjoyed listening to the girls in their open dorm setting. She was becoming accustomed to manifestations of the other students' abilities and Domingo had allied himself as her staunchest supporter.

It was Domingo she was watching in the impromptu volleyball game that sprang up when Dr. Dao had taken them outside to practice using thought energy to bust clouds. Indifferent to the day's planned lesson, the clouds had chosen to dissipate without waiting for assistance and Dao had been totally ineffective in getting the kids back to the meditation room. A sunny early spring day was not to be wasted indoors.

Boomer sprawled on the front steps going through a stack of papers. Carlita sat in the rocker, sorting seed packets for Aimee. Dr. Dao was dragooned into being the game's referee.

Domingo sent the ball toward Ralph, the rangy red-headed boy. When the ball was about three feet from him, Ralph leaped into the air and made a slamming motion with his fist. The ball immediately obeyed and flung itself over the net.

Dao whistled through his teeth. "You are supposed to actually make contact with the ball, Crenshaw."

"I just wanted to see if it would work," Ralph said.

"Heads up, Alix," Dylan shouted. "Jesse's gonna hit to you."

"Not fair. You're giving away my strategy. Stay out of my head, you little creep."

The ball did head to Alix who began to set it up for Johnathan when she suddenly pulled her hands away, letting it drop to the ground. "Oh, yeeech. A slug's crawled on it."

"Yeah, like about a year ago when it was left out."

"Well, I can still feel the slime and it's gross."

"Come on, Alix, you're just 'reading' the slime. It's not really there," Brandy said.

"Hey, Scott, try playing with your eyes closed. See if you can tell what's going on."

Scott closed his eyes and successfully returned one of two shots. The game stopped when they heard electronic cawing from inside the front door telling them someone was at the gate. They all turned toward the drive.

"Can you see who it is, Scott?" Nate asked.

"It's a sheriff's car, I think. Its white with a blue stripe on top," he said.

"It's probably Garner," Theresa said.

"Like that takes ability to know," Brandy replied. "What other cop ever comes here?"

Boomer reached to pull the ranch radio off his belt. He turned the dial to the sheriff's frequency. "You there, Garner?" he said.

A voice came back. "Tell me you have a camera down here, Boomer."

"Sorry, no. Scott spotted you."

"I don't see anyone. Where is he? No, on second thought don't tell me."

"He's about four feet from the front porch. You wanna come up?"

"You people are spooky. You know that. But then I guess spooky is what I want so, yeah, open the gate."

The kids were ranged along the front of the house as Garner pulled around the drive and stopped the car. He paused as he hoisted himself out to look over the array of curious faces. The kids looked like any kid in America in their jeans, sweatshirts, and athletic shoes. It was their eyes that set them apart. It was as though they looked out from a deeper part of themselves.

Boomer grabbed hold of the porch post and hauled himself to his feet. "What can we do for you?"

"We have a couple of lost kids back off Wilhoit Springs. Been looking for them since about 10 a.m. Wondered if maybe...if your kids...you know."

Boomer stabbed his finger in the direction of several kids. "Jesse, Nate, Scott. You didn't happen to bring anything that belongs to them?"

Garner shook his head. "Sorry, the search dog people have the stuff."

"Can't use psychometry then. We'll make do. Let's go, people. Time's ticking."

Garner was pulled in by the stream of kids pushing into the house. In a matter of moments, the kid with spiky hairdo had spread a topographical map of the Molalla area over the huge square coffee table in the living room. Two boys knelt on either side of the map, the rest of the kids fanning out around the table. Nate, a short black boy held up a quartz crystal arrow affixed to a slender cord. He held it perfectly still over the map. He closed his eyes as he concentrated his thoughts. Slowly it began to move gently from side to side, then across the map as though it was searching. It stopped over a point, swinging in tighter and tighter circles. "That must be where they went in," Scott said as he put his finger on the map.

Garner leaned over his shoulder. The kids had pinpointed it. He nodded.

Scott kept his finger on the map and closed his eyes. He started trying to follow their trail with his remote viewing. Nate's pendulum began to swing again. Slowly, it moved in circles, each one a few millimeters larger. Within minutes, it was moving in a straight line from the place marked by Scott's finger to a point that looked like it would be about a mile from where they entered.

"That's it," Scott said.

"Can you give Garner something to look for; a landmark?" Boomer asked.

Scott dropped his head and shook it sadly. "Sorry, it all looks alike. Trees, brush, I can't see anything special."

"That's okay," Garner said as he made a note of the coordinates. "This helps more than you can know." He straightened up and slipped his notebook back in the breast pocket of his shirt. "I'll let you know what happens."

Alyson stepped into his path as he started towards the front door; her expression remote. Although her face was raised towards his, her unfocused eyes seemed to be looking through and beyond him. "Take Roscoe with you. He's needs Roscoe."

While Garner watched, the eyes gradually focused and her face became frightened when she found herself staring up at him.

"Roscoe? Who's Roscoe?" Garner asked her.

She now looked terrified. Domingo darted to stand protectively at her side. The rest of the kids shifted as though they, too, were ready to leap to Alyson's aid.

Boomer came up and gave him light shove from behind. "I'll walk you to the car."

"What was that all about?" Garner asked as they stepped out onto the porch.

Boomer looked towards the gardens. "Don't know."

"Come on, Boomer, what just happened?"

"You were just given some information that may be very important."

"It didn't seem like she knew what I was talking about."

"She didn't. People in trances seldom do. I'd check it out if I were you."

Garner nodded dubiously. "Thanks. I'll let you know the outcome. And, Boomer, you remember...."

"Yeah, if anyone asks, you were never here."

The next several hours found Boomer dogged every step by all the kids. They clung as tightly as the cell phone hanging from his belt. At the door to the bathroom, he whirled and held up his hands. "I'm going in there alone. The first kid that sticks his head in gets flushed. Understand?"

When he pulled the door open to come out, kids fell through like a collapsing wall.

He crossed his arms over his chest. "Can anyone tell me what I am thinking right now?"

He locked eyes with Brandy. They stared hard at each other. Suddenly, Brandy tossed her head and put her fists indignantly on her hips. "That's not very nice, Boomer."

Theresa asked for the whole group. "Well, what is it?"

Brandy crossed her arms and turned to the rest of the students. "Remember how Mel Gibson died at the end of *"Braveheart"*?

It was a mixed bag of reaction. "Drawn and quartered? That's gross." "Geez, I thought you liked us", "Hey, that's great, did you really picture that?" "You are so weird."

Boomer interrupted. "Whoa, whoa...hey," he let out a sharp whistle to silence them. "Does somebody want to tell me just exactly when you saw *Braveheart*? I don't recall that being on our list of acceptable entertainment."

Heads ducked as the kids looked at each other and began hissing at Brandy. "Nice going, blabbermouth." She glared back at them defiantly.

"So who arranged that little showing?"

The kids were silent but couldn't resist taking peeks in the direction of the kitchen.

Boomer turned right and strode off. "Harley!?!" he bellowed. He had just reached the dining room when "Reveille" began to chime. The kids scrambled in, climbing on the benches and even the tables to try to hear as he pulled his cell phone from his belt and put it to his ear.

"Boomer." He flapped his free hand to bring quiet. "Yes, Garner. What's happening?"

The kids focused on the phone trying to intercept the conversation. Finally, Boomer smiled and said, "Hey that's just great. I'm glad that all's well. Yeah, yeah. I'll tell them. Any time. Later."

Boomer made a slashing motion across the air when window-rattling babble erupted as he clicked off the phone. "We will be quiet, people, or you will be told nothing."

Instantly, the room was silent.

"Okay, the kids have been found. They are safe and unhurt. Scott, Nate, Garner wanted me to let you know you were ten yards off. He would like to see greater accuracy in the future."

The kids began to pound Nate and Scott on the back. "Good going." "Awesome, dudes." "Freaks rule!"

Boomer flapped them down again. "Whoa, they're not alone. Alyson, Garner asked the mothers about the Roscoe you 'saw'. It seems one of the missing children is a 7 year old Down's syndrome boy. Roscoe is a special security bear he has. When Roscoe is around, he knows it is okay. And you were absolutely right. He has been taught not to go with anyone who doesn't have Roscoe. He needed Roscoe."

It was Alyson's turn to be hugged and congratulated. Alyson was very uncomfortable in the wake of the lavish enthusiasm.

"Now get your butts moving and get your chores done. Anyone who doesn't have their work done by 5:30 will not get to watch the story on the news."

The level of excitement reached a new peak causing several objects to fly about as the kids scattered. An errant onion wandered from the kitchen chased by Harley while Boomer grabbed a plate sailing off the serving bench. A sharp cry came from the living room. Dao limped into the dining area rubbing his knee.

"I was just kicked by a shoe with no one in it."

Harley reached out and plucked the onion out of the air. "Blame Capt. Boom-Boom. He's got them strung up tighter than Chayote's bow."

Dao hobbled towards the meditation room grumbling under his breath. "I could have been living in a Tibetan monastery surrounded by nothing but silent 80 year old monks. Oh, no, I decide I want to sign up for a program where I can get my ass kicked by a bunch of teenage psychokinetic energy."

The television went on promptly at 5:30 p.m. Absolute silence greeted the beginning of each story followed by mumbling and squirms when it was not about the missing children. Finally the screen revealed an aerial shot of the Molalla foothills and the newscaster's voice began to describe the ordeal of the two children who had wandered away while on a family hike. There was a quick cheer as Garner appeared on the screen and described the rescue. Although there was no direct mention of the part Spirit Wind had played in the rescue, Garner did look right at the camera and say, "For all of those who helped, and you know who you are, thanks."

Boomer was reaching for the remote control when he caught a few of the newscaster's words over the excited chatter of the kids. He clicked the volume up.

"Rhonda Maguire, widow of Christopher Maguire, the late scion of one of Portland's premier conglomerates, appeared in court today in Clackamas County to answer charges of aggravated child neglect and child abuse. Maguire entered a plea of not guilty in the brief arraignment. Maguire's daughter had been removed from her custody and placed under the protection of the state in a juvenile hearing held earlier this year."

"Following the arraignment, a lawsuit was filed by Mrs. Maguire alleging the wrongful taking of her daughter and demanding the child's immediate return. Named in the suit were the State of Oregon, Spirit Wind, Inc., Spirit Wind Ranch and Russell Evanrud, director of the Spirit Wind Ranch."

"Hey, it's about the ranch."

"Why are they talking about us?"

"Shush."

The newscaster's voice continued. "Following her appearance, Mrs. Maguire had these words." Reflexive fear jolted Alyson when the large screen filled with the face of her elegantly groomed mother.

"Spirit Wind Ranch is a purported children's home that is, in fact, a front for the occult. I became aware of the existence of this place when they submitted a request for funding to the Maguire Foundation. An inquiry into the ranch was instituted by the Foundation at my request in an effort to expose its actual purposes. In a retaliatory action, the ranch director, Russell Evanrud, has organized an effort to strike back at me by legally kidnapping my daughter and involving her in practices which go against every principle I have. I intend to use all my resources to eradicate Spirit Wind Ranch and make this man answer for his actions."

An off-screen voice spoke. "And get your daughter back?"

She shrugged a mink-covered shoulder impatiently. "Yes, of course. That's the whole point."

The cameras came up on the newscaster. "Rhonda Maguire currently serves on the Board of Directors of the Maguire Foundation. Created in 1969 by Sean and Meri Maguire, the Foundation provides funding to youth related organizations. Spirit Wind Ranch is a private non-profit facility approved for the placement of gifted children according to juvenile officials at Clackamas County. We'll be back with more news after these messages."

Boomer clicked the television off. Rhonda Maguire's ugly threats had dampened the excitement. As he looked around the room, he saw the staff exchange troubled glances with each other. An uncertain silence filled the room.

Then Harley spoke through the opening between the kitchen and the living room. "What a load of bull pucky. Why doesn't she just fly up here on her broomstick and turn us all into banana slugs? Gimme a break."

A titter began to move through the room as the kids pictured each other as slugs.

"Now, unless you all have developed a sudden desire to slime your way to the garden and gnaw on the plants, I suggest you get yourselves out to the deck because the hamburgers are ready to come off the grill," Harley said, as he pulled the painting back into place.

There was a thunder of feet and some good-natured pushing and shoving as the kids raced from the living room, through the kitchen and out to the picnic tables.

Only Alyson remained motionless, the weight of her mother's image pressing the breath out of her. She had lived amid the devastation her mother wrought. It was something to fear. She watched Boomer closing the doors to the entertainment center. As he turned, she caught the uneasiness in his face and it scared her. The growing sense of safety she had experienced since coming to Spirit Wind fled.

Boomer looked at Alyson and saw her face was as pale and stiff as it had been the day she arrived. When she turned to follow the rest of the kids, there was weariness in the curve of her spine and her feet scraped the floor as if they were too heavy to lift. How had the child survived the poisonous depths of Rhonda Maguire's hell?

He crossed the room to her. "Don't forget my promise, baby." He put his fingers under her chin and lifted her face to look at him. "You're not alone anymore. We're not going to give in no matter how many suits your mother files. She's still going to have to go through me to get to you, remember that."

"Yeah, and if the old Boom gets his butt kicked, I'm right behind him so she'll have to go through both of us and I'm ornerier than anything you're going to find on this mountain," Harley said from the entrance to the dining room, twirling and passing his Bowie knife from one hand to the other.

There was an ear shattering cry as Dao leaped from behind the arch into the room, landing in a kung fu pose. "She will have no chance against my martial art skills." He drew in air, expanding his chest to its fullest as he brought his hands up in front of his face. "These hands are registered as lethal weapons."

The sight of Dao practicing air chops summoned a small giggle from Alyson.

"No, no. He's right, Alyson. I saw him in action last summer when bees swarmed after him. He practically beat himself to death fighting them off," Harley said.

"That's what I mean. I am a killing machine. It took me weeks to get over the whupping I gave myself."

"Come on, I'll grill you a special hamburger. And how about we make a little one for Minnow to share with Ruby?" Harley held out his hand to Alyson.

"What about me?" Dao said as he followed them.

"You who?"

"Oh yeah, cook for the cat but make me have to fight the voracious mob for scraps."

When Alyson was safely out of ear shot, Carlita pushed herself out of the chair. "That woman is muy loco," she said.

Boomer nodded, "Yes, so it would appear. But how? Like a fox or a loon?"

Chapter 7

After dinner, the house was quieter than usual. The kids seemed to have burned off their endless energy during the unusual day. The adults grabbed the opportunity to drift casually into the staff room. They wanted very much to talk about Rhonda Maguire's televised threats.

Harley entered carrying a tray of mocha lattes. He took one himself and sat down in a listing secretarial chair. "So what are we up against, Boomer?" he asked. "I mean, we all know the lawsuit is bogus, even her idiot attorneys have to know that, but what is she really after? Just undermining the credibility of the indictment or does she actually intend to try to get Alyson back?"

Boomer shrugged as he sipped then set his cup back on the table. "I haven't any idea."

Chayote tilted his chair back against the wall and studied the contents of his cup. "What I'm wondering is why does she want Alyson back? Leaving her here would be the perfect way to solve her legal issues. She relinquishes permanent custody to the state, the state drops the charges and the whole thing is over. What's the big deal? It's not like she loves the kid or anything."

Boomer looked at Chayote thoughtfully. "That's a really good question. Why does she want Alyson?"

Aimee came in the room and perched on the edge of the table. "I was pretty sure I remembered but I checked just to be sure. We have never applied for a grant from the Maguire Foundation so what business is it of theirs to 'inquire' into Spirit Wind?"

"It would be interesting to find out if the Foundation is really involved or if the Maguire woman is just blowing smoke." Dao said.

"I think we need to get a fix on what's driving this woman," Boomer said. "I have it on good authority she is not particular about the means necessary to achieve her ends. We need to figure out what her 'ends' are."

Harley grunted in agreement. "And what she means by 'eradicating' us."

Boomer put his empty cup back on the tray. "However, let's set some ground rules. One, keep this off your mind when you are in the vicinity of our telepaths. We don't need Brandy and Dylan picking up bits of information and stirring up the rest of the kids. Two, keep a close eye on Alyson. Until we know why her mother seems so hot to get her back, we don't take any chances. And three, keep your eyes open and your antennae up. Pay attention to the kids. They pick up a lot without knowing what it means, okay? They're apt to be our early warning system. So stay tuned in."

"Speaking of which," Harley said as he picked up the tray of empty cups. "It's time to corral the beasts for another night."

* * *

Alyson had gone to sit on her bed after helping stack the dishes and clean up from the evening meal. The other kids hadn't said a word about what they had seen but she could feel them looking at her when they thought she wouldn't notice.

She was confused and frightened. Could her mother make them give her back? Why would she even try? Her mother had told her for years how much she hated her; how she wished she had never had her; what a monster she was and how she wished she would just vanish. Now in a sense she had vanished and her mother was pitching fits in front of TV cameras as if she really gave a care.

She rubbed her forehead against Minnow's soft kitten fur. An unbearable thought came into her mind. If she was made to go back, she would have to give up her kitten. She wouldn't dare take Minnow with her. Her mother would make sure something happened to him...something dreadful. The thought made her sick at her stomach. She curled her body protectively over Minnow.

A whispering vibration in the air moved around her. Alyson lifted her face and listened. She heard the words just barely tickling the edge of her ear. "Look to your heart."

Her mind lurched around as she tried to understand. The air moved again and a single word formed in her mind. "Breathe."

She sat up straighter on the bed and closed her eyes. The sound of Dr. Dao's voice directing their centering exercises came into her head. "Straighten those spines. Shoulders back. Now breathe deep. Let it go clear to your toes. Count to three slowly as you bring the air in. Count to three as you let the air out. Concentrate on feeling it move in and out. Follow your breath." She breathed, slowly dropping into the darkness filling her. The voice had directed her to her heart. She became aware of sounds coming from deep within her. They were whimpers. Her heart felt so small and frightened. What could it tell her?

"It knows," the voice said. "When it speaks, you must trust it."

Alix and Taylor came into the room. Taylor stopped and looked towards Alyson. There was a shimmer in the air next to her. "Who's that, Alyson?"

Alyson's eyes flew open. She glanced quickly around her. She saw nothing. Had Taylor heard the voice?

Brandy had followed them in, pulling her sweatshirt over her head. She glanced at Alyson as she shook her arms free. "Oh, it's probably just Alyson's guide."

Now Alyson was completely unnerved. The voice was her secret companion. No one else had ever heard it. She kept her eyes on Brandy as she flopped on the floor and began to use the toe of one foot to shove her shoe off the other. "Guide?" she asked timidly when Brandy seemed disinclined to provide further information.

Brandy crossed her legs and reached out to shove her shoes under her bed.

"Yeah. Guide. Spirit guide. You know what that is, don't you?"

Alyson shook her head.

"She hasn't had Carlita's class yet. She won't get that till next year," Alix said, her muffled voice coming from under her bed as she retrieved the flip-flops she used as slippers.

"Oh, yeah, right," Brandy said. "Well…" She scrunched up her forehead as she thought about explaining it to Alyson. "Okay, when we are born, there are special beings assigned to help us throughout our life here. Some are angels and some are spirit guides. Spirit guides were once people like us but they've gone on to the other side. I guess they get some kind of special training. Then they volunteer to be assigned to one of us. They stay with us our entire lives helping us learn the lessons we need in this life and guiding us in finding and fulfilling our purpose."

"Does everyone have a spirit guide?" Alyson asked.

"Sure. It's just that most people don't know they have one or know how to talk to them and listen for answers."

"Only don't bother to ask them to help you with the answers on a math test. Gelly just gives me a lecture on applying myself; that she's not here to do it for me," Katy made a face as she headed toward the bathroom.

"Gelly?"

"Angelica is Katy's guide."

Katy stuck her head back out of the doorway. "I think that's because she flunked algebra the last time she was here."

The conversation was disrupted by the rising crescendo of water running in the sinks, toilets flushing and the comings and goings of the girls as they performed their individual bedtime ablutions.

Joining them, Alyson quickly washed her face, brushed her teeth and slipped into her nightgown. She climbed into bed and pulled the covers up. Her conversation with Katy and the others had raised a tumble of questions in her mind. As they fell over each other, breaking apart and reforming, their droning lulled her into sleep.

Carlita came in to prod the dawdlers into bed and turn out the lights. She was startled to see Alyson already sleeping. It was clear even the image of her mother had the power to inflict trauma on the child. She had been prepared to sit with Alyson as long as needed to ease her terrors. Maybe they were making more progress with the child then they had thought.

While the stragglers were getting into bed, Carlita checked the window locks and the bathroom. "Sueño dulce," she said as she flipped off the lights. One or two voices murmured 'Dream sweet, too' in response.

Back in the living room, Chayote came out of the boy's room. "They're down and out. See you tomorrow," he said as he left for his lodge house. Carlita threw the deadbolt on the doors behind him and waited for Harley to finish locking the doors in the kitchen and classroom wing. He nodded as he came through the dining room. "Ready," he said.

Carlita punched in the alarm code and switched it on. "Lockdown complete," he said as they began to climb the stairs to their rooms.

Boomer had turned on the small television in his room. He wanted to watch the news again. While they did a quick recap on the lost kids, there was nothing in the short ten o'clock version of the news about Alyson's mother. He shut it off and stretched out in bed.

A stack of books were waiting for him to review before they were placed in the library. He picked up the first one and managed a dozen pages before he began to drowse. He put the book back on the pile and switched off the reading lamp.

Chapter 8

"They voted you off the board, Rhonda. Now that your situation has become public they felt they had no choice. It isn't good PR for a foundation that specializes in benefiting children to have a board member who is under indictment for aggravated child neglect and abuse. And they really didn't like you dragging the name of the Maguire Foundation into it," Virginia reported.

"That wasn't very smart of them, was it? If I am no longer on the board, why should there be a board at all? Perhaps it's time for the Maguire Foundation to go the way of the dodo bird."

Virginia ran her hand through her hair, mindless of her recent trip to the salon.

"Rhonda, we've been through this before. There is no way to dismantle the Foundation. Sean and Meri Maguire were not fools. They were well aware of the vagaries of human nature. The Foundation goes on with or without you and with or without the current board. You cannot end it. You cannot undermine it. You cannot interfere with it."

Rhonda's ominous throaty laugh slithered down the phone line chilling Virginia's blood. "Virginia, my dearest advisor, I can do any damn thing I want. And maybe what I want now is to thoroughly embarrass the Foundation."

Chapter 9

On Sunday, spring became the coquette as she hid in her frowsy winter-grey robe. Carlita and Aimee loaded the kids in one of the vans to drive them to their respective churches in town. Harley set to work on the special brunch he planned each week. By 1 p.m., many of the kids would be picked up for a visit with their families. It was a day without schedules and stringent enforcement of rules. Dinner was a casual affair as platters loaded with a variety of sandwiches, bags of chips, plates of fresh vegetables and pans of brownies were left where each person could help themselves whenever they were hungry. The staff worked on lesson plans, graded homework and scheduled the next week. The remaining kids watched movies, played games or curled up with books.

Alyson loved Sunday afternoons. She would take paper and her pencils to the window seat in the library/mediation room. Using a hefty book from the shelves lining the room to provide a firm surface, she would draw for hours curled against the pillows. She loved drawing animals. Today she worked on capturing the gentle faces of the ranch cows and the graceful curves of Casper, the white riding horse. She was so engrossed; she didn't notice the staff occasionally peeking in to assure themselves she was okay.

Day light was fading when Boomer wandered in carrying Minnow. She jumped when he turned on the overhead light and hastily began to gather her papers together, shoving them inside a dilapidated folder.

Boomer kept his eyes turned to Minnow as he scratched the kitten's ears. He was practicing a lesson he had learned from his naturalist grandfather. 'When you enter into the space of another creature, always pause and allow it time to collect itself and prepare to meet you.' It was a lesson that had served him well in the wilds and was equally effective in dealing with the fractious world of teenagers.

He felt Alyson's preparedness when the papers were hidden. "This little guy says there's a tuna sandwich out there with his name all over it."

Alyson's stomach growled in response, letting her know a sandwich would be much appreciated. She slipped off the window seat, carefully sliding her folder beneath the pillows as she went to put the book back. She retrieved her folder, hugging it protectively to her chest as she followed Boomer out into the dining room. It was like being followed by a ghost, he thought.

Although the staff felt her reaching out to them on occasion, the moment was always followed by a hasty withdrawal. Even relying on their sensitivity and skills, it was proving to be a blind undertaking as they struggled to find ways to encourage her to venture forth from behind the protective wall she had built.

The information from the state's investigation had provided them with little in the way of guidance. It was a small handful of bald facts…her father killed in an auto accident when she was two; living with her grandmother until she was four when Meri Maguire succumbed to leukemia.

Once she had gone back to her mother, it was as though she disappeared into a black hole. The only place there was any evidence of her existence had been through the school. Her medical records consisted of only of county immunizations. There was no evidence she had ever been to a doctor, visited a dentist or optometrist. There were apparently no Halloweens, Christmases, Easters, or birthdays. Who had patched up injuries, taken care of her when she was sick or provided comfort when she was frightened was a mystery?

The deeper mystery was what drove Rhonda Maguire to do everything she could to destroy this child and yet appear to be prepared to fight to regain custody of Alyson. In once again working this puzzle, Boomer became so intent on his thoughts; he didn't notice Alyson slip off to put her drawings away.

She was almost back to the dining room when the front door opened and Katy bounded through followed by her mother. She froze when Katy called her name.

"Hey, Alyson. Come and meet my mom."

Boomer turned abruptly in their direction. Mrs. Grinnell caught the movement and looked at him. The cautionary message was plain in his face.

Katy had already grabbed Alyson's hand and was dragging her toward the door. "Mom, this is Alyson. She's my friend."

Alyson looked at Katy in wonder. She hadn't realized Katy thought of her as something as special as a friend.

Mrs. Grinnell smiled and reached out to take Alyson's free hand. She squeezed it warmly. "How glad I am to meet you, Alyson." Her brown eyes were soft as she looked at the girl.

Katy was bubbling over as usual. She was rooting around in the backpack she used when she went home. She stood up triumphantly with a small plastic bag in her hand. "Look at these socks Mom got us." She drew out two pairs of dark blue socks covered with gold moons, stars and celestial symbols. She handed one pair to Alyson. "Aren't they cool? There's one for you and one for me."

Alyson took the socks, looking at them uncomprehendingly. Someone she didn't know bought her something? She clutched them to her chest and looked up at Mrs. Grinnell. Although her lips moved, no sound came out as she said thank you but the miracle of such beneficence swam in her blue eyes.

Despite the warning Boomer had transmitted to her, Mrs. Grinnell couldn't resist bending over and hugging Alyson. "I hope you like them," she said as Alyson breathed in a scent that smelled like love before turning to her daughter. "Come on, kid, give me a hug big enough to last all week."

Katy flung herself into her mother's arms and the two whispered affectionate farewell words to each other.

Although Alyson had witnessed these scenes between many of the kids and their families during her time at Spirit Wind Ranch, she had always viewed them in a disconnected way. Now, with the feeling of Katy's mother's arms still fresh on her shoulders, her heart began to weep.

Boomer, watching from the side, saw her start to struggle to draw in air. The emotional starvation in the child was palpable. He threw out a prayer for help in rescuing Alyson.

* * *

Alyson curled herself into a tight little ball in her bed that night. The pain inside her was almost beyond bearing. It wasn't the physical pain of a beating or being hungry. This pain was savaging her heart. Memories crowded through her as she named her anguish. It was the light of love she saw in the grown-up faces when they came to the ranch to get their children. It was the feeling she experienced when Katy's mother hugged her. It was being loved by someone else for always and never being banished to dark places of hurt.

She thought she might have known that feeling once in the arms of her father but he left so long ago, he was now only an old white shirt in her mind. And there were faint, misty memories of her grandmother loving her, but she had gone away, never to return either. Her mother said they went away because she was such a disgusting, horrible little monster they had been punished by death for caring about her.

Now, as the tears silently flooded her cheeks, she begged the voice to speak the words to the Universe to make her not be a monster; to make her good enough for someone to love.

A whisper of warmth touched her cheek and silent words stroked her pain. "Listen, it calls to you as you call to it." She sensed an answer was out there just beyond her reach. She struggled towards it until she slept.

Chapter 10

The clock said 2:44 a.m. when a bright light hit him in the face. The house alarm had been set off. Instantly, Boomer swung out of bed and jammed his feet into an old pair of moccasin loafers. He grabbed the Magnum flashlight from his dresser as he left his room. At the top of the steps, he could see the front door standing open and caught a flash of white disappearing off the porch.

Behind him he heard Harley, Dao and Carlita emerging from their rooms as he took the stairs two at a time.

Stopping on the edge of the porch, Boomer visually swept the area. A small form emerged from one of the shadows. The moonlight, shining between the clouds, turned the pale blonde hair silvery as it swung in time to her running feet. Alyson!

He leaped from the porch and gave chase. She was barefoot but moving swiftly over the graveled drive as if she were running on softest grass. Abruptly she stopped and he nearly ran her over.

Alyson swung back toward him when he grabbed hold of her upper arm. Her eyes were open, but they didn't see him. Instead, she tilted her head as though she were listening for something. He knelt down on one knee, the rocks painful under it, and held on to her. Suddenly, she stiffened and tried to fight her way out of his hands.

"Alyson, Alyson, it's me," he said softly.

"Boomer?" Her voice was bemused.

"That's right, baby." He felt her shivering in the chilly night. "Come on, I'm going to take you back to bed." He stood up, scooping her into his arms. She buried her face in his neck as she clutched his tee-shirt. By the time he had walked back to the porch, her breathing had shifted into the slower rhythm of sleep and her grip had relaxed.

Carlita was waiting by the door and followed him as he carried the girl to bed. He laid her down carefully. Alyson rolled on her side, her eyes closed and her face tranquil. Carlita took over the duties of pulling the blankets into place and tucking her in. Minnow rubbed against Boomer's bare ankle. He reached down and lifted the kitten onto the bed.

"I will stay with her por el momento," Carlita whispered as she sat on the end of the bed.

Boomer nodded and went back to the living room. Jesse appeared in the door of the boys' side. "Wha's happenin'?" he asked through an enormous yawn.

"Nothing, Jess. Head on back to bed, guy."

The boy was scratching his head. "Thought you were havin' a party without us," he said through another yawn. He disappeared, closing the door.

Boomer flipped on the entry way light. His eyes bulged as he stared at the sight before him. Dao stood poised with a set of nunchuks swinging in his hand. Beside him, Harley held his Bowie knife and his black powder pistol. But the odd weaponry wasn't as boggling as what they were wearing. Dao had on a pair of pale blue pajamas with little yellow ducks dotted over them. Harley's chest was bare above a pair of brilliantly tie-dyed long john bottoms. Boomer covered his eyes.

The two men exchanged looks and then took an enormous stride away from each other. They were both making gagging noises.

"What is that you're wearing?" Harley said as he pointed to Dao's pajamas with his knife.

Dao plucked at his lapel. "My momma made these for me. I tell her I am 48 years old. I got a doctorate in mathematics and a 25 year old son of my own and all she ever says is 'but you still my baby'. What am I gonna do, hurt my momma's feelings? And who are you to talk, what do you call those?"

Harley snapped the waistband. "These were a gift from Buffalo Woman at last year's Rendezvous. They are symbolic of some special moments we shared."

"I think she was making fun of you, that's what I think."

"Will you two go back to bed before you wake up the whole house and what are you doing with those nunchuks? I thought you got rid of those after the last time we had to take you in for stitches." Boomer said, turning to lock the door and reset the alarm.

"That was when I cut myself swinging the katano sword. I didn't need stitches after I knocked myself out practicing with the nunchuks," Dao said.

Boomer motioned for them to go back upstairs.

Harley let Dao go first and followed when he was several steps ahead. "Can you tell me why we keep him? He's totally useless," he said over his shoulder to Boomer.

"I am not."

"Are, too."

"My momma like me."

"Well, she's about the only one."

Boomer flipped the light off on them when they had reached the top of the stairs. He heard Harley's voice coming down. "You aren't going to believe this but the ducks glow in the dark."

"If the fashion police ever catch up with those two, it will be life without parole," Boomer said to himself.

He looked back in the girls' room and motioned for Carlita. She got up and straightened the blankets before coming out.

"You go on to bed," he said. "I'll sleep on the couch, just in case."

Carlita nodded and went to the deacon's bench between the two windows. She lifted the lid, pulling a pillow and a couple of blankets out of it. She dropped them onto the couch.

"Mañana."

Boomer fluffed the pillow and shook out the blankets. He stretched out. In a moment, he was squirming. He reached under the cushion and pulled out a tennis ball, then dug around along the back and tugged out a shoe, a brush and a stick. He settled and the house became quiet.

* * *

Outside, a man lay in the shadow of the boards enclosing one of the raised garden beds. He shivered from the dampness soaking through his clothes while the fire of remaining motionless for so long burned in his joints.

At last the moon advanced so the house's shadow fell over him, creating a dark passageway to the trees. His cold body was stiff and uncooperative as he forced it to crawl towards the safety of the woods. Once he made sanctuary, he leaned against the trunk of a Douglas fir to allow his heart rate to slow. He had been terrified of discovery when the little girl had suddenly come running out of the house.

Using the tree as a support, he pushed himself to his feet, stamping them quietly to return circulation. The night was growing short.

* * *

Boomer was sitting on the stairs sipping his coffee as he waited for the girls to come out for breakfast. He was anxious to see Alyson; to see if she had any memory of what had propelled her into the night.

"Hold still, Alyson," Katy said as she, Alyson and Brandy emerged from the dorm room. "Your band is coming off." Alyson stopped in front of Boomer and Katy slipped the elastic off and began to wind it more securely around the end of the long braid. Although Alyson's face was once again set in its still expression, Boomer detected traces of an emotional storm in the slightly swollen eyelids and pale cheeks. Something had made her cry in the night.

Brandy stopped to wait. She looked at Boomer and her forehead wrinkled as though she was trying to remember something. Then she snapped her fingers. "You won't believe this but I had the weirdest dream last night. I dreamed that Alyson was running away down the driveway and you were chasing her."

Boomer looked sharply at Alyson but she was merely looking at Brandy with mild curiosity. "Where was I going?" she asked.

Brandy shrugged and the three girls headed toward the dining room. "I dunno. You were the one who was running, you tell me."

Boomer was still sitting when Dao came down the stairs, securing an obi around his kimono top. He was talking to himself.

"He gives me any trouble about my pajamas and I am going to publish pictures of him in his long johns on the Web. Significant meaning, my a...."

"Hey, David," Boomer said. "Sit down a minute."

Dao folded himself into a cross legged position on the steps. Boomer looked around for potential eavesdroppers. But the smell of Harley's sourdough waffles with homemade blueberry syrup and crisp smoked bacon had the kids shooting by as if Dao and he were invisible.

"I don't wanna hear nothin' about my pajamas."

Boomer shook his head to clear the memory of them from it. "No. It's about Alyson."

"She remember last night?"

"Apparently not. Brandy picked up on it...thought it was a dream she had. But it looked to me like Alyson had a rough time before it happened, like she had been crying hard about something."

Dao shook his head slowly. "Damn...that hurts. She still doesn't understand she's not alone. That there are people in her corner now."

Boomer nodded in agreement. "Yeah. But she didn't survive by trusting. I think that is going be a long time coming. We just have to be there and wait. I have a more immediate concern now. We have no idea what triggers her trances. She just pops off with apparently no warning she's going and comes back with no idea of where she's been."

"That's the way it is with her type of ability. Look at Edgar Cayce and Eileen Garrett."

"But they entered trances at will."

Dao nodded his head thoughtfully. "I see where you're heading. Can Alyson be taught to control the when of her trances."

"Exactly. We got lucky last night. The alarm went off. But what if the same thing happens during the day when everybody's busy? This is a helleva big mountain to lose one little girl on."

Dao's eyes widened. "That's a scary thought." He sat quietly staring at his folded his hands for a couple of minutes. "Are you sure she was in a trance? It might have just been a somnambulatory nightmare...a sleep walking event brought on by whatever it was that upset her last night."

Boomer shook his head. "I don't think so. When I caught up with her it was like she was looking or listening for something. She came out it just like she has before. And today, it was clear she had absolutely no recall of leaving the house."

"Yeah, I'd say a trance state." Dao was silent a moment. "I'll call a couple of our resource people. I have to know exactly how to guide her; otherwise we might shut her down. She's at the age when so many of them lose their psychic connection."

Boomer nodded soberly. "I know. What a sad twist of fate if, after paying the price she's paid for possessing her ability, we were the ones to end up taking it from her. But I would rather have that happen than to court tragedy."

Dao put out a hand and used Boomer's shoulder to lever himself to his feet. "As my dear departed daddy used to say, "Faith, brother.""

Harley's voice was heard in the dining room. "Everybody full? Okay, I guess Ruby and Minnow are gonna have to eat these last couple of waffles and the rest of the bacon."

Dao leaned over the banister. "If you're feeding my breakfast to that stinkweed and miniature flea transport again, I am seriously going to have to mess you up, rainbow drawers."

"Oh, yeah, ducks? Bring it on," Harley called back.

The cell phone started to ring as Boomer stood up. He pulled it off his belt. "Boomer."

"Boom, it's Garner and I want you to know right off, I'm calling you under duress."

"From whom?" Boomer's voice was guarded

"My sister."

"Sister?"

"Yeah. She went to dinner with the wife and myself last night. She pumped me pretty good about the rescue."

"So?"

"So she wormed it out of me about the help you guys gave."

"And this is a bad thing, right?"

"Uh-huh," Garner sighed. "She's got a problem with missing fingerprints."

"Wanna run that one by again?"

"Sorry, here's the deal. Lacey is a realtor. She sells houses."

"I've heard of them."

"Anyway she's selling this house on the backside of the mountain from you. Now it seems there are getting to be a lot of strange stories going around about it. Although the house is empty, people are claiming to see lights in it at night. She also says that she sometimes thinks that someone has been in it although there is no evidence. It's more like a smell or a feeling."

"So why doesn't she call the law?"

"Actually, I went through it a couple of weeks ago."

"And?"

"It's a typical '70s three bedroom ranch. What can I say? It's totally empty. Only things left in it are the stove, refrigerator, washer and dryer. I saw nothing to indicate anything was going on. I told Lacey that. She agreed and decided the rumors were coming from some bored little old lady who had read one too many Stephen King novels. And then..."

"Let me guess. The missing fingerprints."

"Right. She had a showing of the house and the people who came had a little kid with them who was slobbering on a lollipop. He left a bunch of sticky red smudges on the dryer when he was playing with its door. Lacey came back early the next morning to clean them off and they were gone. The place was spotless."

"So somebody else could have come in. The owners. Another realtor."

"Not likely. The owner is an elderly woman who is in assisted care now. Her daughter lives in Seattle. No other family in the vicinity. Lacey checked the RMLS; they handle those lockboxes they put on houses. They apparently can run a list of everyone who may have gotten the keys out of the box. The last entry was Lacey the night before."

"And now she wants to talk to me about the habits of discarnates and whether nocturnal cleaning is one of the signs for determining whether or not a spirit is in residence."

"Look, Boomer, I wouldn't ask this except once my sister gets an idea, she is relentless. She never quits until she gets what she's after."

"Sounds like she would have made a good cop."

"Inflicting her on unsuspecting criminals would be cruel and unusual punishment, trust me."

"You know the rules about people coming up here. I'll have to meet her in town."

"I told her about that. She's okay with it. She wondered when and where it might be convenient for you to meet."

"Thursday's supply day so that would be a good time. Say 10:30 a.m. at that cafe in the Main Street Showhouse?"

"I'll call and let her know. If there's any problem I'll call you back before Thursday."

"Fine. You gonna be there?"

"No. You're on your own. We got a bunch of DEA agents coming in. They got some bust they want to coordinate with us. Thanks, Boomer. I owe you."

Chapter 11

The ranch was awash in spring fever by Thursday morning. Several consecutive days of warm, sunny weather had the kids operating in slow motion as they drifted through their chores and sat mindlessly in their classes.

Buttery gold light filled the kitchen as Domingo came up from the basement carrying a stack of clean dishtowels. It was his week to help out in the laundry. Alyson was just pouring soap into the dishwasher.

He looked at the clock on the back wall. "Oh, man. We're gonna be late to math class. You know what that means."

"An extra page of problems," she said with a grimace. She flipped the dishwasher door closed, locked it and turned it on. "I'll get the drawer."

The kids were stuffing the towels in the drawer when the back door flew open. Harley and Aimee squeezed through at the same time. Harley was holding his wrist while Aimee kept a tight grip on a paper towel wrapped around his finger.

When they reached the sink, she turned on the cold water and shoved his hand under it. The water ran red for a moment as it washed blood from Harley's index finger.

Aimee caught the kids' wide-eyed look. She grimaced. "Bandito bit him."

Domingo stepped up to the sink to watch as Aimee poured some antiseptic soap on the torn skin. Harley remained stoic but his foot was jiggling in time to the stinging.

"I told you he was feeling bad. It makes him grumpy," Domingo said.

Aimee was scrubbing away at the wound not noticing Harley had his eyes screwed up tight. "What's wrong with him, Dom?"

"I'm not sure. It has something to do with his hip. It aches and he can't sleep good so he's feeling mean."

"Is there something I can fix for him?"

Domingo shook his head. "He tells how he feels but he can't seem to tell me what he needs. I wish I knew lots more about raccoons so I knew how to make him feel better."

"Yeah, I know what you mean," Aimee sighed. "I'm good with people stuff..."

"No you're not," Harley said as he sucked his cheeks in and then blew them out, "You're killing me."

She rolled her eyes at him and pulled his hand out from under the water. She went into the pantry and they could hear bottles and cans clinking around on the medicine shelf. She came back out, pulling the top off an old baking powder can. She was putting powdered sweet clover on Harley's finger when she glanced out the window over the sink.

"Those rotten chickens are in the garden. They're scratching up the peas we just planted," she shrieked. She thrust the can at Harley and shot out of the room.

Harley watched worriedly out the window. "Dom, get out there. She's reaching down their craws to get the pea seeds back. Hurry or we won't have another egg 'til Christmas."

Domingo took off at a dead run.

Harley looked at Alyson. "The way that female acts about her plants you would think she had a lobotany."

Alyson looked at Harley with a completely serious face. She just shook her head to indicate her rating of his joke as she went to the pantry to get the box of band-aids.

Boomer came into the kitchen, shoving a checkbook in his back pocket. He went to the basket on the corner of the counter and began picking out the envelopes to be mailed.

"You about ready?" he asked Harley.

"As soon as Alyson slaps a band-aid on my finger."

"Cut yourself?"

"No, Bandito bit me."

"I wonder if we need to get a tetanus shot?"

Harley was holding his finger out for Alyson. "Nah, I had one just a couple of years ago."

"I was thinking of Bandito."

Alyson giggled.

"Fine, go ahead and laugh at his jokes. I was going to give an excuse to Dao for you but I think you should do an extra page of problems. Teach you whose humor to appreciate."

Boomer motioned for Alyson to hold up while he came over to check the wound. "You might need a stitch or two in that, Har."

"No way, padre. Me and emergency rooms don't get along, remember?"

Alyson tilted her head quizzically.

Boomer read her question. "He fainted last time we took him in."

"You fainted?" Alyson asked as she looked at Harley. She was clearly trying to picture the event.

"Thanks a lot, big guy. Let's just put it on the intercom."

"I won't tell," Alyson said as she maneuvered the band-aid onto Harley's finger. Boomer leaned over and whispered something in her ear. Even though she didn't look up, she added, "If you tell Dr. Dao why I'm late to class."

"He put you up to that, didn't he?" Harley glared at Boomer, "You're a fine influence around here."

* * *

Lacey Emery found it hard to sip her coffee while she was busy turning her head to look from Main Street across the parking lot to Molalla Avenue and back. She had asked her brother to set up this meeting but she wasn't sure she was comfortable with it. Although Kevin said this Boomer was a straight up kind of guy, she was finding it hard to believe considering he was running a ranch for the paranormal. But still if she didn't get to the bottom of the rumors surrounding the Krevitski house, it would soon be unmarketable and she knew the daughter badly needed the money to provide for Mrs. K's care.

A battered blue pickup pulled up in front of the feed store on Molalla Avenue. As she watched, a tall, lanky man dressed as though he planned a return trip to the mid 19th century got out. Lord that was probably him, long red ponytail and all. Kevin was, no doubt, sniggering up his sleeve at her right now.

She breathed a little easier when the man circled around the front of the pickup and stood for a moment on the sidewalk, apparently talking to someone before disappearing from her line of vision.

A second man emerged from the pickup. He came around, giving a quick glance up and down the street before crossing in her direction. He walked with an assured, purposeful stride. Under his windbreaker, his tee-shirt fit nicely over a broad chest while his jeans covered strong thighs. It was an attractive solid looking body filled out by maturity with no apparent running to softness and fat.

He stopped at the mailbox in the center of the parking lot and dropped in a sheaf of envelopes before continuing in her direction. She stood up as he stepped onto the porch.

"Boomer?" she asked. He nodded and she held out her hand. "I'm Lacey Emery, Kevin's sister."

"I'll just get some coffee and be back. You need anything?"

She shook her head no.

In a couple of minutes, he set his cup on the table and pulled out the white wrought-iron patio chair. As he settled himself, she studied his face. It was creased, with deep lines radiating from the corners of his eyes and cutting down his cheeks. There were still a few pock marks from a long ago acne. His once dark hair was liberally salted with grey. Brushed back, it curled under slightly just above his jacket collar.

Boomer folded his broad, capable hands on the table. "Your brother tells me you are having some kind of problem with one of the houses you have for sale. That there are stories about supposedly unusual things happening there."

Lacey decided to match his cool matter-of-fact tone. "That's right. Some of the neighbors have seen lights at odd hours of the night."

"What kind of lights? Like somebody turned on a light in a room or the ubiquitous eerie glow moving from window to window?"

She took umbrage with his implication. "I know you came as a favor to my brother but I have been selling houses for over 10 years. I have run into everything from dry rot to possums nesting in basements to pot plants on the patio, but so far titles were the only things I encountered that were unquiet. There is something unusual going on with the Krevitski house and I intend to get to the bottom of it. Kevin's so het up about your kids' talents, I thought maybe they could help me sort it out."

"Let me explain about my kids. They aren't a bunch of side show freaks to be trotted out when somebody wants to have a private performance of *"The Exorcist"* or to carry on a conversation with dear departed Aunt Maude. Their abilities are tenuous and vulnerable. It's my job along with the rest of the staff to help them gain control of their particular talents and constructively integrate them so they will be able to function in the quote normal unquote world."

"So you won't help me."

"That depends on your expectations. If you are looking for Ouija boards, channeling or séances, the answer is unconditionally no. These kids already are open to unseen forces. Anything along those lines would place them in the gravest of dangers."

"I don't know if I believe in any of that stuff. I wouldn't expect it of you or any of your kids."

"What do you expect, Mrs. Emery?"

"Ms. I'm divorced," she said automatically. "And I don't really know what I expect because I guess I don't really understand what it's all about."

"What what's all about?"

"Spirit Wind, your kids, the whole thing. For example, where do your kids learn that stuff? Do you teach it to them?"

"Generally, their abilities begin to manifest somewhere when they are toddlers, maybe even before, although they are unable to articulate it. It's not uncommon. Probably the majority of children are born with some level of psychic skills. Yet for many, the actual awareness of them disappears by the time they enter school. A good portion of the remaining will lose contact with it by junior high. Very few retain an active awareness and the ability to call upon and utilize their particular talent into adulthood."

"But where does it come from to begin with?"

Boomer shrugged as he took a drink from his cup. "It depends on your particular school of thought. Those with a bent towards theology will tell you it is the language of the soul, the means through which God has had discourse with man since the dawn of time. Psi researchers are also favoring the concept that it is vestigial knowledge left over like our wisdom teeth or appendix from a more primitive time when humans had no language and no written word. That it was a way of tapping into what Jung termed the great river of collective unconsciousness to find the means to survive. As we developed and created language, the written word, tools and ways of understanding and controlling the world, it began to fall into disuse until we no longer recognize or acknowledge it."

"But you have to admit, most people don't accept such things as being real."

Boomer smiled. "Most people aren't aware they actually do believe. Think for minute, how many times have you heard people say 'My gut told me', 'I had a hunch', or 'I should have listened to my feelings'. Everyone has had flashes of déjà vu. Let's take your business for example, have you ever picked up the phone and called someone to see if they were interested in selling their house and found out they had indeed been thinking of it?"

Lacey felt the color rising in her face. "Yes, I have."

"What made you make that call?"

She shifted uncomfortably. "It was just an impulse...I mean, I never thought about it...maybe, I had overheard something..."

"Maybe your thoughts were connecting with someone else's on a level you simply don't recognize."

"But science should be able to..."

"To what? Weigh, measure and dissect these things? Tell me; what instruments can decode a thought? Or track the trajectory of an unspoken intent? Or follow the flight of a dream?"

"That's very poetic." She looked at him with the feeling she had glimpsed something she wasn't supposed to. Somewhere in this tough man was a very tender stratum. It piqued her curiosity.

It was Boomer's turn to shrug uncomfortably. He placed his empty cup on the table. "So back to the original problem. How about I bring a few of the kids out one morning and just let them walk through the house to see if they pick up any information?'"

She reached for her day planner and opened it. "What would work for you?"

"Saturday starts the kid's spring break. So we can either do it tomorrow or wait until after they're back to schedule it."

"If you don't mind, I'd like to do it as soon as possible. Much longer and the damage may be irreparable."

He stood up. "Give me the address and we'll see you there about 10:30 a.m. tomorrow."

She pulled out a business card and scribbled the address on the back of it. "I'm looking forward to it....I think," she said as she handed the card to him.

Her face was thoughtful as she watched him cross back to the pickup.

Chapter 12

Aimee's mood was definitely pissy when she came out of the ramshackle building that served as her apartment above and the gardening center below. She didn't know why those stupid chickens were allowed to run free when they were never going to be eaten. The kids couldn't bear the thought of one them going to the great chicken coop in the sky by any other means than dying peacefully of very advanced old chicken age. And Harley could just stuff his arguments about how they helped by eating bugs. They much preferred her tender little sprouts and freshly planted seeds. They would even settle for a plump, perfectly ripened tomato. Oh, yeah, there was the fertilizer they provided, but Blossom and Clovis provided plenty of fertilizer and nobody thought it was inhumane to keep the two milk cows from running free in the garden area.

She pulled her work gloves on and slammed her bucket of gardening tools down at the edge of the herb bed. The bucket struck something causing it to catapult into the air and land a few inches away.

She saw the handle of a knife sticking up; its blade embedded in the grass. She bent down and picked it up. It was a small hunting knife. It's vintage decades old. The handle was covered with well worn black leather while the blade was narrow and very thin from countless sharpenings. She turned it over curiously. She didn't recall ever seeing anyone with it.

Growing voices from the other side of the house let her know Chayote was returning from a totem seeking trip into the woods with the four older kids.

He stopped the kids with upraised arms at the front porch. "The Wednesday after spring break I want a 5 page paper on what you perceive to be your totem. I expect some research on the meaning of your totem and why you have chosen to take it into your life; what you expect to learn from your choice and how it may guide you in the future. You will also be graded on your spelling and grammar."

The groans started as soon as he lowered his arms.

"What if we haven't figured out our totem? Do we still have to do a paper?" Ralph asked.

"Those of you who found no totem can do a 10 page paper on why you have been rejected by the spirit world and what you must do to seek propitiation from them."

"Geez," Ralph said as they turned to enter the house. "Anyone got a totem they can loan me for a week?"

"Chayote," Aimee called when the kids had disappeared. She waved him over when he turned toward her. "Do you know whose knife this is?"

He took it from her and examined it carefully. Shaking his head, he handed it back. "Where'd you find it?"

She pointed to the ground by her bucket. "Here."

Squatting, he scanned the ground, then lifted the bucket and set it aside. Under it was several small piles of cut herbs. Aimee knelt down and studied them. "Lobelia, comfrey, yarrow. Look," she pointed to the wilted plants. "Whoever cut these knew exactly which part of the plant to harvest and which was at the correct stage of growth for maximum potency."

Aimee stood up and leaned over to examine the herb bed. She reached in and picked out several more cut plants. 'Skullcap and yellow dock." She laid them beside the plants on the ground. "Tranquilizer, antiseptic, anti-spasmodic, blood purifier...somebody is treating a pretty broad range of health issues."

"Moon harvest," Chayote said. "It was a full moon last night."

Aimee sat back on her heels. "Cameras. I wonder if Jesse ran a tape last night." She jumped to her feet. "Let's find out." She started toward her apartment.

Chayote motioned in the other direction. "Ah, Aimee, the house is still that way."

"I know," she answered over her shoulder, "but I have a notebook I need to get."

Aimee, Chayote and Jesse were in the computer room when Boomer came into the house. The air was redolent with the smell of Carlita's enchiladas, burrios, and tamales. He sniffed appreciatively as his stomach reminded him he hadn't eaten this morning.

"Boomer," Aimee's voice was excited as she called to him from her place next to the television monitor. "I think we may have some answers."

"Great," he said. "Anyone want to remind me what the questions were?" The area was littered with calendars, Aimee's notebook, and a stack of video tapes.

"Our herb thief was here last night, only something happened that scared him off."

"That must have happen when..." Boomer stopped abruptly. He didn't want to discuss last night in front of Jesse. Apparently, Aimee and Chayote hadn't been informed of Alyson's incident. "So show me."

Jesse rewound the tape and played it through. Boomer saw the shadow emerge and perform as before. Only this time, as the shadow hovered over the herb bed, there was a ripple like static across its blackness and then it vanished. Boomer checked the time on the video. It said 2:44 a.m., exactly when Alyson had left the porch.

"Now, look at this," Jesse said. He fast forwarded the tape until the time said 3:37 a.m. The whole area had become obscured by the shifting shadow cast by the house. Jesse paused the tape and enlarged a portion of the picture. The outline of what could have been a person creeping along the ground appeared very, very faintly. It was only an instant before it was gone. Jesse fast forwarded it again and caught once more what may have been a human being diving into the dark woods.

Aimee, Chayote and Jesse looked at Boomer expectantly. "Okay, so we know for sure whoever is taking herbs is human. But it still doesn't tell us how our security is being jammed and why he or she is so interested in stealing herbs," Boomer said.

"True," Chayote said, "but Aimee's kept a log of the previous thefts. I think maybe we might be able to pinpoint the next time the thief would strike. We could set up some kind of trap and maybe catch whoever it is in action."

Carlita's voice interrupted the discussion. "It is eating time."

"I'm starving. Let's eat first, and then resume this discussion later," Boomer said.

But later never happened as Aimee and Boomer had classes to teach. Then Nate took a tumble out of one of the old apple trees requiring a trip to the emergency room in Silverton to have a badly swollen wrist x-rayed. Fortunately, there were no broken bones; just a nasty sprain.

After splinting it, the doctor scribbled out instructions. "Ice, elevate, and one of those comfrey poultices would be good," he said. "I'd write a pain prescription but I know how you folks are about drugs. Aimee probably has something that will help for a couple of days."

He ripped the sheets apart and handed one to Boomer. "And congratulations on a new record. We haven't seen anyone from Spirit Wind in three months. We were beginning to think you had left the area."

Boomer folded the sheet and jammed it in the pocket of his windbreaker. "Nah. With the wet weather, they haven't had as much opportunity for self-destruction. Now that's its drying out, keep a cubicle ready. We'll be back...and back...and back."

The doctor leaned against the nurse's station. "Can I ask a question, Boomer? Do your kids ever 'see' in advance some of the things that are going to happen and maybe attempt to prevent them?"

Boomer shrugged. "They're kids. They tend to take all but the most serious of any prescient warnings the same way they take me or you saying 'don't climb the apple tree, you could fall and hurt yourself'. In other words, it doesn't matter if the warning is from a human or the cosmos; they're gonna push the boundaries thinking it isn't meant for them. Or they change something thinking that will make it different. Like they sense they will get hurt if they climb the apple tree so they climb the cherry tree instead. They don't recognize that it is the act they are supposed to avoid not just a specific kind of tree."

"So what's Nate's ability?"

"He's a dowser."

"One of those people who find water with sticks or metal rods or something? I saw a clip on the news one time about someone who made his living doing that."

Nate came out of the cubicle with Chayote. His splinted wrist rested in a blue sling. "Hey, Boomer. Chayote says he will rattle me to make my arm better. "

"Aimee sticks one of her poultices on you and Chayote rattles you, you'll be a new man by morning."

"That's not your dowsing arm, is it?" the doctor asked.

"Kinda," Nate said. "Sometimes you need two hands when you're looking for stuff."

"Like water?"

"Nah," Nate waved off the idea with his uninjured arm. "I look for good stuff like treasure and lost kids and money and cool stuff."

"So how does it work?"

"First you gotta know what you're looking for cuz what you're hunting tells you how you have to do it."

"Give me an example."

"Well, say you lost your watch," Nate said as he pointed to the doctor's wrist. "You wouldn't wanna use a forked branch because wood doesn't pay any attention to metal. You would use something metal like a rod and then as you scanned it around, when you got close, you would feel the metals talking. Maybe they like each other so they pull together and you feel it. Or maybe they don't like each other and they push apart but you can still feel it. Then you find your watch."

"Which would you use for looking for people...wood or metal."

"Neither. You use a crystal. Crystals are real, real sensitive to energy and they like to follow it."

There was a noise behind them as another patient was brought into the treatment area. The doctor sighed as though he was genuinely disappointed their conversation was being interrupted. "Back to work, guys. No tree climbing for a while, Nate. See you probably sooner than later."

The wipers intermittently flicked the misty rain from the windshield as they drove up the drive. The windows of the house were bright as they pulled into the parking area.

Boomer could see the silhouettes of heads looking out and disappearing in the direction of the front door. An impromptu welcoming committee was being formed for Nate.

A rush of warm air and light enveloped them as Taylor flung open the front door. Mixed in the air was the smell of cocoa and popcorn. Harley was obviously serving up his own healing remedies.

The remainder of the evening sped by as Aimee applied poultices to Nate's wrist and Chayote, having changed into his shaman shirt and necklaces, performed a healing ceremony using his gourd rattles. The swelling had greatly diminished by the time Aimee massaged a lotion of St. John's wort and arnica onto Nate's wrist and replaced the splint to protect it during the night. Harley slipped a small piece of uncut amethyst under the elastic bandage. "That'll help you sleep and keep the pain down," he said as he adjusted the sling around Nate's neck.

Jesse and Alyson gathered up the used cups and bowls and carried them to the kitchen.

"Look," Alyson said as she put the cups in the sink.

"What?" Jesse asked.

"The glasses. They are all laid down."

"Helga must be back. She's always worried about the glasses getting knocked over and broken. She just doesn't understand about plastic."

"Helga?"

"She's Canute's wife. They originally homesteaded this place back in the 1860's I think it was. Anyway, they still hang out here."

"Ghosts?" Alyson looked around as though she expected something to suddenly appear behind her.

"No, they're discarnates. People whose bodies have died but their spirits stick around for a while. Ghosts are different. We don't have any of them."

Alyson edged closer to Jesse. "Does anyone ever see them?" she asked taking quick nervous peeks over her shoulder.

Jesse was rinsing out the cups. He handed them to Alyson to put in the dishwasher. "I've been trying to get pictures of them using some of the techniques I've been reading about. No luck so far."

Jesse washed the bowls and stacked them in the dish drainer. "Actually, it's pretty neat having them around. I got really sick last year. Strep throat and I felt like I was going to burn right up. I was having a really hard time sleeping. I kept having these really weird dreams and my throat would get dry and wake me up when I tried to swallow. Then it was like somebody put something super cold on my forehead. It felt good and next thing I know I had slept a long time and when I woke up my throat hardly hurt at all. Carlita told me it was Helga who had stayed with me. It's kinda like having your grandma take care of you only you can't see her."

He took a few swipes of the counter with the dishcloth before tossing it over the faucet. "Come on, that's good enough."

Jesse bounded into the living room. "Hey, Boomer, Helga's back. The glasses were all laid down."

"That's good. Welcome back, Helga," he said and the kids echoed him. "Helga! That reminds me. We've got a little practice field trip tomorrow for Alix, Taylor, Johnathan and Alyson."

"What are we going to do?" Alix asked.

"We're going to drive around the mountain and walk through a house."

"A haunted house? I wanna come and try out some of my equipment," Jesse said.

"I sincerely doubt that it is haunted. It's just an empty house for sale but it's close and will give the four of you a chance to practice picking up information."

"I like where I get to practice better," Brandy said as she headed towards the girls' room.

"Where's that?" Alyson asked Taylor.

"She and Dylan get to go to one of the malls like Clackamas Town Center or Washington Square. It helps them listen to lots of people and practice filtering out and focusing in on one person's thoughts." She suddenly giggled. "Hey, Boomer, remember when you pretended you were Santa Claus last year at Washington Square?"

"Oh, yeah," Dylan said, "that was so cool."

"Tell me," Alyson begged. She had uncovered an insatiable desire to know people's stories. It was like reading living books.

"Well, we were at Washington Square, only we weren't there for Brandy and Dylan to practice. We were doing Christmas shopping. And while we were there, Brandy started to hear this one person's thoughts. She was trying to figure out how to steal some stuff, but she was really upset and scared inside. So Brandy kinda followed her and listened to her. She was a momma with two little kids and she had no money and she wanted really, really bad to give her kids something for Christmas so she figured she would just have to steal something for them."

Theresa took up the story. "Brandy told Boomer she was afraid this girl would get into lots of trouble and go to jail and then the little kids wouldn't even have their momma for Christmas."

"So Boomer goes up and tells her he's Santa Claus and he's got a whole bunch of elves that need some training and would she mind helping them out."

"You could see she thought she had found a real nut case," Jesse laughed.

"He told her that each of us had to buy some presents for someone and could we buy them for her kids?" Theresa said.

"So we took her all over the mall and bought lots and lots of stuff for the kids. She got more and more excited and happy. And we bought stuff to decorate a tree and some Christmas stockings. And Carlita got a gift card so she could buy food."

"It was so much fun. Maybe we can do it again this year," Taylor said.

"Yeah, well, we got a while before we need to worry about it. Everybody hit the hay now. Alix, Taylor, Johnathan and Alyson, be ready by 10:15 a.m.," Boomer said.

Chapter 13

He sat crouched under the tree and watched the lights in the house go out room by room. He looked across to the lodge house. The night had turned drizzly so there would be no fire in the pit tonight.

Kip had been hiding in the hills for almost six months before he realized this place was some kind of kids' home. He had always carefully kept to the far side of the ridge to prevent awkward encounters and possibly unpleasant consequences. But one of his trackings had brought him to the crest of the hill rising up behind the ramshackle collection of buildings. Hiding in the shadows, he had watched the inhabitants go about their activities. It had stoked the loneliness in him but the price of human companionship had come to cost too much. He satisfied himself by coming to watch them now and again.

One day when he saw everyone load up in the two vans and leave, he sneaked onto the ranch. He wandered around, peeked in the windows and looked in the sheds. That was when he had discovered the marvelous herb beds. He had been wildcrafting what he could find but the beds had given him a whole pharmacopoeia. He took to creeping in and getting a slip here, a start there, to plant but many of the herbs needed to be well established before they produced the necessary potency. Sometimes the need could not wait and he had to sneak in rather more often than he liked in order to get the supplies he needed.

That was what had brought him to huddle in his camouflage poncho under the trees. In his fright last night he had left the herbs he had cut. The necessity for them had not gone away just because he had almost been caught. He would have to risk going in again. He only hoped that if they had found his handiwork, they would assume he would not be making another foray so soon.

Chapter 14

When his cell phone rang just before 10, Boomer assumed it was Nate's parents returning his call about the fall. He was taken off guard when a woman's voice breathed his name into his ear.

"Mr. Evanrud, how kind of you to take my call at this hour."

The voice jangled a memory but he couldn't place it. "Who is this?"

"Someone who wishes to make a business proposition with you."

"Lady, if you are selling something, I'm not interested."

"Actually, I was thinking more of an exchange. I have something you can use and you have something of mine that I want back."

The quarter dropped and he knew who was on the other end of the phone. "Ms. Maguire."

"Oh, no. I much prefer to go by Mrs. Maguire. I'm afraid I'm just not one of those liberated women. You see I like having other people take care of all those unpleasant little details that can cause one to age."

"So what are you doing making your own calls?"

"I had intended for my attorney to call and present my little proposition to you but unbelievably, people often have scruples about what they will and will not do."

"Yes, I am sure that must come as a shock to you, Mrs. Maguire."

Her laugh had a throatiness some might consider sexy. It grated on Boomer's ear. "I do have scruples when they suit my purpose."

"Cut to the chase, Mrs. Maguire. What do you want?"

"I want to offer you a considerable sum of money in the form of a grant from the Maguire Foundation in exchange for you convincing the court it would be in everyone's best interests if Alyson was returned to me."

"Everyone's best interests? You mean your best interests, don't you?"

"Well, of course. Who else's matter?"

"You have nothing I want, Mrs. Maguire. Least of all your money. Goodbye."

"Whales? Why am I seeing whales? Oh, dear, I seem to be looking down a gun barrel at the whales. Did you do something naughty, Mr. Evanrud?"

Boomer's hand tightened so hard around the little cell phone the plastic pieces creaked in protest.

"Oh, I really must look into that. You see I have learned nearly everyone has a skeleton or two they would pay dearly to keep hidden in the closet. And would you look at this, here I am offering to pay you instead. Life is full of little ironies."

"Good night, Mrs. Maguire."

"Just remember, Mr. Evanrud. I did give you a choice."

He pushed the disconnect button and found his hands were shaking when he tried to clip the phone back on his belt.

Only two people had been on the dock that day and one of them was dead. By what means did Rhonda Maguire acquire information?

He went back downstairs and double checked all the locks and the alarm. It did little to assuage his foreboding.

* * *

"Simon, darling, it's Rhonda. I do hope I am not calling too late. I have a little job for you. I want you to find out everything you can about a man named Russell Evanrud. That's E-V-A-N-R-U-D. I am afraid you will just have to start from scratch. All I can tell you is his name and that he is now the director of someplace called Spirit Wind Ranch in Molalla."

"Why how perceptive you are, yes, that is the place I have sued and he is, indeed, the odious man I spoke of in my interview. I want every dirty detail you can find out about him, most particularly if he ever had anything to do with whales. You see, I believe Mr. Evanrud may have done something quite shocking and I want the proof in my hands ASAP."

"Oh, yes, that was a lovely bit of work you did on my dear friend, Carl. It always makes me feel so good when I can verify my little insights. Carl and I are going to share a much closer working relationship in the future thanks to you. Well, ta-ta, darling, and remember, I do mean ASAP."

Chapter 15

There was an edginess to the day as the sun warily watched the clouds pile up above the Coast Range. The wind carried a sharpness sending the kids back to grab jackets and sweatshirts before they piled into the van for their trip around the mountain. Boomer turned his face into the briskness using it to clear his mind. Ghosts had drifted through his sleep as the graves of old memories opened and closed turning the past into dark dreams and bad sleep.

Sitting on the stoop of the white house, Lacey looked serene in a padded ivory jacket quilted over with cranes. The sun caught copper glints in her cropped dark brown hair as she bent over the large drawing tablet in her lap. She looked up as the van pulled into the driveway, her hand holding the pencil poised over the pad. She watched Boomer turned in his seat to talk to the kids he had brought. The sunlight on the window obscured her view of them.

Boomer swung out of the van and walked toward her. Although his stride was as sure as yesterday, she saw his face was tired and shadows lurked in his eyes. "As far as the kids know, we are here strictly for a practice session. They know nothing at all about this house or any problems associated with it."

"And you don't want me to say anything that might unduly influence or cloud their impressions."

Boomer's expression let her know he was pleased with her perspicacity. "Precisely."

"Understood."

He turned and waved his arm at the van. She heard the van side door slide open. Four kids peeked around the back of the van and then came to stand next to Boomer. They looked at her with shy curiosity. She felt herself startled at the ordinariness of the kids. They were just young teenagers. She wasn't sure what she had been expecting. Maybe kids who were Goth with green dyed hair and multiple piercings.

"Kids, this is Lacey Emery. She's the lady who is selling this house and who has been kind enough to let us use it for practice."

"I'm glad you came. Would it be inappropriate for me to come in with you? I promise to stay out of the way." The kids just shrugged so Lacey looked to Boomer for guidance.

"You can stay with me."

Lacey nodded and, tucking her drawing tablet under her arm, she went to the door and opened it. Boomer herded the kids into the house and then leaned against the jamb of the open door. Lacey looked at him in surprise. She thought he would at least go in the house with them.

She watched closely. The kids milled around in the living room. A sturdily built, blonde girl was lightly running her hand over the walls and along the window sills. She glanced at Boomer and shrugged as if to say nothing much here. The boy with the wire-rimmed glasses stood still in the middle of the room. He closed his eyes and remained stock still for several moments. When he opened his eyes, it was clear he wasn't sensing anything of interest. The slender brunette was conferring with the blonde. They wandered towards the dining area trailed by the boy. The youngest looking of the four, an undersized girl with waist length pale blonde hair, brought up the rear.

As they stood by the door, Lacey could hear the hum of voices. There seemed to be a growing undercurrent as if they were learning something. Lacey leaned through the door as far as she could; trying to decipher the voices coming from the kitchen/laundry room area. Then the boy stuck his head around the corner of the dining room.

"Boomer, Alyson is in a trance."

Boomer stepped into the house and followed Johnathan around to the kitchen. Alyson was standing beside the dryer, her hand resting lightly on the top. She had a remote expression and her blue eyes were glazed over. Lacey had followed quietly. She was startled when she saw the girl. It reminded her of a friend from college who had been epileptic. She would get the same blank expression just prior to a seizure. She glanced quickly at the rest of the kids. They didn't seem alarmed. They were watching with interest. Boomer went to the girl and squatted down in front of her, observing her closely.

Tears were welling up in her eyes and her lower lip was trembling. Although she didn't seem to see him, it was as though she sensed Boomer's presence and spoke to him.

"They hurt and they don't know why. They're so frightened. They need him. He's scared sometimes. He's all alone." She stopped to gulp air.

"Who is it, Alyson?" Boomer voice was very gentle and low. "Can we help him?"

But it was slipping away. For the first time, Alyson was aware that she had gone into her 'other place' as she thought of it and she felt herself leaving it. She also felt a terrible pang as though the place she had gone was somehow needful to her. Then it was gone. She found herself looking into Boomer's face. She hurled herself into his arms. He felt her shaking. As he held her, he knew something different had happened this time. She had always come out of her trances disengaged, not knowing where she had gone or why. But this time it was as though she had brought something back with her. In a few moments, it passed. Alyson pulled away and drew a deep breath.

"Okay, baby?"

She nodded.

"Why don't you go outside with Lacey? Maybe she will show you what she was drawing."

Lacey started. She had been so engrossed by what was happening, she had forgotten about the drawing pad she still clutched.

"Alyson LOVES to draw," the dark haired girl said. "She's good, too."

Lacey held out her hand to Alyson. "Oh, it's always so much fun when I get to meet someone who likes to draw."

When Alyson and Lacey were outside the house, Boomer leaned against the counter. "Okay, anybody else pick up anything?" he asked.

"Well, it's a man but only in the bathroom and around here," Taylor said indicating the washer and dryer.

"He's doesn't live here. It's like he comes here for a reason and leaves," Johnathan said. "I get the feeling he's like sneaking and kinda scared every time he comes here."

Alix was lightly stroking the top of the washer. "I know this is gonna sound really weird but it's like I have felt him before."

"You mean like it's somebody we know?" Boomer asked.

"Not exactly. More like maybe I touched something of his once. It's just kinda of feeling I have."

"Well, maybe you'll remember. Anything else?" The kids shook their heads no. "So who's hungry? Anybody for McDonald's?"

The whoop echoed through the empty house.

The kids stopped short of running over Lacey and Alyson. "Hey, we're gonna go to McDonald's, Alyson. Come on."

The three kids leaped off the stoop and were hurtling for the van when Boomer's voice stopped them. "Anyone got anything to say?"

They halted. "Thanks for letting us come. Bye, Lacey," Alix said. "Yeah, it was neat," said Taylor. "Thanks," Johnathan said.

Alyson stood up more slowly. She hugged the drawing tablet. It was what real artist's used. Not just sheets of notebook paper. Reluctantly she handed it back. "Thank you," she said in her shy soft voice and followed the rest of the kids to the van.

When Lacey heard the van door slide shut, she turned to Boomer. "She's so fragile. Like she would break in a breeze."

"She's a lot tougher than you would expect. She's survived the mother from hell."

Lacey's eyes widened. "Ohmigod, is that Rhonda Maguire's daughter? I saw her on the news a while back. What a horrible woman!"

Boomer felt a prickle across his neck as he flashed to his phone conversation the night before. "Yeah. She's a piece of work." A shadow passed through him and momentarily darkened his eyes.

Lacey sensed it and it made her uncomfortable. She briskly changed the subject. "So did they find out anything?"

"They picked up some information. There is no discarnate or ghost in the house. It's just a house but the kids seem to have the impression that someone may be sneaking in to use the bathroom and laundry."

"But how? The doors are always locked and the only keys are in the lockbox. I have checked a couple of times with the lockbox computer and they show no one is opening the box for other than accounted for showings."

"Maybe somebody has a key from when Mrs. Krevitski still lived here. A caretaker, handyman, former neighbor."

Lacey shook her head. "Wouldn't matter. I had the locks changed to deadbolts, both front and back, when Mrs. K went to assisted living for that very reason. We couldn't be sure who might have had keys and I didn't want to take any chances."

"Well, it feels like a simple case of somebody breaking and entering. I guess that would put it back in your brother's turf. Give him a call and see what suggestions he might have."

"Yeah, I will after he's done with whatever he working on. A wounded bear would be easier to talk right now."

"Must have a tough case."

"No, he's preoccupied when he has a tough case. When he acts like this it's because he is working on a case that he believes is not valid or appropriate. So be forewarned, if you answer the phone and someone starts barking in your ear, it's Kevin."

"Thanks for the heads up. Well, if I don't get those kids some food, they are going to start eating the upholstery. Hope we were of some help. See you."

"Thanks for taking the time and coming," she said to his retreating back. She hugged her drawing pad to her chest as she watched the van back out and drive off.

* * *

The kids were barely stopping to breathe as they devoured hamburgers, fries and shakes in the big corner booth at the local McDonald's. Boomer found his mind drifting towards his late night conversation. Not good with a sensitive like Johnathan and particularly Alyson in close proximity. He pulled it back and fixed his attention on the large rodeo picture framed in boards covered with branding iron symbols hanging above the entrance to the restrooms. He was trying to decipher each brand when Alyson spoke.

"She's a real artist, did you know that?" she said quietly examining her half-eaten hamburger.

"Who's an artist?" Alix asked as she reached across to dip some French fries in Alyson's ketchup.

Alyson set her hamburger down. "The lady at the house. She told me she went to the art school in Portland; at the museum I think she said. And she's taken lots and lots of classes at other places."

"She is, huh," Boomer said tuning into the conversation.

Alyson's face took on a misty, faraway look. "Maybe someday I can take an art class."

"Would you like to study art, Alyson?" Boomer asked. It was the first time she had ever expressed a desire for anything since she had been at Spirit Wind.

She looked up startled as though she didn't realize she had actually spoken out loud. The flash of apprehension showing in her eyes stabbed at Boomer's heart. Every time he thought they were gaining ground, he realized it was only in micrometers.

An idea began to form in Boomer's head as they drove back to the ranch.

The instant the kids got out of the van, they announced to the others that they had gone out for lunch, setting off a round of whining and kvetching by those who hadn't been involved in the trip.

Boomer put his hands over his ears as he went into the house. He intended to round up a cup of coffee and hide out in his office until it was time to teach his class. His brain felt as cluttered as the living room.

By the time he had gotten his coffee, the kids were starting their afternoon classes. He could hear Carlita working with the younger students in their Spanish studies. The mid-teens were in math, being dragged screaming and kicking through geometry by Dao, and the older students were outside in the plant shed with Aimee who was proceeding with her reverse genetics lesson. The class was trying to unravel groups of tomatoes from their cross-bred state and take them back to the heirloom varieties they had once been.

Boomer opened the door to his office. The sun, momentarily shining through the window, washed the room in cheer. The area closest to the window held the desk and filing cabinet Aimee used to keep the ranch financial records and grant information. Near it was the ranch's business computer. As always, it was perfectly neat with the wood surface of the desk gleaming in the sun. Notes and reminders were pinned in tidy rows to the bulletin board attached to the side of the filing cabinet. By contrast, his own area was awash in papers, scattered files, stacks of books, magazines and what else he couldn't even begin to remember. He sighed as he looked at the mess. He would have to get on it soon or Aimee would drag him in by ear one day to get it cleaned up and organized so it could begin its descent into entropy once again.

He groaned when he couldn't even find a place to set his coffee cup. "No time like the present," Aimee's favorite saying, echoed in his head as he went to get the big trash can from the hall outside the classrooms.

The sorting and dumping proved to be a soothing activity over the next hour. He got folders back into their appropriate hanging files; pitched a mountain of junk mail; sorted magazines and catalogs into stacks to carry across to the staff room and put in the cubbies. He noted with amusement that none of Aimee's gardening and herb magazines were among the collection. She had no compunction about scavenging through his desk when she knew they should have arrived.

He was just hauling the trash can back to the hall when his cell phone rang. He nudged the can back against the wall with his leg as he answered. It was Garner but his voice sounded thin and stretched.

"Boomer, don't ask questions. Just get the kids out on the lawn and open the gate...now."

The tone in Garner's voice electrified all of Boomer's nerves. Something was wrong...very, very wrong. His reply was succinct. "Done."

He stepped across the hall and pushed the fire drill button twice. It emitted two short bursts. He crossed the dining room to the computer room in a dozen long strides and hit the button to open the gate. Around him the kids were racing out the exits to gather under the maple tree. He could hear Carlita and Dao clapping their hands and saying, "Move, move, move."

Harley came out of the kitchen, his expression a question.

"Trouble is about to pay a visit," Boomer said softly. "You know what to do."

Chapter 16

They were all in position as the sheriff's car pulled around into the parking area. It was followed by a SWAT van and an unmarked white car.

Kevlar vested officers poured out of the van, hoisting their guns. They hesitated when they viewed the people standing under the budding branches of the old maple tree.

After watching the arrival for a moment, Boomer looked hard at Brandy, mentally calling her name. She caught it and gave him a quick look. He thought his question. She listened and then leaned toward Jesse and whispered it. Jesse kept his eyes fixed on the action in front of him but he gave an almost imperceptible nod.

A man wearing a dark blue windbreaker with DEA emblazoned on the back got out of the unmarked car and strode up to where the officers had collected.

"What are you doing? They're suspects, now let's make it clear who's in charge here." He was motioning for them to raise their guns.

"They're kids, sir," one of the officers said in a low voice.

The man swung around to study the group. "Holy shit," he said. "Did we hit a time warp getting here?"

He stared at Harley in his customary attire standing with his feet apart and arms crossed over his chest. Chayote, wearing his fringed buckskin shirt and pants, was standing an arm span from Harley in an identical pose. His long grey streaked hair lifted and fell in the light wind, the feather he had twisted in it fluttering. The kids were huddled behind them, eyes wide with fear-tinged curiosity. Carlita and Aimee stood on either side of the kids and Dao had taken up his position behind them.

Boomer stood between the clustered Spirit Wind inhabitants and the front porch, his eyes dark with anger. He looked at Garner whose face was a mask of frustrated misery. Garner met his eyes once. In them, Boomer could read his anguish.

"Do you have a reason for being here? Or did you just want practice terrorizing kids?" Boomer asked in a flint hard voice.

The man pulled off his aviator style sunglasses as he walked towards Boomer. He was reaching inside his windbreaker. "I'm Agent Harmon with DEA. I have a warrant to search this place. We have reason to believe this place is a front for drug dealing."

The man didn't miss the surprise that swept over Boomer's face. It wasn't the reaction he was expecting. Normally this was the point when people got pale, started licking their lips and began looking around for an exit.

"Drugs? We don't have drugs here. What the hell made you think we have drugs?"

The man jerked his thumb in the direction of the kids. "You got teenagers, you got drugs."

Boomer bounced the analogy back at him. "You got cops, you got brutality."

"That's a pretty broad statement, Mr. Evanrud."

"Exactly," Boomer said keeping his eyes fixed on the officer.

"Okay, we have a little more than that." He turned around and signaled the officer who was standing beside the unmarked car. The officer turned to open the back car door. He motioned to someone sitting inside. A man got out. He looked around nervously.

"We've got him," the officer said to Boomer.

"Congratulations." Boomer looked the man over. He was wearing an expensive suit with a color coordinated shirt and power tie. His wing tip shoes were highly polished and would have carried a nice price tag as well. The man's skin was pasty and he kept wiping his nose with a large white handkerchief. He wore designer sunglasses which he kept on even though the sun had now dodged behind a cloud, dimming the afternoon light.

"Come, come, Mr. Evanrud, you do know this man."

Boomer took the time to deliberately study him once more. "Can't say that I do."

"Well, we'll see if your story changes when we get through searching." He turned around to motion the other officers forward.

Boomer spoke from behind him. "Search away. Just remember, this is a state certified home, approved and inspected annually, and it's those kids' home so you better feel real sure of yourself before you go in there and trash it. Understand?"

The agent just gave a glance over his shoulder at Boomer's implacable face before leading five of the SWAT team up the stairs. He turned and spoke to two of the remaining officers. "Keep them covered."

The two men exchanged glances. It was clear they were not happy being ordered to keep their guns at ready around children.

Kip came over the ridge, staying well hidden in the shadows of the trees. He had caught the sound of police radios squawking. If there was a danger of discovery, he wanted to be prepared. He was startled when he saw the county car, the SWAT truck and an unmarked car parked helter-skelter in the big gravel area in front of the house. Seeing the kids and staff standing on the grounds was even more alarming. He crept stealthily closer until he was within ear shot but, he hoped, carefully out of view. He huddled behind a tree to watch. Even though they knew nothing of him, he regarded them as part of his world.

The search team stopped at either side of the open front door. They readied their weapons and then moved through the door in a swift synchronized movement. The exit they made a moment later was much more free-style, with two leaping to the far side of the porch, three leaping off the porch and the sixth dashing for the porch railing.

All eyes were drawn to the door where a small black animal sporting a broad white stripe waddled slowly out, pausing at the top of the stairs. She was oblivious to the guns aimed at her as she sniffed the air.

"Ruby!" Domingo shouted as he began to lunge towards the porch. Harley caught him.

"Steady, Dom," he said as guns swung around in their direction.

"Don't let them shoot Ruby!" he wailed as he wiggled in Harley's grasp. Taylor and Alix began to cry while Brandy and Katy emitted little screams as they covered their faces with their hands.

A long moment passed as the officers searched their minds for the appropriate procedure to govern this situation.

Garner abruptly strode up to the porch and picked up Ruby. He turned and met the sharply disapproving look of Agent Harmon. "Maybe you would like to search the skunk for contraband before I give her to the kid," he said as he held Ruby out. Harmon took an involuntary step back. His lips tightened but he jerked his head in the direction of Domingo.

Garner crossed to Dom and handed over Ruby. He ruffled Dom's hair and gave a quick smile to the rest of the kids.

Harmon motioned to the officers to reassemble around the door. "Any more surprises, Evanrud?"

Boomer's stance was an obdurate wall. "Guess you are going to have to find out, Harmon."

Under the tree, Kip let out a breath he didn't realize he had been holding and felt his muscles relax. He looked with admiration at the stolid Boomer. He was as unyielding as the mountain he stood on.

The agents again did their armed sweep into the house. Once they were inside, they stood looking sharply around. Harmon motioned for two of the men to go upstairs. They began the climb, carefully keeping their backs to the wall and their eyes on the landing above.

"Scope out this floor and the basement, if it's clear then we'll start. I'll stand watch," he said to the remaining three. It was only a few moments before the two men who had been sent upstairs came to the top of the stairs and announced it was empty.

"What you got?"

"Four bedrooms, two baths, some storage."

"Then do it," the man at the foot of the stairs said.

They holstered their guns and one went to the left and the other to the right.

"We got two dorm-type rooms, one for boys and one for girls, living room, computer room, what looks like a library, kitchen, pantry, dining room, some classrooms and offices at the back. Basement has laundry facilities, rec area and storage," one of three agents said as they returned from checking each room.

The agent pointed to one of the men. "You start in the girls' room." He pointed to another. "You start in the boys' room. You do the basement. I'll start with the kitchen."

Upstairs, an agent entered a room. "This must belong to the Hispanic woman," he thought as he looked around at the walls painted the colors of a sunset. It contained a bed covered with a bright woven spread. A large armoire stood against the wall behind the door, the turquoise paint on it faded and chipped as though it were very old. A low bookcase against the wall to the left was topped with what appeared to be a shrine. There was a picture of the Virgin Mary, several tall candles in glass with religious symbols on them, a carved crucifix and a well-handled rosary resting on a Spanish language Bible. The small nightstand next to the bed had a paper shaded lamp and a stack of magazines, also in Spanish. A comfortably worn purple lounge chair sat angled near the window with an orange and yellow afghan folded neatly over the back. Everything was spotless.

The man opened the doors of the armoire. One side was fitted with drawers and the other a closet. He reached in to riffle through the hanging clothes. He snatched his hand away almost instantly. It felt as though someone had sharply slapped it. The door on the armoire swung closed.

He reached out to open the door again, but it refused to give. It was as though someone was standing on the inside holding it shut. He'd pull and it would pull back. A strange feeling began to crawl around his shoulders. There was no one in this room but him. Abruptly, he decided this room was clean and he would move on to the next.

At the opposite end of the landing, the agent entered Boomer's room. It was like entering an aquarium. Painted in the blue-grey greens of the ocean, one wall was fitted with floor to ceiling shelves. They were filled with dozens of whales...orca whales. There were carved wooden representations in the style of the Haida and Tlingit tribes. There were photos. One large one of a breaching whale was beautifully framed. A tiny brass plaque attached to it was engraved with the word "Minowah". Another small whale had been created entirely of black and white seed beads. There was an ivory tusk, yellowed with age, depicting a scrimshaw whale. There was even a Beany Baby® whale.

The tallboy dresser appeared to be hand constructed of cedar and the drawer fronts were carved with swimming whales. The wood framed mirror above the dresser had been made by the same hands as was the headboard to the single wide bed and the small chest sitting at the foot of the bed. He'd start with the chest.

The agent lifted the lid and found it contained quantities of old notebooks. He picked one out and flipped it open. The handwriting was distinctly feminine but he couldn't make heads or tails of what it was about. It appeared to be field notes of some kind. There were measurements and cryptic numbers, dates and times. The dates were more than 25 years old. There was an air of mustiness coming from the chest as though it hadn't been opened for a long time. He put the notebook back and began to paw deeper into the chest when he heard a sound, like the clearing of a throat.

Jumping to his feet, he looked around the room. He caught a motion out of the corner of his eye. He swung around to face the dresser, his hand automatically clamping over the gun butt.

A woman's face appeared in the mirror. Ash blonde hair waved back from an attractive face. She smiled sweetly as she looked him right in the eye. He whipped around to look behind him. There was no one else in the room. An involuntary tremor ran through his body. He couldn't get out fast enough.

Downstairs, the agent going through the girls' room was feeling foolish as he poked through drawers filled with girly under things, the occasional romance novel, CDs, makeup, brushes, barrettes, and jewelry. He patted along beds topped with assortments of stuffed animals. Finally, the patting down of one bed yielded the feel of something solid hidden under the mattress.

Outside under the tree, Scott had been standing with his eyes closed, following the activity in the girls' room. He saw the man toss back the bed coverings and lift the mattress to reveal a purple diary. He leaned over and whispered to Katy. She opened her mouth in horror. "But that's private property," she hissed back. She closed her eyes tight and focused her thoughts on her book. Ralph looked at Katy. Mischief danced across his face. What was the point of having abilities if you didn't have fun with them? He closed his eyes and envisioned the boys' room.

As the agent reached down to pick the book up, the cover opened and snapped shut, almost catching his hand. He jerked back; hesitated a moment and then started to reach again. The book opened up to snap at him. The book kept opening and snapping until the mattress flopped back down and covered it. He stared at the bed for a long moment but the show seemed to be over. He carefully swept his arm through the air above the bed, feeling for wires. Nothing. He got down on his hands and knees and swept his arm under the bed, then along the sides. If there was a trick to what had happened to him, he couldn't find it. He suddenly comprehended the term "creeped out".

The agent examining the boys' room reached down to throw back the covers on one of the beds. The comforter on the bed next to it began to ripple and roll as though it was alive and grooving to an unheard rhythm. It fell quiet just as a soccer ball shot out from under another bed. The ball stopped in the center of the room. Then spinning around it rocketed across the floor and through the legs of one of the beds. He could hear it bouncing up and down under the bed as though it were doing a victory dance. Then the room was quiet. The agent drew a deep breath and became aware his heart was pounding. "Okay, okay, game's over," he said to himself. "Drugs, you're looking for drugs."

He moved to the other side of the room and got down to look under the bed the soccer ball had come from. A grubby athletic sock lay on the floor. As he bent over to examine the underside of the bed, the toe of the sock lifted off the floor and slowly undulated upwards. It stopped when it was level with the man's face. Suddenly, the toe spread in a good imitation of a cobra's hood and struck at his face. He fell backwards and scrabbled to his feet. The sock slithered out from under the bed and crawled across the room to coil itself in front of one of the clothes hampers. Cold sweat stood out on the agent's forehead as he looked warily around. It was the first time he had ever felt endangered by dirty clothes and badly made beds.

In the kitchen, Harmon started his search with a close study of a bulletin board to the left of the door. It had a neatly typed listing of the month's menus. Next to it were two grocery lists. One was headed Costco and the other Local. The items listed were in different colored inks as though they were noted at different times.

The upper cabinets were glass fronted, their interiors revealing exactly what one would expect in a kitchen. He flipped open the solid front lower cabinets. They contained the usual array of pans, baking equipment and kitchen miscellany. The drawers didn't prove any more interesting with their contents of silver, pot holders, trivets, dish cloths and towels.

Harmon opened the door and flipped on the light in the room at the end of the kitchen. Wide shelves held institutional sized cans, organized according to content, the tops dated with month and year in felt pen. Then, he caught sight of the disparate containers collected on one shelf. His mouth curved into a nasty smile. Now they were getting somewhere. He picked up a baking powder can marked 'sweet clover'. He popped the lid off and sniffed. It smelled like clover alright. He pulled out a large oatmeal box labeled 'lavender'. He recognized the smell from the potpourris his wife bought. He pushed it back on the shelf. He shivered slightly. The air was getting chilly.

He investigated several more containers. The one identified as bergamot had a deep earthy smell. A hand drawn skull and crossbones on the front of a canning jar caught his attention. Below was the word pyretheum. On the back of the jar was a label with directions on how to mix for an insect spray. As he pushed the jar back on the shelf he realized his hands were shaking and he was shivering uncontrollably. It felt as if he were standing in the middle of an Arctic ice floe.

Almost simultaneously with his realization of the cold, he felt someone was standing behind him. He swung around and confronted…nothing. But he couldn't stop the sensation he was not alone in the room now the temperature of a super freezer. He had to get out of here before he got hypothermic. He stumbled out of the pantry.

He was at the base of the stairs, stamping his feet and blowing on his hands to warm them when the rest of his team began to reassemble. He could feel their edginess. Somewhere a door slammed. It sounded like the kitchen. The men all jumped. He drew his gun and, signaling to one of the others, they eased their way back into the kitchen. The pantry door was now firmly closed. Harmon approached it and slowly turned the knob, then swiftly thrust the door open. The pantry was empty of anyone. Harmon reached his hand into the room. There was no coldness now.

Suddenly the light turned out and the door slammed in their faces. Harmon started to reach for the knob but stopped. He knew there would be no one in there. The agent with Harmon leaned over and whispered. "Excuse me, sir, but can we get the hell out of here? This place gives me the heebie-jeebies."

Harmon was disinclined to argue with him. "Yeah. Let's move out."

The team left the house with a speed that did not enhance their machismo image. Harmon led them around to the far side of the SWAT van.

"Anyone find anything?" he asked.

"Nothing I'd like to talk about at headquarters, sir," one of the agents said. "Did anyone else feel like we weren't exactly alone in there?"

The other men shifted their weight and glanced at each other. Finally, one of the other agents spoke up, "Yeah, it was almost like the house was haunted or, er ...something."

"Or just very well booby-trapped to make it appear as though it were," Harmon said.

"Excuse me, sir, but if that was all tricks, these people belong in Vegas."

"Well, you suggest that to them. Let's see if our star informant can help us out."

Harmon came around the truck and motioned for the man in the suit to join him. "So, Mr. Bowman, tell me a little more about your business dealings here. This is a pretty big place. Lots of places to stash drugs. It would sure help us out here if you could give us a more precise location about where you and Mr. Evanrud transacted your business."

The man's expression lit up with eagerness. "It's inside. I could take you right there if you want me to."

Boomer reacted. He moved to stand in front of the steps and crossed his arms over his chest. "I don't think that would be a good idea, Harmon. Your warrant doesn't include him."

Challenge to his authority brought out the worst in Harmon. He swung on Boomer; ready to point out suspects didn't give orders to anyone, least of all him, when an unfamiliar voice spoke. Harmon turned his head to see a short girl push through the clustered kids and duck between the two men. She was moving as though she had no awareness of her surroundings. And the voice coming from her was deeper, darker than he would have expected. It was the voice of a woman, not a girl.

"Well, my dear Carl, caught with your hand in the cookie jar. Whatever will the Board say when they find out you have been helping yourself to the Foundation funds?"

Harmon started, "What the hell? Hey, you, young lady, get back there."

Boomer grabbed his arm. "Don't. She can't hear you when she's in a trance."

Harmon lifted a skeptical eyebrow. "Trance? Do you honestly expect me to believe that?" He attempted to shake off Boomer's hand.

Boomer held on. "Didn't you do any research on this place? We are a special facility for kids with psychic abilities. Alyson is a trance clairvoyant. If you break it before she comes out of it naturally you may harm her."

Harmon looked at the girl. She did appear to be in some kind of altered state. He also caught the involuntary step back Bowman had taken. Okay, let the kid have the stage for a minute.

Alyson stopped in front of Bowman. "But you know what a good heart I have, Carl. I wouldn't want to see you end up in jail for such a paltry bit of money. However, I do think you should have to pay in some manner for my protecting your good name."

Bowman took another step back. "Shut her up. She's a freakin' freak. Keep her away from me!"

Harmon's interest in what Alyson was saying became acute when he saw Bowman's reaction. Although he had missed a few sentences while Bowman was squalling, he now focused carefully on what she was saying.

"So all you have to do, my darling, is to convince the DEA that you have been purchasing your lovely white powder from a man named Russell Evanrud at this place outside Molalla called Spirit Wind Ranch. Why you'll be a hero… you'll be my hero."

It was eerie to hear such seductive words and tones coming from the girl.

The man wiped his mouth with his handkerchief. He seemed fascinated with what was being said to him the same way people are always fascinated with disaster. He whimpered under his breath. "How do you know? You weren't there. No one was there."

The voice coming from Alyson ignored him and continued. "So you just go in and sing your little song for them. They're just going to love the tune, don't you think? And then all you have to do is to make sure they find something. It doesn't have to be much. Just enough to bring the place down around Mr. Evanrud's ears."

The smile Alyson was giving the man was pure evil.

While the kids were watching Alyson, Brandy suddenly caught a flash of the man's thoughts and saw what he did not want seen. She leaned over to whisper to Katy and Ralph. They gave each other a long look and then lifting their right hands, they focused on the man.

He began to twitch and jerk. "Don't touch me. Get your hands off me." He was swatting at something invisible.

Harmon and the other agents looked at each other. It appeared their witness was dissembling. Boomer looked past them and saw Katy's and Ralph's focus. His mouth twitched in a hint of a smile.

The front of the man's jacket opened up revealing a pale yellow silk lining. He tried to pull it closed. Something was edging out of the interior pocket. It looked like a small glassine envelope containing white powder. Just as the man grabbed for it, it flew out of his pocket, hovered before Harmon's face before dropping to the ground just in front of the agent's boot.

Harmon stared at it for a moment before leaning over and picking it up. He turned it over in his hand, studying it.

Before he could say anything, a small gasp caught his attention. He looked down at the girl still standing in front of Bowman. It was obvious even to Harmon she didn't understand what she was doing there. She cast a quick scared look at him. Boomer stepped forward and touched her arm. "It's okay, Alyson." He looked across at the group and gave a small nod to the heavy-set woman. She hurried across the lawn to wrap an arm around the girl's shoulders, turning her and leading her back to the rest of the kids.

Harmon looked at Boomer. "I suppose you have an explanation for everything that's happened here today."

"I have an explanation but I don't think it's anything you would want to put in your report, Harmon. I've always found bureaucracy pretty closed minded."

Harmon looked past Boomer to the house. As he watched, the old rocking chair on the porch began to move slowly back and forth as though someone was rocking in it. A strange sense of disorientation swirled through him. There was only one way to deal with the situation. He went to familiar ground.

"Carl Bowman, I am charging you with the crime of possession of cocaine, obstructing justice by the presentation of false information, and

I'll work on coming up with a few more before we get back to the agency. You have the right to remain silent, anything you say can and will...."

One of the other agents had placed Bowman's hands on his head and was carefully patting him down. He pulled up the man's pant legs and pulled glassine envelopes out of the top of each sock. He handed these over to Harmon before pulling the man's arms down behind his back and clamping the handcuffs on him.

They hustled him back into the white car. Harmon went around to the driver's door and opened it. He gave Boomer a long look before slipping his sunglasses on and getting in. In just a couple of minutes, the area was empty except for Garner's car.

***

The bubble of tension enclosing them burst, leaving everyone feeling limp. Only the man hiding above them on the hillside remained taut as he tried to see the face of the girl who had so boldly spoken, but he could only get glimpses as she remained in the midst of the kids beginning to mill around in the yard.

Where had she gotten that voice? Kip knew it. It was smoother, more polished than the one that was echoing in his memory, but it was definitely a voice he recognized from the past.

As the kids began to scatter, he realized the vulnerability of his position. Carefully edging his way back through the dappled shadows of the trees, he escaped over the rim of the hill and vanished in the woods. He moved automatically; a maelstrom of memories bubbling in his brain. He ignored the dark phantasms rising and jostling for his attention. Instead he kept his mind focused on the brief moment of seeing the back of young girl with waist-length pale blonde hair. He looked up at the Douglas firs gold dusted with the spring sun and sensed time moving in a vortex. Past, present and future were circling towards each other. What rode in their wake?

***

Garner offered to go with Boomer to see the condition of the house before allowing the kids back in. They were surprised at the lack of signs of the search.

"It's almost like they weren't really looking," Garner said. "And they were so very hot to rip this place up when we left the station."

"Maybe it was the kids," Boomer answered.

"Listen, Harmon would trash his own grandmother's house if he thought there was a chance to put another notch on his bust record."

Although the kids had stopped at the door when Boomer had motioned to them, they couldn't resist pushing and jockeying for a chance to peer inside and consequently were spilling into the entry.

Boomer knew better than to try to hold back the human tide. "Okay, people, go and check your own stuff. Let me know if anything is missing or damaged."

The noise level escalated as they split up with the girls heading past the stairs to their dorm room and the boys whooping and running through the living room.

Boomer started to climb the stairs. Garner trailed him. They began with Carlita's room at the far left. It was immaculate. They opened the door to Dao's room. The bare simplicity of the Zen-like room was undisturbed. Next door, Harley's rustic room was equally free of any sign of intruders.

At his own room, Boomer drew a deep breath before reaching out to push the unlatched door open. He winced when he saw the lid to the chest still standing upright. One of Laurel's notebooks was lying as though it had been dropped. Oblivious of Garner stepping around him, he squatted in front of the chest and tenderly picked up the old spiral, carefully smoothing its cover before placing it neatly on the others stacked inside the chest.

Garner was drawn to the collection of whales occupying the shelves. He methodically surveyed the shelves, studying each piece. "What's with all the whales?"

Boomer shut the lid to the chest before standing up. "I was a marine biologist, specializing in orcas."

Garner gestured toward the large photo. "That one's beautiful."

Boomer joined him in front of the shelves. He stroked a blunt finger along the edge of the frame. "Minowah was the matriarch of the pod I researched."

"Minowah?"

"It's an Indian word. Means 'moving voice'."

"So why'd you give up whales for spooky kids?"

Boomer turned away from the shelves as though he was checking out the rest of the room. "Things happen."

Garner remained silent as he finished looking over the shelves. He spotted something almost hidden by the numerous whale figures. Tucked way back in the corner of a shelf was a photo, a Polaroid. A young woman with dark, curly hair spilling over the shoulders of a red and black plaid shirt was kneeling in a canoe, laughing into the camera. Not beautiful but with an aliveness that still radiated in the fading picture.

Garner thought the water and shoreline in the background looked like one of the sounds in Washington State.

"No damage," Boomer said. He swung the door wide and Garner knew it was an order to move out.

Downstairs the kids were strewn across all the flat surfaces in the living room.

"I hope it bit him," Katy was saying.

"Who got bit?" Boomer asked.

"That guy that was trying to read my diary. That's PRIVATE."

"How would he have gotten bit?" Garner asked.

"I made my book bite at him." Katy put her hands together and simulated the opening and closing of the book's cover.

"I wonder where the guy was in our room when I turned Jesse's sock into a snake," Ralph grinned.

"Snake?" Garner was skeptical.

"Yeah. I saw Jesse's sock under his bed this morning when I was looking for my shoes. So I made it act like a cobra." Ralph used his hand to show how he made the sock rise up and strike.

The noise level began to increase as the kids vied to each tell what they had done to make the agents' visit uncomfortable business for them.

Harley leaned through the opening behind the picture. "Coffee's ready."

Boomer motioned for Garner to follow him. In the kitchen, Harley was pouring out three mugs. He sat the pot back on the warmer and handed a cup to Garner and Boomer, then lifted the third for himself. "I think Canute handled whoever was searching the kitchen," he said.

"Canute? Have I met him?" Garner asked

Boomer pulled his lips back from his teeth in a grimace at the coffee's heat. "Don't know."

"Okay, I don't recall being introduced to anyone named Canute. Is he new around here?"

Harley sat his cup down and began to fiddle with the knobs on the two wall ovens. "Nah, he's been around here a long, long time."

"So you keep him hidden or something when I come around?"

Boomer shook his head. "Nope." He took another sip of coffee. "Might be here right now."

Garner looked around the kitchen. "I don't see any…..oh, no. You're not going to tell me he's a…a ghost?

"Discarnate," Harley said from behind the refrigerator door. "Ghosts aren't real."

He emerged with several large white paper-wrapped packages of meat.

"I'm confused. You guys, of all people, are telling me ghosts aren't real."

"You explain it to him, Boomer. I need my kitchen to fix dinner for the howling mob."

Boomer motioned Garner to follow him to his office. Garner collapsed in the overstuffed armchair. "Okay, skip the dissertation on ghosts and dis..dis-whatevers. Talk to me about what happened here today. Who's got a hard-on for you and the ranch? And how does the Maguire Foundation fit in?"

"You must have missed the news a while back. Rhonda Maguire."

"Rhonda Maguire? Of the Maguire fortune? What does she have to do with you? Not an old flame I hope."

"I've met moray eels that were more attractive and a lot friendlier. No, we have custody of her daughter, Alyson."

Connections begin to form in Garner's mind. "Let me guess, she wouldn't be that little one who gave the, what do you call it, reading of Bowman."

"Exactly, which brings me to a question we need some help with. Alyson was removed by the court because her mother criminally neglected her when she wasn't physically and mentally abusing her. Yet, ever since she was handed into our care, the Maguire woman has been bent on getting her back and obviously doesn't care how she does it. I want to know why. Think you can help with that?"

Garner slipped his coffee thoughtfully. "Yeah, I think I can. At least I can give it a try. I assume you want to keep my snooping under wraps."

"Nothing official...yet."

The door of the room opened and Jesse poked his head around it. "I got it." He swung his arm around the door and waved a video tape in the air. Boomer motioned him in.

"I made a copy to keep but there's some really good stuff on here, like Harmon getting in your face and them pointing the guns at Ruby," he said as he handed the tape to Boomer.

Boomer reached out for it. "Good. Thanks, Jesse."

Jesse turned to leave and then stopped still facing the door. "Ah, when you got a minute, Boomer, I got something I want to show you. Something I spotted in the tape. It might have to do with that...ehm." He hesitated. He wasn't sure what Boomer did or did not want to have Garner hear. "Other problem we've had around here," he concluded.

He turned his bright blue eyes on Boomer and saw that he had caught his message.

Boomer nodded. "Okay, after dinner."

"What other problem," Garner asked after Jesse had left the room.

"Oh, just varmints," Boomer said vaguely as he held the tape up and looked at it. A grim smile formed on his face. "I wonder what the Maguire Foundation will make of this."

Chapter 17

Virginia Thornley strode up and down her office, keeping her face turned towards the window, avoiding the photocopied letter sitting precisely centered on her desk. Too much emotion was surging through her, overriding the cool legal-trained part of her brain. She needed to burn off some of it before Rhonda arrived. One of them had to maintain a level head and that had never been Rhonda.

She finally stopped and stared out her window at the city skyline. What a devil's bargain she had made when she first decided to become Rhonda's mentor and ally.

How long had it been now? Nearly eighteen years ago, she realized with a start. Rhonda had phoned their office for an appointment to look over a pre-nuptial agreement. She had caught the call because she was the only woman associate. When Rhonda had mentioned her intended's name, she hadn't been able to get her in fast enough.

As they sat in the small back room office she first occupied, Virginia had quickly ascertained Rhonda was not in love with Chris Maguire but with his world of money and power. Drawing on her own heritage of belonging to one of Portland's old families, she had used that knowledge to leverage herself into the girl's life by offering to guide and teach her the requisite skills for moving in the Maguire world without embarrassing herself.

In return, by retaining Rhonda as one of her clients, Virginia had gained stature in the law firm. Her tie-in to the Maguire family had quickly moved her out the back office into a partner's position. But the last nine years had been tough. Once Rhonda had gained the Maguire power, the world either turned precisely as Rhonda dictated or someone was going to pay dearly.

A cloud passed over the face of the sun and for a moment turned her window into a mirror reflecting back her image. The expensive suit and immaculate grooming gave her slightly dumpy figure and pleasant face a patina of elegance, but not beauty. She suddenly realized how much she resembled her own mother at middle-age. Although surrounded by the accoutrements of a successful career, she could just as easily been on her way to lunch with the ladies. "The fruit doesn't fall far from the tree after all," she murmured

Was that the case with Rhonda, she wondered? She had met Rhonda's mother only a couple of times in the early days. Virginia closed her eyes and searched her memory. A woman's image floated to the surface. The lineage of Rhonda's beauty had been evident in the mother's own good-looks. On those few occasions, the woman had orbited Rhonda making sure the limelight stayed firmly on her daughter. Maybe that was the origin of Rhonda's overweening self-centeredness.

She pressed her hands against her temples. The stirring of a migraine was beginning to pressure her eyes. She couldn't afford to give in to the pain. Rhonda was on her way and she would need every bit of her mental acuity to try to get her to see reason.

She had just swallowed medication to ward off her headache and was chasing it with a long drink of ice water when the door to her office flew open. She winced as she heard it cuff the corner of her antique French lady's desk standing behind the door. She didn't have to look to know that the moments of silence were due to Rhonda automatically posturing in the doorway. It was such a habit, Virginia could easily imagine Rhonda posing and waiting for applause as she slid into the delivering doctor's hands. She chose to ignore it.

She carefully sat her Waterford drinking glass on the tray next to the silver pitcher of iced water. She didn't look at Rhonda until she has crossed the expanse of Imari carpet to her desk and seated herself in her leather chair. She was relieved to see her hands weren't shaking as she folded them on the desk top over the letter. She leveled her grey eyes on Rhonda.

As the sun again illumined the office, she was surprised to be able to pick out flaws in Rhonda's perfect face. She could see a tiny network of fine lines radiating from the corners of her blue-green eyes and two just barely perceptible vertical lines between her eyebrows. The hard set of the woman's mouth thinned it unattractively.

"And what is your explanation for this?" Rhonda said as she flung a crushed envelope obviously containing the original letter on top of the copy already on Virginia's desk.

A cloud of Rhonda's *Bal á Versailles* perfume enveloped Virginia, momentarily increasing the pressure in her temples. But there was something else mixed in the scent. Was it the smell of fear?

She suddenly relaxed and casually brushed the envelope aside. "That, my dear Rhonda, is the result of your monumental self-absorbed stupidity," she said as she fixed a cold eye on the woman now seated in one of her pale yellow leather client's chairs.

Rhonda swept to her feet with all the hauteur of an insulted queen. "And that is the last time you will ever even consider addressing me in such a manner. You seem to forget that you are just an employee, a hired hand. However, as of this moment you are fired. I've warned you, there are any number of law firms who would crawl through fire to represent my interests."

Virginia reached out and picked up the envelope. She waved it in the air. "As of right now, without Alyson, you don't have any interests to be represented."

* * *

Rhonda drove home hard and fast. If anyone had gotten in her way she would have mowed them down without a qualm. She brought her forest green BMW sports coupe to a shuddering stop just scant inches from the garage doors. Not in memory could she remember such a helpless rage with no one to vent it on.

She managed to get herself in the house and headed instantly towards the array of crystal decanters on the antique trolley. Even though there was an assortment of the finest liquor available from Glenlivet to Absolut vodka, she ignored the bottles and reached up to open the door to the little refrigerator skillfully hidden behind a gilt framed mirror. She pulled out a bottle of Evian water. Popping the top off with the sterling bottle opener, she took a long draught.

Turning, she surveyed the room. It was not a comfortable or comforting room. That was not her interest. Rooms like that were for dowdy little women who shared their lives with loathsome children and loutish men. Her space was the setting of a queen.

It had been a grand day when she was finally able to rid herself of those "oh, so charming chintzes" and "warm woods" installed by her mother-in-law. Virginia was responsible for suggesting she would endear herself to Chris' mother by asking her to decorate and furnish the house given as a wedding present while the newlyweds were off on their three month honeymoon. She had abhorred the coziness the minute she stepped foot in the house. She had never pictured herself as a homebody eager to spend a quiet evening reading by the fireplace.

Even when Chris had been killed, she was held back from making the changes she wanted. Virginia had harped to her over and over again to wait; to keep up the pretense of the grieving little widow because it would only be a matter of time before it would all be hers and then she could do whatever she wanted without once encountering the disapproving eyes of the Maguire family. So she had waited and chafed under the waiting. But at last, it had come. At 4 a.m. in the morning, Virginia had phoned her to relay the news of Meri's death. She remembered Virginia starting to yammer instructions at her on what she should do to make the best impression before the media and shore up her relations with the network of wealth the Maguires had been part of. The words had shrunk to only an irritating vibration in her ear as her mind exulted, "The Queen is dead. Long live the Queen."

She had ordered the work to begin on her house even before she made her way to the West Hills for her performance of the 'tragedy beset young woman' with only the Maguire millions to aid her in her life's struggles.

Now she gazed on the delicate gilded chairs and divans, covered in the richest of brocades and thickest of velvets. The icy blue walls, the mirrors in their gold scrolled frames, the ormolu clocks and fragile statuary evoked a sense of Louis XIV's royal reign. She looked at the chair where she always held court. It had once belonged to another queen. She tasted again her disappointment when she first saw it. The material in the seat was thread bare. Although the antiquarian had pleaded with her to understand the intrinsic value of leaving the piece as it was, she had been adamant in demanding it be recovered. She could not abide anything worn looking even if it had been Marie Antoinette's ass that had done the wearing.

Her anger was being eroded by an unfamiliar and unsettling feeling of panic as she began to walk through the house. She paused in the large entrance hall and stared into her dining room. The walls, covered in pale pink brocade were the perfect backdrop for the enormous dining table overlaid with an Alsace lace cloth. Huge vermeil vases supported sheaves of roses. The candelabras had purportedly journeyed to her from some long ago ransacked cathedral. In a vast storage room off the kitchen was her exquisite Limoges china, heavy sterling dinnerware and dishes, and Baccaret crystal glassware. Someone had once commented the only thing missing from her dinner parties was a liveried courtier standing behind each chair. The remark had pleased her enormously.

She spun on her heel and quickly strode toward the back of the house. The Maguires may have contained her when they were alive, but they were dead. It was all hers now and god help anyone who thought they could take it from her. She just needed the right ammunition and a plan to cause the most devastation. It was time Simon reported in to her.

Even though she was aware of how scrupulously punctual Simon was, she was still pacing the length of the marbled entry way as she waited for the clock to strike 2 p.m. The doorbell rang exactly as the clock chimed. She saw Simon's elephantine shape through the heavily etched glass as she jerked the door open.

"You better have something good for me," she said without preamble. He lifted a thick manila envelope. She acknowledged it by leading the way to her office. Simon Quirin made little noise as he followed her. He had a curiously light step for a man so ungainly in appearance.

Rhonda flung herself into the chair behind her desk. The back rose and flared around her giving the impression of a baby blue leather throne. Simon made his steady way to the matching loveseat, seating himself with great care to prevent it from splintering under him. He then set the envelope on the low table in front of him, precisely aligning it with the edge.

He straightened up and, placing his hands on his knees, began his report. "You were quite right about the whales, Mrs. Maguire. Mr. Evanrud was at one time an up and coming marine biologist. His specialty was the orcas inhabiting Puget Sound."

Rhonda leaned forward eagerly receptive to Simon's every word. She was actually rubbing her hands together in anticipation.

"His observation of a pod H provided a wealth of information for researchers during the time he was connected to the University of Washington. He was considered to have an almost mystical ability in his communication with and interpretation of the creatures' social structure and interactions. He was well on his way to becoming one of the premier experts in the world when he abruptly left it."

A malevolent smile settled on Rhonda's face. "So he did shoot Keiko. Give me every single deliciously gory detail."

Simon shook his head. "I'm afraid Mr. Evanrud left due to a personal tragedy. It seems the woman he had loved and lived with for over five years drowned in the sound just a couple of months before they were to be married. She was carrying his child at the time of her death."

Rhonda fell back in her chair deflated. "I don't suppose there were any suggestions of foul play?"

"None. Apparently the young woman in question was a researcher in the field of raptors, eagles to be precise. She had fallen from one of the nests while recording and banding baby eaglets a year before she met Mr. Evanrud. She sustained a rather bad head trauma. According to our informants, Mr. Evanrud was very instrumental in her rehabilitation and in helping her continue her own work. The autopsy report stated the young woman had developed an undiscovered brain tumor as a result of the original accident and the pregnancy had possibly exacerbated its growth. She was canoeing, a habit of hers I might add, when she apparently had a grand mal seizure and toppled into the sound, thus drowning."

"Are you sure you uncovered everything? What about gossip, rumors, that sort of thing?"

"It appears there was only great empathy and regard for the man during his loss. Even former colleagues who admitted to jealousy at his tremendous success could not fault the man, his methods or his life; only his success."

"Shit," Rhonda said under her breath. The last thing she wanted was some tragic hero mourning his precious lost love. That would not serve her purpose at all.

"Anything else," she asked in a flat voice.

Simon looked at the envelope and shook his head. "I am afraid your Mr. Evanrud has always erred on the side of morality and honorability."

Rhonda pushed out of her chair and began to stride back and forth in front of him. "Come on, Simon, nobody's that good. What about women? You can't tell me he's been celibate all these years."

"No, but none of the ladies would speak about their time with him." He twitched a shoulder. "In fact, one of them was quite rude and graphic in her declining to discuss him."

"Why, are they afraid of him or something?"

"Mrs. Maguire, in my experience when a woman perceives she has been wronged by a man, she is most eager to provide all manner of evidence to substantiate her sense of outrage. Women who have enjoyed something they consider special seldom share it with anyone; least of all someone they sense could be an enemy."

"Sum it up, Simon."

"I have nothing to give you, Mrs. Maguire. The man is no saint but neither is he more of a sinner than the average person who tries and sometimes fails in life."

Rhonda stalked to the French doors. A spring squall was pelting the glass with hail. Her own emotions were splintering apart and bouncing through her mirroring the small ice pellets skittering about on the flagstones of the patio. She couldn't afford this loss of focus. To quote one of the phrases in the letter "time was of the essence".

Simon watched her as she stared out the door. She was literally vibrating with emotion. "I am sorry, Mrs. Maguire. While we can usually find the dirt so desired by a client, occasionally we find what we found with Mr. Evanrud. No dirt; only a gathering of dust from walking this planet nearly 60 years. However, I am aware of your situation and am not without sympathy to it."

Rhonda turned back to look at him. As he sat there with his too small head balanced on his oversized body, she became aware of how much like a spider he was. With his vast web of contacts, he had long been society's primo investigator. His work was impeccable while his discretion was legendary. His number was in everyone's Blackberry® ready to be dialed should a competitor need persuasion to accept the terms of a buy-out or a soon-to-be ex become more amenable to a divorce settlement. It had also been rumored he could direct one to those whose means were a little less acceptable in polite society but equally effective in achieving one's goals.

She returned to her chair. "Talk to me."

Chapter 19

Lacey sat in a chair in the staff room; a drawing tablet balanced against the edge of the table. Across from her Alyson was bent over a similar tablet focused on her pencil's motion. Lacey had been sketching Alyson at work but now she simply sat and watched her for a moment before looking around the shabby room.

Although she had been coming twice a week for nearly a month, she still found herself feeling off center at times. From its outward appearance, it was not unlike a couple of the camps she herself had attended as a kid, yet, there was always the sense of invisible currents flowing around her when she was here. She found her perceptions challenged by the kids and staff. It wasn't as much what they did, although she had been startled when one of the boys had held out his hand and the salt shaker had slid down the table to him, it was the air of normality with which they all lived as though this was the real world and anything outside the gate functioned under a handicap.

Conversations took on a surreal feeling when she reviewed them outside the perimeter of Spirit Wind Ranch. She thought of the day she had gone to the kitchen to get water for her lesson in watercolors. As she stood filling the pint jar, she had watched three glasses standing in the drainer lay over on their sides.

Harley had emerged from the basement with huge cans of stewed tomatoes and corn in his arms.

"Did we just have an earthquake," she had asked him.

"Nah," he said. "It was probably just the thundering herd."

"No, nobody went by, but I just saw those glasses lay down," she said as she pointed to the drainer.

Harley had hefted the cans on the counter as he casually replied. "That was Helga. She has a thing about the glasses. She's always afraid they're going to get broken if they are standing upright."

That brief exchange had launched Harley into a discussion of the difference between discarnates and ghosts. She learned that discarnates were apparently viable spirits who had moved out of their bodies at death but continued to remain on earth for any number of possible reasons. Ghosts, on the other hand, were like images impressed on a particular place or time and usually the result of a tremendous burst of human emotion such as in the case of murder. Ghosts apparently faded away over time much like a photo left too long exposed to the light. They were annoying at best and alarming at worst but did not actually exist.

As Lacey looked back at Alyson, she wondered briefly how she would ever be able to work that bit of knowledge into a conversation with one of her real estate clients.

Alyson laid her pencil down and looked up at Lacey, her eyes unfocused for a moment. A frisson of alarm ran through Lacey as she wondered if the girl was going to go into a trance like she had at the Krevitski house. Then Alyson shook her head and gave Lacey a shy smile.

"I drew this one for Boomer," she said softly as she turned the tablet towards Lacey.

It was a carefully rendered shoreline complete with a cabin and dock backed by a line of trees. The detail showed a canoe tied to the dock while a stand was supporting what appeared to be a pair of binoculars. Everything was in perfect proportion. What was unusual was the perspective. It was drawn from a low angle as though being viewed from the level of the water.

"I'm sure he is going to like it very much. You have done a beautiful job, Alyson," Lacey answered as she passed the tablet back.

Alyson lovingly stroked her hands over the edges of the paper. "It is so wonderful having real artist paper to draw on. And this." She touched the wooden artist box Lacey had filled with drawing pencils, charcoal, kneaded eraser, a small pad of sand paper, pastels and watercolors. Her expression was reverent.

Inwardly, Lacey was shaking her head. Although, Boomer had told her to spend whatever was necessary, she had spent less than $100 to provide the supplies to give Alyson her first lessons. The box to store them in had been her gift. All that Maguire money and the child had scrounged through garbage cans to find trash to use in expressing her talent. And it was a genuine talent. As Lacey had told Boomer after the first lesson, if she had possessed such a natural, if untrained ability, she would never found it necessary to get her real estate license to support her art 'habit'.

She glanced at the round institutional clock above the staff cubbies. The hour always went so fast.

"If the weather will let us, let's you and me go find some flowers in the woods the next time I come. We can practice using the pastels."

"Oh, yes," Alyson said. She was very carefully pulling the drawing sheet away from the adhesive at the top of the pad. She laid it aside and lifted the protective cover back over the remaining paper.

Lacey looked at the tablet. It was still less than half used. "Are you practicing, honey? That doesn't seem to be disappearing very fast."

Alyson flushed. "I don't want to use it up," she whispered, laying her arms protectively over the tablet.

Lacey reached across the table and took the girl's hands in hers. "Alyson, you use that drawing pad up and we'll get you another. You use up a hundred drawing pads and we'll get you a hundred more. The same thing with your pencils, pastels, paints. You're not going to do without as long as Boomer and I are around, okay?"

Alyson's clear blue eyes met Lacey's dark brown eyes. She drew in a breath and then nodded. Lacey squeezed her hands. "Good, and that reminds me, I brought you something." She turned and dug around in the canvas bag she carried back and forth to the ranch. She drew out a small spiral bound sketchbook. "Here. This is what artists carry around with them all the time. Anytime they see something they want to remember, they make a sketch in it. It's to keep their ideas from getting lost. So I want you to put lots of ideas in here to show me when I come back next Tuesday."

Alyson took the sketchbook and immediately hugged it to her chest.

Lacey glanced at the clock again. "You better get to your next class, sweetie. I'll put these in your room, okay."

Alyson looked at the clock and sighed. She could spend all day drawing and never miss going to Chayote's Oregon history class but she dutifully stood up and took her books off the end of the table.

"Uhmmm, could you give this to Boomer, please," Alyson asked as she pushed her drawing across the table.

"Don't you want to give it to him yourself?"

But she was already out the door. Lacey stuffed her own drawing pad into her bag. She slid back the top of the long wooden box she used to carry her pencils and put them in along with her kneaded eraser and pencil sharpener before adding it to her bag. Standing up, she swung the straps over her shoulder and was reaching across the table to get Alyson's pad and artist box when Boomer wandered in the room.

"Harley's got fresh coffee if you want a cup before you head back to town."

"That sounds great. I had a showing at 8:00 a.m. this morning so I'm down at least a pint on my caffeine."

She dropped her bag on the table and picked up Alyson's things to put away in the dorm room while she got her coffee.

When she returned with a mug in her hand, she found Boomer leaning over the table, his hands planted on either side of Alyson's drawing. There was tension in his stance. He heard her and asked, "Who drew this?"

"Alyson did. She said it was for you."

Lacey walked around the table and sat down in the chair she had occupied earlier. The atmosphere had an uncomfortable feel to it now. She didn't know why but she sensed the drawing had triggered something negative in Boomer. Her hackles rose defensively. "It is an excellent piece of work with the unusual perspective handled extraordinarily well." Her sharp words seemed to break something in the air.

When Boomer looked up at her, she could see amusement in his eyes. "Getting a little overprotective, aren't we?"

Lacey had the grace to give an embarrassed grin. "That's possible but it looked like you didn't much care for something she poured her heart into this morning."

Boomer sat down in Alyson's vacated chair. "Let's just say I was taken aback more than anything. Even after all my years here, I am sometimes confounded by what these kids are able to perceive."

"I take it you know this place…that it isn't something Alyson simply made up."

Boomer picked up the drawing and gazed at it. "Yeah, I knew this place."

It was clear from his tone he was not going to elaborate on the place or its meaning to him.

"How'd you end up here?"

"You mean Spirit Wind?"

"As the director of, how does my brother put it, of a 'spooky kids' school?"

Boomer shrugged as he carefully set the drawing aside. "It was one of those one-thing-led-to-another situations."

Lacey took a sip of her coffee and kept her eyes on Boomer silently demanding more explanation.

Boomer turned his own cup in slow circles as he thought about his answer. "I was educated and trained as a scientist. I was in research for a while. Then just like John Lennon warned us, life happened while I was busy making other plans and I left. I knocked about for what turned into a decade doing physical labor...construction, truck driving and so on. One day I realized I missed academia and I was ready to go back in some capacity. My brother-in-law taught music at a private school. He got me on in the science department teaching biology. I genuinely enjoyed the challenge of pouring knowledge that wasn't wanted into minds that weren't willing."

He paused and took a sip of coffee. "That was when I met my first 'spooky' kid. He was a telekinetic like Ralph and Katy. I became aware of his abilities when he spent an entire class having the paperclips on my desk crawl out of the container, down the front of the desk and across the floor like so many ants. One of the girls in the class got hysterical. Meeting with his parents over the incident gave me insight into the dilemma of families trying to cope with extraordinary children. What do you do with them?"

"Gifted children, you give advanced studies and ship them off to college when they are 12. Developmentally delayed students get tutoring and programs designed to help them bridge their handicaps. But what do you do with a kid who can move lunch trays from across the room, or possesses information he has no ordinary way of knowing, or rushes out of class to call his mother because he can hear his fallen great-grandmother crying for help seventeen miles away?"

There was commotion as Harley's class came back in the building. Lacey kept her eyes fixed on Boomer so he wouldn't leave her in the middle of the story.

"The obvious solution is to shut them down, which most of their parents were attempting to do. But that felt wrong to me...like telling a natural singer to keep their mouth shut or," he gestured towards the drawing, "an artist to put their pencil down."

"So, I following my training, I began to research the phenomenon and how it should be handled for the benefit of all. Eventually I met Dr. Wheatcroft and his wife, Jesse's parents. He's an anthropologist and she's a documentary filmmaker. They specialize in studying peoples who have incorporated what we call the paranormal into their everyday lives."

"Like gypsies or aboriginals?" Lacey asked

Boomer nodded. "From their studies they had developed the concept for a facility based on tribal customs and traditions to not only educate young people with psi skills but also to help them keep their gifts intact while learning to control and utilize them in their adult life." Boomer held his hands up. "Spirit Wind Ranch."

Although she still had questions, the eruption of students from the classrooms told her it was lunchtime. She hurriedly got up and slung her bag over her shoulder. She had a 1 p.m. meeting with some people who wanted to list their house.

Lacey spotted Alyson hovering outside the room. She put her hand out and gave the drawing the smallest of shoves towards Boomer. "Someone needs some feedback…positive if you don't mind," she said quietly. The warning glint in her eye was unmistakable.

Leaving the room, she stepped over book bags, jackets and notebooks as she maneuvered her way through the kids who were descending on the food exactly 'like a plague of locusts', she thought. She sidestepped Harley who was coming through the kitchen door with a huge platter of toasted cheese sandwiches.

"These kids could give sharks lessons in staging a feeding frenzy," he said as the sandwiches were already being snatched up.

She decided to preserve life and limb by leaving through the back door. She stepped down onto the bricked patio and drew a deep breath. There was green in the air today; a combination of tender new leaves, lilacs and forsythia blended with the damp tilth in Aimee's meticulously planted gardens. A soft breeze was stirring, pulling in the scent of the firs and nature's own plantings in the hills behind the house. A sense of tranquility scudded through her.

It made her wonder when she would keep all those promises to herself about learning to meditate, keeping a journal, and finding a bunch of roses to bury her nose in; to quiet the combative spirit she lived with.

She had arrived in the world pugnacious. Her mother always claimed she had been hard to deliver because of the chip on her shoulder. She had inherited her family's deep intolerance to injustice, but while they approached it from the quiet arena of service, she had been a throwback to some forgotten ancestor whose tactic was much more direct.

In Lacey's way of looking at things, service was fine but there were definitely times when a well-placed fist could also bring results. She had scrapped her way through school, always ready to knock a bully down or verbally slap those who took pleasure in using a perceived superior position to hurt and belittle someone who wasn't able to fight back.

Even though it had been a long while since she had actually participated in fisticuffs, the red river of anger in the center of her being would still send her into battle when ignited.

Already the pleasant smells and sights of the spring day were receding as she thought about Alyson. Abusing that child was like slapping around a newborn kitten. Lacey searched her memory as she summoned up media images of Rhonda Maguire. What few she had paid attention to flashed across her mind. Stunningly beautiful but even in the newspaper photos, the coldness was evident, like she had a diamond in place of a heart.

She wondered what exactly the child had lived through trying to survive the freezing atmosphere of her mother. She had queried Boomer about it when he had talked to her about giving Alyson lessons, but he had no information to share.

"We don't ask," he had said. "It's up to Alyson to open the door to that information when she is ready."

"But shouldn't she be getting counseling to cope with the trauma?"

"What Alyson needs is not coping skills. She obviously has enough of those to have allowed her to survive. What she needs is healing. We have been addressing that since the moment she was placed with us. Carlita spends time every day bathing her spirit in prayer. Harley pampers her with special treats all the time. David Dao is teaching her to recognize the truth of her being and its importance in the scheme of things. Chayote has created a dreamcatcher with a special medicine bag to call out protection from the spirit world. Aimee has dug a healing hole for her. Whenever Alyson gives up a bit of her pain, Aimee takes it there and buries it so the natural cleansing of the earth can replace it with growth."

"And you?"

"I'm looking for someone who can help open the door to her deepest dreams."

"And that includes what?"

"Teaching her whatever it is artists are taught."

"That's it?"

"That's it."

It seemed too simple an answer for a situation as complex as Alyson's. Lacey had probed deeper. "How can you be sure I am the one who should be doing this? It seems to me you really should be looking for someone who has an art therapy degree; who has been taught to use art as a healing tool."

His enigmatic answer still made little sense to her. "You have everything we need."

Pondering once again on that statement, she was unaware of being watched as she crossed the graveled drive to her car.

Chapter 20

On the ridge overlooking the ranch, two men were seated on an old fallen log. One watched the woman through field glasses. She was tall and her slenderness was on the athletic side rather than the willowy. She walked with the long strides of a woman who spent minimal time in skirts and heels. Her hair was close cropped and her clothes had an elegant no-nonsense about them.

The second man noted the time of her leaving in a notebook. In the two weeks they had been working, they now saw her pattern. She came Tuesdays and Thursdays at 10:00 a.m. and left usually a few minutes after 11:00 a.m. Today was an exception; it was nearly noon when she emerged from the back of the house.

When her car had driven around the shielding spit of forestland and vanished, the man with the binoculars set them aside. He leaned back slightly as he zipped up his regulation jacket. The dampness of the woods kept the air just cool enough to be chilled if not moving. The other man reached down behind the log and lifted up the large heavy thermos and shook it.

"There's probably enough for two more cups," he said.

"I'm getting hungry. You?"

The man nodded as he focused on pouring coffee into their commuter mugs.

"I'll go get the chow from the rig."

He stood up and realized his butt was numb and damp from sitting on the log. He shook his legs and then swung one over the log. He started down the trail they had created in their trips back and forth.

Hidden and so far undiscovered, the man who staked this portion of the land as his home listened to the progress being made down the hillside. Kip wondered if the two men who wore the Forest Service uniforms were really connected with it. They seemed so oblivious to how easy it was to track them as they came and went daily. The sharp snap of fallen twigs and the silence of the birds and animals as they passed through gave him a constant aural map of their activities.

His own father had worn the Forest Service uniform for nearly 30 years. Having grown up in these hills, his father knew them the way most people know their living rooms. In their frequent escapes from home, he had passed on his passion and knowledge of the land to his son. It was his father who had taught him to move as silently as a bobcat through the rugged brush. At his father's side he had learned to forage for food and discovered the vast richness of nature's table. Many nights they had feasted on tiny wild strawberries or huckleberries, depending on the season. He had been taught how to find and identify mushrooms and to whip up tasty salads with Miner's lettuce mixed with the tender tops of emerging fiddlehead ferns. And his father had taught him the healing hidden within the land.

"Whatever happens to you out there," his father had said as he swept his hand in the direction of Portland and the many towns strung along Highway 213, "you can always come back here and find what you really need."

He could still see his father stroking the bark of an old Douglas fir; then squatting to pick up a handful of the forest floor. "We were created in the earth and when our time has run, we'll return to it. It's in-between we lose sight of how much we need to touch her. If you ever find yourself being knocked around like a balloon in a high wind, then head for the hills. They won't forget you or fail you."

The time came when his life exploded. Left with nothing but ashes scattered around his feet, he followed his father's wise words and dragged himself back. The mountain had whispered his name as it welcomed him home.

The topography of the land had changed in the nearly two decades he had been absent with many of the big landholdings now divided into smaller occupied pieces. But they still sat on the perimeter of the vast, rugged forestland. He had located some of the overgrown old roads and hiked the hills looking for a safe place to hunker down.

After several weeks of wandering and camping out, he had stumbled on the old travel trailer alone and abandoned in a draw. He had closed in on it by circling it over and over, each round bringing him a few feet closer. He hadn't forgotten that well-guarded and often booby-trapped marijuana patches dotted the forest. Many locals noted September, not by the turning of the seasons, but by the buzzing Drug Enforcement Agency helicopters crisscrossing the mountain looking for the ready-to-be-harvested crops.

If the trailer had been brought in by an entrepreneurial dealer, the forest had reclaimed any signs of his agricultural efforts. A check of the inside showed it had been abandoned for some time but was still serviceable. All he had to do was clean it up, move a few field mice out and stock it. He had spent nine months here with no one the wiser.

Living forbidden had sharpened his instincts to a feral awareness. When he had first heard the men making their way up the side of the mountain, he had panicked. He had dragged his creatures away from the old trailer and into a shelter he had built deeper in the woods. There he had hidden them behind brush. The animals, too, had sensed the strangers and cooperated by staying silent and still. But as he tracked and watched the men, he realized they were only interested in the ranch.

They would arrive shortly after dawn had lit the way and leave prior to darkness falling. They watched and recorded whatever they saw in a notebook. It occurred to him they were not really with the Forest Service but were using the uniforms to justify their presence on the mountain. Now, having observed enough to know they wouldn't be down now until dark, he decided to risk doing a little snooping himself.

He waited until the man returned. Once he heard him reach their lookout place, Kip slipped down the side of the hill, avoiding their trail. He came out on the remains of the old roadbed where their parked vehicle sat. Only a few yards away, his motorcycle was sitting camouflaged.

He peered through the Suburban's windows and was not surprised to see none of the equipment normally found in the back of Forest Service vehicles. There were no shovels, picks, axes or collapsible buckets. There should have been rain gear, blankets and first aid supplies and maybe a live trap. The only things in this vehicle were two athletic bags sitting side by side in the back.

He'd confirmed his suspicion these people did not work for the Forest Service. They were here on another mission entirely. He wondered if it had to do with the dust-up that had taken place a few weeks back when the DEA had put in an appearance. Maybe the ranch wasn't as innocent as it appeared from his observations. Someone else seemed to be under the impression there was something worth keeping surveillance on. But why?

He turned and strode off into the woods. He needed deep country to do some deep thinking.

Chapter 21

It was one of those perfect late April mornings when Lacey pulled her car into the Spirit Wind parking area. The sun poured warm from a clear blue sky. The gently moving air gathered the scents of the lilacs, violets, hyacinths and the young green maple leaves, blending them into an invigorating potpourri that made every living creature giddy with life. The swallows, sparrows, and robins were turning aerial cartwheels over the tender grass. The blue jays hopping about in the branches of the trees provided a raucous commentary. In the paddock, Casper was racing about, kicking and bucking from sheer exhilaration. It was the kind of a day when Oregonians pitied all those who didn't live within the cradling arms of the Coast and Cascades Ranges, watched over by their grande dame, Mt. Hood. Eden was here and life's possibilities stretched all the way to the horizon.

Lacey ran up the front steps. She could hardly wait to head up the ridge. Alyson was sitting on one of the dining room benches, her drawing tablet and art box beside her. Barely stepping inside the door, she held her hand out. "Come on, girlfriend, it is so beautiful outside. We have to get this on paper."

Boomer came through the archway, a stack of envelopes in his hand. He spotted Alyson gathering up her things and Lacey at the open door motioning for her.

"What are you two up to?" he asked.

"We are heading to the hills. Nature drawing. There are some wildflowers just begging to immortalized," Lacey said.

Boomer opened his mouth as though he were about to protest. Lacey's dark eyes skewered him with a clear message, 'Don't you dare go there.'

"Be careful. Keep a good eye on her. By the way, your brother's coming up in a little bit."

Lacey rolled her eyes. "It's such a great day, don't mess it up. Come on; let's get out of Dodge before the heat arrives."

Alyson finished gathering up her supplies and hurried to the door. Lacey grabbed her hand and pulled her along as they raced towards the green shadows of the hill.

The men watched them running across the open area between the barn and the corrals. The two females paused for a moment at Casper's paddock. The older one whooped and they both applauded as the white Arab raced around the field, dipping and shaking his head and occasionally turning his heels to the sun.

The man with the binoculars kept a careful eye on their progress as Lacey showed Alyson how to imitate the horse by kicking up her heels.

"This may just turn into our lucky day. It looks like the broad is about to deliver our paychecks," he said. "Come on, come on; bring the little darling home to papa."

He lowered the binoculars when he lost sight of them as they reached the place where the hill began its ascent. Even though the men couldn't see them, voices breathless with giggles were steadily coming in their direction.

The men stood and, following the plans they had been refining for more than two weeks, moved away from each other to be able to approach their quarry from either side.

"Oh look, Alyson. It's a trillium. Let's sketch this," Lacey said and she knelt a short distance away from the plant. "Now we have to be careful. Trilliums don't like their toes stepped on so we can't get too close and crunch the earth around it. Okay, now the first thing we do is study the shape of the leaves and petals. Notice everything about a trillium comes in threes; three petals, three little leaves under the blossom and three big leaves below them. Inside, it has three stamens. That's how it gets its name. Everything is threes."

As Lacey and Alyson concentrated on reproducing the delicate flower on paper, the rest of the world faded from their awareness.

***

Kip was just placing a tuna can full of water in the hawk's cage when he felt something cross his neck making the hair stand up. He quickly fastened the cage and stood up, pulling the heavy protective glove off his hand as he scanned the area.

The sensation came again. Something was very wrong somewhere. He threw his glove down and ran back to his trailer. The area was empty and silent. The feeling was intensifying; it crawled around his spine. He swung right and then left. "Where, where, where…" the question echoed in his head. He heard a branch snap. Suddenly he knew it had to do with the men. He sprinted for the hill overlooking the ranch.

***

Lacey had moved from the ground to sit on a fallen log so she could occasionally reach down and guide Alyson's hand in laying down the pastel colors. She had just leaned away from Alyson when a hand clapped over her mouth and a bulky arm encircled her waist pulling her up and over the log.

The drawing tablet and art box scattered as Alyson whirled around. She became a small terrified animal scrabbling backwards from where Lacey was struggling with the man. A second man swooped down on Alyson, grabbing her around the middle and hauling her up into the air. Her arms and legs flailed helplessly.

Any intent to approach by stealth was discarded when Kip looked up and caught a glimpse of one of the uniforms with the child struggling in his arms. As he saw her, the mountain instructed him, "not as cat but as bear." He deliberately crashed up the mountain making as much noise as he could. Both men froze, tightening their holds.

***

On the ranch side below, Boomer was strolling back from the feed shed, the clipboard with the barnyard supplies list swinging loosely in his hand. Aimee had the three mid-teen kids with her in the garden.

There was a crunch of gravel as Garner's county car eased its way through the shade of the trees and pulled to a stop beside Lacey's neat maroon Hyundai. Garner opened the door and stepped out. He automatically resettled his utility belt and adjusted his gun before giving a wave to Chayote sitting in the middle of the older kids, each sporting a different painted face. Chayote's too, was painted. Turning, he spotted Boomer heading his direction. He strode toward him, the gravel grinding under his regulation boots.

One of the girls working with Aimee stood bolt upright. She had what Garner would have called a "frozen in the headlights" look. She seemed to be intently focused on something. Garner didn't know why but it made his cop instincts leap to the surface. Then she shrieked. "Boomer, there's something terrible going on. I can hear fighting."

Garner couldn't hear anything but Boomer reacted instantly. He sent his clipboard skidding into the timbers of the raised bed and was instantly poised for flight. "Where, Taylor?" The girl had her eyes closed as she threw her hand out in the direction of the hill rising up behind the barn.

Boomer was already running in the direction she had indicated. Garner ran after him. Aimee immediately started to push the kids towards the house.

***

Coming up from the other side, Kip broke through the brush and leaped onto a log. Startled by the intrusion, the man holding onto Lacey loosened his grip just enough so she was able to move. Swiftly, she twisted and drove her elbow into the man's stomach, knocking the breath out of him. When he let go of her, she swung away from him and came back around, delivering a solid roundhouse punch to his jaw. He staggered back and lost his balance when his feet tangled in the creeping blackberry vines.

Kip dove from the log towards the man holding the girl and grabbed the man around the throat, using his arm as a lever to cut off the man's wind. In a few moments, the man had to drop Alyson to try to free himself from the grip that was threatening to render him unconscious. Being heavier, he was able to wrest out of the suffocating hold. He swung around and lowering his head like an enraged bull, he charged into his attacker, sending them both tumbling over the log.

Lacey immediately dropped to her knees to sweep Alyson into her arms when the man she had knocked down regained his footing and lunged to grab a fistful of her hair, but the cropped style slipped through his fingers. Before he could grab for her again, Lacey had jumped to her feet, snatching up a broken chunk of branch. She whirled on the man and swung it hard at him forcing him to step back. She advanced and swung it again. There was a loud pop as she connected with his arm. He howled in pain and stumbled away clutching his elbow. As she prepared to pursue him, still swinging, they heard pounding feet approaching them from the ranch side of the hill.

The two men broke off to head down the mountain.

Just as Boomer, Garner and Chayote sprang into view, Kip pulled himself painfully up to sit on the log. He was bleeding from his mouth and already there was the beginning of bruising along the outer edge of his left eye. He winced as he swung his right leg back over the log.

Lacey yelled at her brother, "That way," pointing down the backside of the hill with the chunk of wood she still held.

Garner leapt the log and followed the sound of the men running down the hill.

Chayote raised the tomahawk he had grabbed from his lodge house and rushed the man on the log. He stopped with his arm still upraised when the man just looked at him, using the back of his hand to wipe blood from his mouth.

"Dibs on the scalp," Lacey said as she knelt to catch Alyson in her arms.

As silence settled, the adults heard the raggedy sound of Alyson's breathing. Lacey could feel the girl's chest cave into deep wheezing as she tried to draw in air. Lacey looked up at Boomer frightened.

"We've got to get her help," she said.

The man pushed off the log to slide down beside Lacey and Alyson. Boomer tensed but made no move. Kip took Lacey's right hand and placed it on Alyson's diaphragm. He placed her other hand on Alyson's back. Keeping his hands over Lacey's, he instructed her. "Very gently push in. Give her lungs something to work against. Now release. Match the movement to your own breathing. When you breathe in, release. When you breathe out, push." Watching Lacey, Kip realized she was still breathing too fast herself. "Slow down. In. Out." She found her body obeying his quiet commands.

He kept his hands in place until she had captured the rhythm he wanted. He let go and took Alyson's hands. Turning them up and resting them in his own hands, he used his thumbs to slowly trace circles on the girl's wrists in the same cadence as Lacey's breathing. He ducked his head so the child looked into his eyes. He held her gaze as he used his mind to send calming emanations to her.

By the time, Garner had retraced his steps up the hill, Alyson was breathing calmly and steadily. She and Lacey were restoring the pastels, pencils, and other items to the art box.

"Lost'em. They had a rig parked at the bottom of the hill," he said.

Kip had moved up to sit on the log and was rubbing his right knee. He definitely wrenched it when he and the girl's assailant had gone over the log. "CYQ 237," he said.

"Come again," Garner said.

Kip looked up, the bruised swelling around his left eye beginning to obscure his vision slightly. "White 2002 Chevy Suburban, license number CYQ 237. Bogus forest service decals."

"You're right." Lacey sat back on her haunches. "The two creeps were in uniforms."

Chayote looked severely at Kip. "You knew these guys were hanging around up here and you never reported it to anyone?"

Garner dropped his hand so it rested on his gun's butt. "Just who are you by the way?"

"A thief, I'd say." Boomer's words caught everyone off guard. They all looked at him. His face was severe as he kept his eyes fixed on Kip.

Kip's back straightened slowly. He lifted his head to look Boomer in the eye. The face looking back at him was unbending. The two men stared at each other.

Then Kip let his focus move beyond Boomer and settle on the gold dappled green light filtering through the trees. No matter how noble his purpose, he had stolen the herbs. He would answer without complaint.

As Boomer watched, he saw the man's eyes reflect the mountain's light. Then the light died away.

Kip slowly rose from the log. His voice was low. "I have animals down there in the woods," he said as he nodded his head towards the place where his trailer was hidden from view. "Injured animals I'm caring for. Please release them so they may have some chance of survival rather than being condemned to dying of starvation and thirst."

Lacey had stood up as she watched the exchange between the two men. Alyson now stood up as well and backed up against Lacey.

Garner reached behind him and pulled his handcuffs from his utility belt. He flipped a practiced wrist and they opened. He moved purposefully to Kip. "Place your hands on your head."

Kip obeyed and Garner swiftly pulled one arm behind his back, snapping the cuff on, followed by the other.

Lacey was stunned. This man had come to their assistance. If it wasn't for him, heaven knows what would have happened to her and Alyson. She looked into his face. It was bleak and drawn in the places not marred by the fight. But it was his eyes that caught at her heart. They were not angry or surprised. It was almost as though he expected punishment for coming.

Lacey began to quiver with anger. It wasn't right, fair or just what Boomer and her brother were doing. She needed to move and move now or she was going start smashing faces again. She reached down and grabbed the art box and drawing tablet. Then taking Alyson's hand, she began to pull her down the hill toward the ranch.

"Where are you going?" Garner said to her retreating back.

She whipped around, dark eyes fiery with her rage. "Back to the house. Children shouldn't be exposed the acute stupidity of men," she spat back at him.

She continued on, pulling Alyson after her.

"Want me to stop her?" Chayote asked. He turned preparatory of giving chase.

Garner sighed. "Not if you don't want to find that tomahawk buried in your skull. Lacey in a temper is not something you want to face alone, even armed."

He looked around the area and then grasped Kip's upper arm and started to push him after Lacey. "I need to get this radioed in. I'm sorry, Boomer, but this place will be swarming with deputies. Better get ready."

As Kip was led passed Boomer, he looked at him. "Don't forget the animals. They don't deserve to die like that."

Lacey and Alyson were nowhere to be seen when they reached the bottom of the hill although Lacey's car was still parked beside the county vehicle. As the men reached the gravel area, Lacey walked out on the porch and stood with her arms crossed. She said nothing but her face was white with suppressed fury as she watched the men's progress towards the county car.

Garner reached down to open the door.

"Take the cuffs off," Boomer said.

Garner straightened up. "What? But you said this guy…"

"I know what I said. However, I think we have bigger problems than worrying about some guy who was occasionally getting herbs to use on animals in need of help."

Kip had been standing rigidly beside the car keeping his eyes focused on nothing. Now he slowly turned his head to look at Boomer.

"That's what you took them for, isn't it?"

Kip nodded.

"Get the cuffs off of him and get on the horn, Garner. I want to know who was on that mountain and what they wanted with Lacey and Alyson."

Garner pulled the key out and released the locks on the cuffs. He stuffed them back into his belt as he went around the car to use his radio.

Boomer reached out to grab Kip's upper arm and steer him towards the house. "You need some patching, son," he said. Kip was totally confused as he limped along beside him.

It was four hours later when the chaos subsided. Deputies had swarmed the mountain. The wilderness gave up her secret witnessing reluctantly. The only solid evidence was the recovery of the large silver thermos the two men had carried back and forth to the mountain during their weeks of spying on the ranch. Handling it carefully with latex gloves, deputies slipped it into an evidence bag and stored it in the back of one of the cars.

At the door, Boomer had met the detective who was to coordinate the interviews. He volunteered the use of the staff room to conduct them in private.

The detective flipped open his notebook. "Looks like there's just three eyewitnesses according to Garner. His sister, Lacey, one of the kids and some guy he doesn't know. Nobody else saw anything?"

Boomer shook his head. "By the time, we got there, they were out of sight."

"So how'd you know something was going on up there? Garner said one of the kids heard the fight and alerted you."

"That's right. Taylor McKenzie was in class with our botany instructor, Aimee Justice. They were working in the herb bed there," he said indicating the second raised bed over, "when she heard it start."

"You want to show me exactly where?"

Boomer led the way and stopped by the bed. His clipboard was still lying on the ground. He bent over to retrieve it. "I'd say about here."

The detective stood still and listened carefully. All he heard were the sounds coming from the immediate vicinity. "You say the kid was here? I'm sorry but we have about six people up in that spot right now and I don't hear a thing."

"Taylor's clairaudient."

"Clair what?"

"She has the ability to hear things from great distances. Things the rest of us wouldn't hear."

The man scribbled in his notebook.

"So the kid tells you she's hearing some kind of fight on the mountain and you three take off, right?"

Boomer nodded.

"But by the time you get there it's all over. The assailants have fled. So you didn't see anything."

"That's right."

There was definite doubt in the man's acknowledging nod. He was still making notes as he followed Boomer back to the house and was shown into the staff room.

Lacey volunteered to go first. Boomer closed the door and went in search of the mystery man. He found him with Jesse in the computer room. The two were bent over a computer casing; its innards strewn around the metal skeleton. They were talking in techno speak, a language of which Boomer had only a vague understanding. But it was evident from the enthusiasm in Jesse's voice, he had at last found someone worth communicating with.

"Careful, Jess," Boomer said. "This is the guy who jammed your systems. You don't want to be giving away all your secrets."

Jesse looked up. He was practically dancing with excitement. "Yeah and he told me exactly how he did it and it was so easy. See our spy cameras are digital and he was using an analog system to...."

Boomer held up his hand. "Spare me the grim details."

Looking at Jesse, Kip's expression became shuttered. "He's right, Jesse. Allowing the wrong people access to your proprietary work can be very harmful. Sometimes fatal."

Kip stepped gingerly out of the room and went to sit on the stairs. He straightened out his right leg and rubbed his knee. He looked in the living room and saw it crowded with kids. He did a quick count, coming up with eleven plus Jesse in the computer room. That made twelve. The girl from the mountain was nowhere to be seen. She would make thirteen.

Boomer had gone to sit on the couch. Easing his way back, he stopped and reached around behind him. When he brought his hand up, Kip was surprised to see a sleepy skunk in it. Boomer handed the skunk off to the Hispanic boy who was sitting on the floor watching the deputy who was watching them.

The skunk yawned showing a set of small white teeth, then wriggling out of the boy's arms; she stretched and shook herself awake. She began a slow waddle out of the room. As she came close to the stairs, she stopped and lifting her nose, smelled the newcomer. She followed her nose to the side of the stairs and looked up at Kip with bright eyes. He reached through the balusters and lifted her into his lap. She sat up and put her paws on his chest as they exchanged breath, then she settled down in his lap and permitted herself to be stroked.

The kids were roaming in a restless state. The air was thick with emotional turbulence. A red-headed boy was wandering back and forth holding a tennis ball in his hand. Every few steps the ball would rise straight up out of his hand and fall back into it. Kip watched closely but couldn't catch the movement that propelled the ball up. Abruptly a book which was sitting on the edge of the large, square coffee table rose straight up in the air, turned a complete circle and fell to the floor.

Boomer calmly leaned over, picked it up and tossed it back on the table. As he did, a heavy pillar candle began to slide along the fireplace mantle, knocking into the photos and knickknacks sitting on it. Boomer spoke as he watched. "Alright, people, calm down." The candle stopped.

Several of the kids were huddled around a boy who showed a mixed ancestry of Caucasian and Asian. The boy was sitting with his eyes closed and would occasionally whisper something as the other kids listened.

"Scott, you better not be in that room," Boomer said sternly.

The boy's eyes popped open and he looked at Boomer. "I just wanted to see what real detectives do."

"We'll get Garner to arrange a field trip for that. You stay out of there, understand?"

The boy nodded a little sulkily.

Lacey emerged from the staff room and crossed through the dining room. "Next," she called.

Boomer shot the man a look. Kip used the railing to pull himself up and carefully set the skunk on the floor. He looked at Lacey who was pointing in the direction of the staff room.

It was a very long hour as the detective led Kip over and over his story. Kip was truthful about everything except his name, address and reason for being on the mountain. Finally unable to shake his story or anything else out of him, the detective let him go with a strict warning to stay available if they had any further questions.

The detective followed him from the room. As Kip paused, the detective veered around him and headed through the dining room. Kip leaned against the wall outside the room and drew a deep breath. The air was rich with the smell of browning meat riding on a wave of warm cinnamon. He could hear the detective begin to argue with Boomer about talking to the girl. Kip lost the thread of the conversation as he recognized he was drained to the point of collapse. He heard water running and realized his mouth was parched. Pushing away from the wall, Kip went left towards what appeared to be classrooms. He was looking for an exit and he found it around the corner of the staff room.

As Kip threaded his way through the garden beds, he was relieved to see all but two of the county cars were gone. He wouldn't have to circle out of his way to get to his home base and he was grateful. His knee felt as though glass shards had lodged themselves between his thigh and leg bones. He had a smashing headache beating in time to the throbbing in his bruised eye. The inside of his mouth was so dry the cuts in it were sticking to his teeth. When he grimaced at a jolt to his tender leg as he stepped in an unseen low spot, he tasted fresh blood on his tongue.

Kip pushed on. There was enough daylight left to bring his animals back to the trailer. He hoped there was enough of him left to do it.

Chapter 22

With the assistance of Scott's remote viewing, Boomer had little trouble finding his way over the ridge and through the woods to the trailer. He approached it, remembering to give space, but there were no signs of anyone. He slowly circled it. The area was immaculate. A small bench made from a half log with thick branch legs sat next to the metal steps leading into the trailer. On the back side of the trailer was a carefully constructed shelter of split logs. Boomer lifted the latch to the door and pushed it open. Sunlight entered through two screened windows.

There were cages inside; some with animals. He moved quietly and studied them. There was a baby bobcat whose eyes hadn't been open long playing with a carved wooden mouse in its bed of soft moss and cedar chips. A Cooper's hawk, balancing on a bandaged foot, turned a sharp golden eye on him. An owl sat on a roost, its eyes blinking and unfocused. In a large pen was a dog, some sort of shepherd mix, a back leg heavily bandaged. Ribs and backbone stuck pitifully through its rough coat. Still the dog managed to lift its head and give a welcoming thump of its tail.

Along the end of the shed was a built-in table. Arranged neatly in shelves above it were dozens of books all pertaining to wildlife, herbal medicines, animal anatomy, and animal care. On the shelves below were bandages, suturing packets, medical instruments, salve bases, and an eclectic collection of cans, not unlike their own collection of herbs at the ranch. A thick notebook lay open on the bench. Boomer looked at it. There were daily entries pertaining to each patient. It named the treatments, herbals and medications administered as well as recording the amounts of food and water each had consumed and who was urinating and defecating on schedule.

Although the smell of animal was in the air, it was a clean fresh smell. The man was meticulous. Boomer eased his way out and quietly relatched the door. He turned and surveyed the small herb bed laid out behind the shed. He suspected some of the starts had been unknowingly donated by Aimee. He went back around the trailer and sat down on the bench. He leaned his head back and let the warmth of the sun lull him into a state between wakefulness and sleep while he waited.

Boomer sat upright when the trailer door creaked open. The man leaned out. Taking a hold of the door handle and holding onto its jamb, he gingerly put his weight on his leg as he stepped down. A tee-shirt was flung over one bare shoulder. Boomer observed him and thought he saw a little too much rib and backbone on the man as well.

Looking to the south, the man pulled the shirt over his head. Boomer stood up alerting the man to his presence. The man turned to face him. His face was haggard with circles under his eyes almost as dark as the bruising on his face. His mouth was puffy and he was being protective of his right knee. But he pulled his shoulders back and lifted his head, readying himself for whatever he thought Boomer would hit him with.

"You look like hell," Boomer grunted.

The man's attempt at a faint smile ended in a grimace. "I've had better mornings," he said. "How's the girl?"

"She's good."

Kip nodded his head and shifted his weight carefully.

Boomer stood straight with his feet apart and his arms crossed over his chest. "Would you be willing to come to the ranch and help us try to figure out what happened yesterday?"

"Maybe, depends."

The silence stretched as the two men stood taking the measure of each other.

Finally Kip spoke. "I have a question for you…Boomer, isn't it?"

Boomer nodded.

"Would you have come and released them?"

Boomer looked down at the ground and shook his head. "Nope."

Kip sucked in air as though he had been struck.

He leveled his gaze at the younger man. "I'd taken them back to the ranch and made sure they got the care they needed until they were ready to be released." His face bespoke the truth of his statement.

Kip shaded his eyes and looked at the sky. "I've got a couple of midday feedings. We better get going."

By the time they had climbed up one side of the ridge and down the other, Kip was limping badly. A sheen of fine sweat covered his face and he was shaking from his blood sugar bottoming out.

When they reached the front steps, Kip had to lean heavily on the railing to get up them. The child he had helped yesterday stood in the doorway, holding a piece of rolled up paper. Boomer paused to introduce them.

"This is Alyson. I believe you two met in the middle of the woods yesterday. Alyson, this is Joe…Joe Meek."

Kip shot Boomer a look. Boomer shrugged. "As good a name for a mountain man as any. Unless there's something else you'd like us to call you."

Kip answered by smiling at the girl. "Hello, Alyson."

"Alyson, would you take Joe back to my office. I'll be along."

The girl smiled shyly and turned towards the back of the house. Kip followed the waist-length pale blonde hair. He saw the staff room where last night's interview had been held but Alyson went to her left, opened a door and held it. Kip went through and looked around. The room was a study in contrasts. The desk just inside the room was mounded over with files, magazines and papers. The other desk, closest to the window, gleamed in its bareness. He saw the overstuffed chair, hobbled to it and sat down.

Alyson came to stand by him for a minute. He realized she was a very pretty child on the cusp of blossoming into a woman. Oddly, something about her seemed familiar to him. She spoke in a barely audible voice, "Thank you for helping me yesterday." She thrust the paper she had been carrying at him and before he could respond, she was gone.

He carefully unrolled it and found a drawing on it. It was a beautifully rendered depiction of the little draw his trailer sat in. He was stunned as he studied the details drawn from the perspective of the ranch side. There was the half log bench, the side of the animal shelter, the herb bed and flying overhead a hawk.

Boomer came into the room a few minutes later carrying a large tray. He paused as he looked over Kip's shoulder. "I see Alyson has drawn you a picture. Looks like she got it pretty much right."

Kip looked up at him. There was uneasiness in his expression. He wondered if the spying had been going both directions without him knowing it. "How did she know about all this?"

Boomer motioned to Kip to move the drawing out of the way so he could place the tray across the arms of the chair. It was laden with a large platter of scrambled eggs, pancakes, a pile of sausage and bacon, thick slices of toast, a pitcher of huckleberry syrup, a small dish of butter, a glass of orange juice and two large cups of coffee; one of which Boomer took for himself.

"Eat. You've got as many ribs showing as the dog." Kip looked up from the tray. "Yeah, I snooped today. It seems to happen in these parts," Boomer said. Kip looked at him warily. Something very weird was happening here. It set all his defense systems on high alert. He picked up the orange juice and took a tiny sip. It stung the inside of his mouth but not as much he had expected. He took another swallow.

Boomer reached across the desk and picked up the drawing. He sipped his coffee as he studied it. "It's uncanny, isn't it, how she can put on paper so accurately something she's never seen. I know. She did a drawing for me last week of a place I left over 25 years ago. Every detail was dead on."

Boomer sat the drawing down; swung his chair around and gazed out the window. He glanced back at Kip and noticed he was just sitting there looking at him.

"No more talking now," Boomer said. "You need food in you more than anything. Eat."

Kip obediently tucked into his food but his mind was retrieving memories from last night. In his emotional and physical overload, he had seen things and not questioned them. Today they stood out in sharp relief: the book, the candle, cease and desist orders to a boy who was right in the room with them, a girl who could draw pictures of someplace she had never seen, an Indian complete with war paint and tomahawk. He wondered if he dare ask the question looming at the forefront of his mind. "What was this place?"

There wasn't much left on the plates when Kip finally leaned back and sighed with satisfaction. "Thank you and my compliments to your chef."

Boomer grunted as a reply and got up from his desk to take the tray. He was pleased to see the color had come back into the man's face and his hands had quit shaking "More coffee?"

"It would be much appreciated if it's not too much trouble."

Boomer was soon back and handed over a fresh cup of coffee. "You always that stubborn?"

"I came, didn't I," Kip said with an edge of defensiveness.

"I was referring to our walk over here. I would have sworn half a dozen times I was going to have to drag your unconscious body back but you just kept putting one foot in front of the other." A glint of admiration showed in Boomer's brown eyes.

Kip decided to capitalize on it. "At the risk of sounding ungrateful for the hospitality, what is this place? Who are these kids and why are they here?"

Boomer circled around his desk and sat in his chair. Putting his feet up on top of the clutter, he folded his hands over his midriff. "Spirit Wind Ranch is a school facility for psychically enabled kids."

Kip's expression was skeptical. Boomer smiled at the familiar reaction and rolled out his standard explanation of the school and the kids. Kip asked sharp, probing questions.

The conversation was interrupted by a small commotion as two women entered. One of them was the tall woman who had acquitted herself so admirably in the woods yesterday and was now holding a basin and a large bottle. The other was shorter with long blonde hair carelessly clipped to the top of her head. Both barely glanced at Boomer before fixing their eyes on Kip's face, scrutinizing it carefully.

Kip became acutely uncomfortable. To cover it, he stood up. The women exchanged quick looks when they noticed him avoiding putting weight on his right leg.

"This is Lacey Emery. I believe you two met yesterday and Aimee Justice, the keeper of the herb beds you have occasionally raided."

Kip flushed but looked at Aimee directly. "That was wrong of me. Your beds are magnificent. My own are too young to provide the variety and potency I needed sometimes. If you will figure out the value of what I took I will gladly make restitution. And you have my word, for whatever worth you may give it, I will not do it again."

Aimee crossed her arms over the front of her bib overalls and stared back sternly. "Boomer says you used them in caring for injured animals."

"Yes," Kip said as he continued to look unflinchingly into Aimee's blue eyes.

"Did they help?"

"Immeasurably. There are a number of wild things out there who owe their life literally to your skills as an herbalist and the gifts of your garden."

"They work on people, too. Go put these on," Aimee said as she unfurled the material she had been clutching. A pair of shorts hung from her hand; the electric green background covered over with brightly colored lizards of every kind.

Boomer looked down and shook his head. "I don't even want to know who those belong to," he muttered.

"We need to examine that knee," she said shaking the shorts in the direction of his leg.

Kip started to protest. "It'll be fine…"

Boomer looked up at him. "Son, these women are on a mission so the way I see it is you can voluntarily change into the shorts or be pants'd right here and now."

Kip held out his hand to take the shorts. Aimee directed him to the restroom. When he returned, they sat him down and propped his leg on a straight back chair. Lacey began applying a cool compress of comfrey to the knee.

Aimee examined the bruising around his eye and mouth. "Not much of a fighter, are you?" she said as she pulled a small container of salve out of her pocket.

"Not as good as some people, for sure," he said looking at Lacey.

Aimee lightly patted the salve over the bruising around Kip's eye and at the corner of his mouth. "What's in it?" he asked.

"Calendula petals and elder leaves."

He nodded. "Good stuff."

"Especially if you use it four times a day," she said handing it to him. Aimee glanced at the clock on the wall. "He's all yours, Lacey. I have to take class for somebody who claims to have an important meeting but is, in fact, just sitting around and sucking up coffee." She swept out of the room.

Lacey continued to wet and apply the compress for some minutes. Finally she pulled it off and dropped it in the basin.

She picked up the large bottle and poured herbal oil into her hand. Rubbing them together she began to massage Kip's knee. He jumped at the sudden sensation of intimacy and his muscles tightened as her hands began to methodically work their way up from below his knee to midthigh.

It was exactly the reaction one of her first childhood rescues had shown when she touched him. It took months of gentle stroking, talk and reassurances before the little dog had become her adoring companion. She looked up through her lashes. The man had his eyes fixed on the window with a look that said his mind was absenting itself from the moment. Was it a female's touch he was uncomfortable with or was it just human contact?

As she massaged, she experienced the sensation of someone unseen placing their hands over hers. They were slowing her speed and adjusting the pressure on her fingers. As she followed the unseen guidance, she felt a warm tingling feeling rising in her palms. She oddly was able to visualize the structure of the muscles, ligaments and bones. For some reason, she began to think of a soft blue light washing through the tissues cooling the bright red inflammation and she actually felt the changes in the knee.

The squeaking of Garner's utility belt alerted them to his approach. He paused in the doorway, holding the coffee he had collected from the kitchen with one hand and using his other hand to stifle an enormous yawn.

Lacey stopped her massage to glower at her brother. She hadn't forgiven him yet for being so willing to slap the cuffs on their rescuer.

He looked blearily down on her. "Cut the bug eyes, Sis, it was one long night." A movement caught his attention. It was a glimpse of a blonde woman straightening up from beside Lacey and smiling at him before vanishing. He was staring at the empty space now. His voice took on a peculiar sound as he asked, "Who was that?" Everyone looked at the place in the air where he was staring.

Lacey looked up at him. "There's nobody here but us." She suddenly looked at Boomer as she remembered the sensation of someone guiding her hands.

"Tall, blonde, attractive?" Garner was also looking at Boomer.

"Friend of the ranch in a manner of speaking," Boomer said, a small smile pulling up the corner of his mouth.

"Discarnate?" Lacey said in a barely heard whisper.

Kip was trying to decipher what they were all talking about when he felt a touch on his forearm. It was cool and squeezed in what felt like an affectionate greeting. Glancing down, he actually saw depressions from slender fingers in his skin. Simultaneously, a voice he thought he should recognize spoke in his head. "It's so good to see you again, Kip."

It didn't alarm him. He had grown up with the legends of the mountains and the ancient peoples who once walked them. Sometimes in the still of the night, he and his father had heard voices as though the mountain men still hunted over the land. Once when they had hiked through the Dickey Prairie area, they had come into a place that turned them back with cold warning. His father said it was probably a burial ground for the Molallas still guarded by unseen spirits.

While he was not disturbed, Lacey was licking her lips nervously and Garner definitely looked disquieted as he crossed to the chair at the other desk. He kept watching the place he had seen the woman as though she might unexpectedly reappear.

"So?" Boomer said indicating he was ready to get to the business at hand.

"Well, the good news is we know who they are. The bad news is we will probably never be able to lay our hands on them."

"Why?" Lacey asked.

"Those were some heavy duty people you tangled with yesterday. Pros based out of Las Vegas. These guys have more identities than the entire population of Molalla. They were somebody's hired guns."

"Damn, I knew I should have broken his head instead of his arm," Lacey said.

"Whose and why?' Boomer spoke everyone's thought out loud.

The silence in the room grew as the four adults grappled with the question.

Kip suddenly sat forward in his chair. "Lacey, describe to me exactly what you heard and saw from the time you came up the ridge until you were grabbed."

Lacey recited the facts as Kip looked hard into her eyes. "So they were not in sight when you and Alyson arrived."

"Right."

"And you were drawing for what twenty, thirty minutes before you were grabbed?"

Lacey nodded.

"Then you or the little girl was the target. Had to be."

Garner was leaning in his direction. "I may be just too tired but I'm not following."

Clutching his hands together and steepling his index fingers, Kip began to punctuate the air as he talked. Lacey temporarily lost the thread of his statements as she watched his hands. They were so beautifully masculine. They looked hard yet when he had put them over hers, the touch had been incredibly tender.

Something kicked her in the thigh of her crossed legs. Her brother had caught her staring. He gave her a knowing look out of the corner of his eye. She deliberately shut her mind off to everything but Kip's words.

"Because of the whole way it went down. These guys have been up on the ridge for over two weeks. They watched the ranch through binoculars and made a lot of notes, like they are studying the habits and schedules at Spirit Wind. Plus they went to the trouble of acquiring regulation Forest Service uniforms and driving a rig appearing to be regulation so if anyone stumbled on them…a hiker, a poacher, whatever, no one would question their right to be there."

Garner nodded, his attention now strictly on Kip.

"Second, when they heard Lacey and Alyson coming up the ridge, they had plenty of time to hide if they didn't want to run the risk of anyone mentioning them being there."

"And they did hide," Lacey replied.

"Where you couldn't see them but they could see you."

"Probably," Lacey nodded in agreement. "They certainly were well-positioned to surprise us."

"They were in no danger of being discovered, so why attack unless one of you was the target."

Garner leaned back in the chair. "The logic's there, alright"

Boomer's hand hit the desk with a crack causing the other three to jump. "Alyson," he said softly. Then more loudly, "Alyson."

Garner and he locked eyes. "Rich mother," Garner said.

"Rich mother who wants her back big time," Boomer said.

"Why would she do something as stupid as try to kidnap her? Why not just come get her?" Kip asked. 'You said the kids were all here at the choice of their families."

"That's right, every kid except Alyson. She was placed with us by court order when they removed her from her mother's custody for long term abuse and neglect."

"Didn't she have any other family?"

"They're mostly dead, from what the court was able to determine," Boomer said.

"Her father?"

"Father, too," Garner said. "He was killed in auto accident about eleven years ago. Hinky circumstances, too. The driver of the car was his long time assistant. When the paramedics got there, the father was dead already. The assistant was dying but he made a deathbed statement." Garner fished in his pocket and pulled out a notebook. He flipped through the pages until he found what he was looking for. "He told the paramedics to 'tell her I did it for her.' There were a lot of questions at the time but they were never able to make any connection. It was finally concluded that the assistant was one of those repressed types. You know almost 40 years old, still lived at home taking care of ailing mother. No social life. Developed a crush on his boss' wife and built a fantasy world around her. Acted on his own twisted reasons."

"Father's parents both dead. Grandfather died before she was born. Grandmother when she was about four years old," Boomer added.

"What about the mother's family?"

Garner shoved his notebook back into his shirt pocket. "Records on the mother have been fairly well obliterated. My guess is whoever her family had been; they didn't measure up to the world she was stepping into so she erased as much as she could. Without some deep digging, it appears she drew her first breath the day she got married."

Lacey leaned back on her hands and looked over the edge of the desk at Boomer. "That still doesn't tell us why? Why does Rhonda Maguire want her daughter back so badly she would go these extremes?"

The name hit Kip in the chest like a blow. "Who?"

"Rhonda Maguire," Boomer said. "One of nature's less likeable creations. She married into the Maguire fortune. Alyson is her daughter."

Kip felt stunned as he struggled to take in the information. "Alyson is the daughter of Chris Maguire?"

Boomer looked at him curiously. "That's right. You knew them?"

Kip swallowed hard and grabbed a tight hold on his flailing emotions. "I was at Oregon State the same time Chris was. We were in the same dorm for a couple of years until his mother got sick and he left. We kinda hung out together…you know, two geeks," he answered.

Lacey's eyes widened as she looked at him. Geek? He thought of himself as a geek? She looked at the thick dark hair waving back. The face was as chiseled as any cover boy on one of those romance books. She was fascinated with his hazel eyes and their constantly changing color like the ocean. And although he was a little thin, it didn't detract from the strength in his arms and broad shoulders.

He felt Boomer's eyes appraising him. "Like a lot of people, we lost track of each other after college. It must be pushing fifteen years or more since I last saw Chris. I had no idea he was dead."

"It was pretty big news when it happened," Garner said. "Media was all over it for days."

"I took a job out of state after college," Kip said.

Although Garner was watching him with askance in his expression, Boomer nodded and looked away.

"What state?" Garner asked.

"California. Silicon Valley." Nevada had come later.

Garner seemed satisfied. Silicon Valley had been the gold rush of the late twentieth century.

Kip was grateful when Lacey jumped up from the floor. "I got a showing I'm going to be late for."

Kip followed suit. "If there's nothing else, I've got feedings." He grabbed his jeans off the back of the chair and headed for the restroom. He returned to the office long enough to lay the folded shorts on the chair. "Thank you," he said to Boomer and turned back to the door.

"Whoa," Boomer said. Kip turned around, his face wary. Boomer pointed to the arm of the chair. "Don't forget the salve and your drawing."

Kip flashed a quick smile in relief and picked them up. He shoved the container in his jeans pocket as he left. Boomer noticed with satisfaction he was walking much better.

"So what have you learned about him?" Garner asked as he pushed to his feet.

"He went to Oregon State the same time as Chris Maguire."

"Stick to spooky kids, Boomer. You'd make a lousy detective."

"Maybe we're not looking for the same things."

Chapter 23

Lacey stopped the car and waited for the gates to swing open. Then turning the wheel she swung to the left and headed back to Sawtell Road. It was time somebody figured out what was motivating Rhonda Maguire and following a twitch in her instincts, she thought she knew where to look.

Fortunately, her clients hated the house on sight and she was able to quickly send them on their way with a promise of looking up more possibilities in the next day or so. They were barely out of the parking lot before she was in her car and heading to Highway 213 and Oregon City.

Two and half hours later she climbed the stairs to her apartment overlooking Molalla Avenue. She balanced the sheaf of copies she had gotten from the courthouse and the tall caramel latte she'd picked up at Hot Shots in one hand while she unlocked the door. She kicked it shut with her heel and crossed to set everything down on the coffee table. She glanced at her answering machine. The light was flashing. She punched it while she went to change into jeans and a paint stained Mexican wedding shirt, her favorite at home outfit.

There were only two messages. The first message was from her sister-in-law, Bernice, wanting details on her ordeal and the second was a friend who wanted to know if she was going to the Women's Council of Realtors' luncheon and, if so, could they carpool?

Lacey ignored the messages as she went back to curl up on the couch. She picked up the papers, tapped them together on the table and began to read. When she finally laid them down, she had the answer to one big question. She unfolded herself and went to get her phone. She punched in the number written on a list tacked to the wall and returned to the couch.

While she waited for an answer, she picked the copies up again.

"Boomer," the deep voice rumbled.

"I know why Rhonda Maguire wants Alyson back. I went to the courthouse this afternoon and got copies of all the wills…Sean Maguire's, Chris Maguire's and Meri Maguire's. It's a little complicated but the bottom line is that all those Maguire millions are Alyson's. Rhonda only gets access to the money as long as she is the legal guardian of the girl. Without Alyson, Rhonda's got a reservation in line at the Union Gospel Mission."

"So we're talking some really high stakes here."

"High, high stakes."

"And a player who's got the nothing to lose and everything to gain." There was a pause. "Come on back to the ranch and bring those papers if you don't mind. I think you need to be in the staff powwow tonight. I can offer you dinner among the savages by way of compensation," he said.

***

Boomer sat alone long after the rest of the staff and Lacey left just before 9 p.m. For a while he could hear the familiar sounds of the house settling down for the night. Then he heard footsteps upstairs as Harley, Dao and Carlita retired for the night.

They had debated having Alyson stay with Carlita one more night but decided against it. At this point, Alyson believed she and Lacey just happened to be in the wrong place at the wrong time. It was important to keep her believing it was a never-to-be-repeated event.

He played and replayed endless scenarios in his head trying to determine what would provide the safest environment for Alyson. Should she stay or should they go back to court and have her placed elsewhere for her protection? If they did that, would Alyson understand it was for her best interests or would the fragile shell of security she had begun to develop be shattered, perhaps irrevocably?

The minute hand was moving past 11 p.m. when he heard Meri's voice. "Go to bed, Russell. Answers come easier with a good night's sleep."

"Yeah, maybe. I just wish I knew what was best for Alyson."

"Alyson is where she's supposed to be."

He rubbed his eyes wearily. "But can we keep her safe?"

"When you've done all you can, you must go with faith."

"That's Carlita's strength, not mine."

"You've dwelled in purgatory for many years. Perhaps it's time you forgave yourself for that day."

He shook his head. "Can't."

"Or won't?"

Boomer closed his eyes. "The first time I ever saw whales was with my grandparents on a California coastal headland. As I watched, it was like my chest split open and a part of me jumped into the water with them. I was 9 years old and from then on all I did was eat, sleep and dream whales. Every night I prayed to be the one who would be able to open the communication lines between us and them. I wanted to be the one who would save them single-handedly."

"And your prayers were answered, weren't they," Meri said.

"Yes, by Minowah. Every success I owed to her. It was she who patiently taught me their ways, helped me interpret their language. That wise woman of the sea gave me everything her great heart could…and I blamed her and the pod for Laurel's death."

"You were overwhelmed by your loss. You were not thinking clearly."

"Even now, I can see her beyond the end of the gun barrel; feel my finger on the trigger and the acid of reprisal burning in my mouth. If Laurel's dad hadn't arrived and stopped me, I would have pulled the trigger."

"But you didn't."

"I broke faith with everything I was, everything I believed in that day. I broke faith with her. She knew…she saw the darkness in me…the vengeful executioner who wanted bloody retribution. She led the pod away and I never saw them again."

"She long ago forgave you for being only human."

Boomer looked at the place where the air shimmered when Meri spoke. "I wish I could believe that."

"Perhaps it's time you went back and asked her yourself."

There was a cool serenity coming from the place of Meri's voice. It soaked up some of the tension Boomer felt twitching through him.

He lifted one of the pages still spread on the table in front of him. "You did a good Last Will, Meri. At least you protected her from being dropped off a bridge somewhere."

"I just wish I had been able to do a better job of protecting her from her mother after I left life. The safeguards I arranged failed and that is my personal grief. Go to bed, now. She is well guarded tonight. Between myself, Helga, and Canute, a chilling welcome awaits anyone who breaches your security."

Boomer smiled tiredly. He got up from the chair, gathered up the papers and stuck them in his cubby before turning out the light and heading for bed. The last thought in his mind as he fell asleep was if Rhonda Maguire needed Alyson so much, why had she so maltreated her?

Chapter 24

"Why, my dear Virginia?" Rhonda said the next morning with a laugh that was a harsh imitation of the one once described by a columnist as lilting. The two women were sequestered in Rhonda's office. The rest of the house was crawling with attorneys, appraisers and photographers as they prepared a detailed inventory of the items currently in Rhonda's possession.

Virginia stood in the open French door smoking a cigarette; a habit she had once thought she had given up forever. "Yes, Rhonda. Every year we sent in requests for tuitions and now you're saying you never sent her. Why?"

"Yes, all those boarding school fees the attorneys so graciously handed over without question."

"What was the point? You certainly didn't need the money."

"It wasn't about money; it was about keeping them from sticking their snoopy noses where I didn't want them. If the Maguire attorneys thought Alyson was safe in the bosom of some swank girl's school, they were not going to be checking up on the little monster and interfering with my plan."

"Plan?" Virginia crushed her cigarette out at the base of one of the fig trees planted in huge antique Greek urns. Then she caught the full implication of Rhonda's words. "You mean you planned to do those things to Alyson? For God's sake, why?"

Rhonda had been studying her reflection in the carved Venetian mirror over the Italian marble fireplace but now she whirled on Virginia, "Because it was supposed to be mine, not go to some snot-nosed beast."

"Alyson had nothing to do with how the Maguires chose to leave their fortune. Why take it out on her? She's was scarcely more than a baby when all that happened."

Rhonda caught her shocked expression. "Oh, don't give me that 'mommy's such a monster' look. Actually, I had two very good reasons. One, the little horror had this really nasty habit of getting all glassy-eyed and popping off with information that she had no business knowing. A revolting little trick my late, unlamented mother-in-law taught her, no doubt."

She crossed back to her chair. "Second, I had to think about my future, didn't I? The day she turned eighteen I would have been out on my ear. But it occurred to me that an emotionally disturbed person would require a guardian…a lifetime guardian. And statistically, it is amazing how many children subjected to long term abuse are quite incapable of functioning well as adults."

Virginia had moved to the loveseat and was now staring at her, the revulsion plain on her face.

"Are we all horrified, my dearest Virginia? Is that so different from what you did to me?"

"What I did to you? I taught you how to move in the Maguire world. I taught you a shrimp fork from a dessert fork. I taught you art, music, appropriate small talk. I taught you who to trust and who to avoid. I took an uncut stone and polished you into a gem."

"You latched onto me like a leech. From the minute I called you to look at the pre-nuptial, you sank your claws into me so I could drag you right up the ladder with me."

"I was born on that ladder, girl, and I kept it under you when you had played a little too loose and reckless. You were about two heartbeats from being hauled into divorce court for your little fling with what's his name…Gary, the Happy Humper."

"So it's Saint Virginia now; always looking out for the little people."

"You were plenty glad I was looking out for you the day you showed up hysterical because Chris not only had suspicions, he had private investigators that had gotten the goods on you. My advice kept you married to all that Maguire money, didn't it."

"Your advice landed me with a freak that ended up with all the Maguire money. God, if I had known that, she would have been one of those 'tragic' crib deaths."

"And don't you think Chris didn't know that? Why do you think she was never left alone with you?"

"Well, it's all her fault. She was supposed to end up drooling and vacant-eyed in a padded cell. Not be romping around on some cowboy's ranch having the time of her life."

"I don't think Alyson is having the time of her life, Rhonda. You may not have broken her but you can bet you did plenty of damage. She's going to pay every day the rest of her life for your 'plan'."

"Shall we get out the violins?" Rhonda leaned back in her chair and looked out the window. Her perfectly manicured nails tapped on the desk top. "Plans…it's so important we plan for the future, isn't it?" she murmured.

Virginia felt the world tilting. She had always known Rhonda had a dark side but she had never grasped the full extent of the woman's embodiment of evil. The air in the room became thick and hard for her to get into her lungs. She had to get out. She stood up.

"I don't know what you are up to now, Rhonda, and I don't want to know. You're on your own from here on. Find one of those other law firms you threatened me with for years. I want nothing more to do with you."

Rhonda's laugh cut across Virginia's nerves. "I'm afraid you are going to have to stick with me, dear mentor. As you so aptly pointed out a while back, without Alyson I have nothing to be represented anymore so I am not likely to find a replacement."

"That's your problem, not mine."

"Oh, but it is your problem. Think about it, Virginia. Think of all those letters you wrote on my behalf about boarding school fees and other special needs for Alyson's care and well-being. Your complicity, dear heart, is on file with the Maguire law firm. Any direction I'm going, you're going as well."

Virginia knew the devil had come to collect.

Chapter 25

It had been a long night for Kip. He had walked back to his trailer in surging waves of emotion. Shock, anger, grief and revelation roiled though him. He did the mid-day feedings and then sat for a long time with the dog, the drawing beside him. He fought the desire to rush back to the ranch and find the daughter of Chris.

Synchronicity had brought him here; there was no doubt of that. Beginning with the soul-trashing events that had driven him out of Las Vegas and back to the mountains; then the mountains themselves who had unerringly guided him to a small abandoned trailer near a ranch where a girl named Alyson Maguire had been sent.

But now what? What should he do? What was he supposed to do? He listened for the answer; his heart straining through his shirt. There was only silence.

Mid-afternoon found him once again climbing the ridge. Below he could see the woman Aimee with four of the older kids working in the gardens. There were several kids sprawled under the blossoming cherry tree with the Indian. He leaned forward and strained his eyes. Yes, one of them had waist length pale hair. He sat down and watched until everyone had vanished into the house for the evening.

Standing up, Kip groaned as the long hours of not moving had stiffened his knee. He made his way down to the trailer. He prepared the evening feedings, getting the animals settled and shut in safely for the night. In the trailer, he fixed himself a peanut butter sandwich, washing it down with bottled water. He had put the drawing on his wall. Now and again he lightly touched it with his fingers as though he could somehow use it as a medium to communicate with the girl.

As dusk settled on the land, he thought of the one thing he could do; he could watch. The ridge that ran along the flank of the ranch was its key vulnerable spot. The two goons had used it without detection. If one plan failed, would there be another?

He also knew he could find out if other plans were in the works but it meant crossing back into the burned territory of his heart. He reached for his cell phone and then hesitated. Just as he was about to put it back, he saw again the terror in Alyson's eyes as she swung her face towards him when he had come over the log. He felt again her body suffocating. This wasn't about the past; it was about the future, someone else's future. After keying in the code to block his number showing up, he punched in the number he had sworn he would never dial again as long as he lived.

The phone rang and rang. He was just about to click off when she answered it. The voice was the same; soft, breathy and vulnerable. It instantly opened his mind's eye to the memory of her. The fall of silky chestnut hair, the huge brown eyes fringed with long lashes, the sweet oval of her face and the slender body with its aura of voluptuousness walking towards him as open as a trusting child. He had loved her with a passion that had ultimately consumed and destroyed him.

"Steffi?"

"Omigod, Kip! Kip, where are you? Are you here? Please, Kip, I can explain everything. I can make it right. Come home, I need you so much."

There was a surge in his chest but it did not produce the searing pain he had endured for so long. It was more like the burn of scarred tissue being stretched.

"I need to talk to Mike, Steffi. Where can I find him?"

"Please, Kip. It wasn't Mike's fault what happened. He just had a problem. He's better now. He truly is. He won't do it again. Can't you just forget about all that?"

Forget about all that? Forget that Mike's betrayal had cost him the premier security technology company he had spent 15 years building? Forget that his reputation and the respect of the industry he had been foremost in had been completely destroyed? Forget that he had left Vegas with his heart and soul in a body bag? Forget that even at this moment, Steffi was still justifying her brother's actions with no acknowledgment of the price he had paid? His heart went silent.

"I don't care what Mike does or doesn't do. I want information and he will have it." There was cold steel in Kip's voice. "Is he still in with Red Sedgewick's people?"

"Yes." Steffi's voice was very small. It was her little girl act that had so disarmed him for the seven years they had been together.

"Thanks. That's all I needed to know."

"But what about us? Don't you want to see me?"

"No, Steffi, I don't want to see you. Your brother killed the man you knew." He clicked off the phone.

He got up and went to the narrow shelf which served as his bed. Reaching under it, he pulled out the brown leather bag he hadn't touched since he stuffed it there. He hefted it onto the table and unzipped it. Dust puffed in little clouds. He just hoped the batteries were still good in his laptop.

He opened the computer up and pushed the power button. It began to hum. He fished around in his bag and pulled out a couple of jewel cases with the CDs he had burned during his last days in Las Vegas. He popped one of them into his computer and activated it from the touch pad. A few taps of his finger and he had the numbers he wanted. He reached back in his bag and pulled out a cord. One end he plugged into the back of the laptop and the other end he pushed firmly against the back of his cell phone. He typed in a few commands. Nobody would be able to track his number or location. He punched in the number he read on the screen.

The phone only rang once when one of Red's many minions answered. "State you business."

"Mike Witten."

"He's busy. Call back later."

"Tell him it's Kip and I want to talk to him now."

There was a rumble of voices and then rustling as the phone was handed off. Kip also heard the faint clicking start. He smiled grimly to himself. 'Let the search begin,' he thought.

"Listen, you dumb bastard, I was just on the phone with Steffi. She's hysterical. I warned you before if she got hurt what I would do to you." Good old Mike, bombastic as ever.

"I'm holding a CD, Mike, just one of many which contains a great deal of information regarding certain events that took place during your employment with Securitx. I can burn off about ten of these in a few minutes and overnight them to a few of the casino dons. So ask yourself, are you ready to spend the rest of your life hiding in the Sierras?"

For a couple of seconds, Kip could only hear harsh breathing through the phone.

"You're bluffing. I cleaned out those computers myself."

"Each system had a backdoor to another system that recorded every keystroke, every click of the mouse, the face of every person in front of them. You're alive, Mike, because I chose to let you live."

"What do you want?"

"Did Red supply a couple of thugs to kidnap a little girl out of Oregon in say the past couple of weeks?"

"Come on, Kip, you know better than that. We don't mess with kids. That's a one way ticket to the big house."

"Well, somebody did and my sources say they were pros from the city. I want names…the right names, and I want them two minutes ago. Oh, here's a hint. One of them is probably sporting a new cast on his right arm."

"And if I get you what you want?"

"Deliver the goods and the debt's paid. Blow me off and I'll choose your day of reckoning. My promise."

"How do I get a hold of you if I can come up with names?"

"Contact the Clackamas County Sheriff's office and ask for a deputy named Kevin Garner. Give the information only to him directly."

"You'll hear about it, right?" A click terminated the call.

***

Mike swung around to the bank of computers covering the entire back wall. 'So where is he?"

The young man in an oversized tee-shirt hunched in front of the monitors was pushing keys frantically. Finally he stopped and looked at Mike. "According to the signal, he is in a satellite somewhere over India."

***

Kip put the computer away. He pulled on a sweatshirt and got his heavy waterproof anorak out of the narrow closet. He stuffed another bottle of water and a granola bar in one of the pockets. Then picking up his flashlight, he left for the ridge. He knew from his short time in the ranch's computer room they had a good inside alarm system. He would make himself part of the outside system.

The sky was pale in the east when Kip made his way back to the trailer. The glowing dial on his watch told him it was just after 6 a.m. He could grab a couple of hours sleep before he needed to care for the animals. Back in his trailer, he dropped his coat and flashlight on the table. Setting his alarm for 8 a.m., he flopped on his bed, pulled the sleeping bag over him, and fell instantly asleep.

His eyes felt full of sand when the alarm woke him. He pulled himself out of bed and went to the sink. Pouring some bottled water into his hands, he splashed his face. He felt generally grimy. It was time to sneak off tonight for a shower. He hoped no one had bought the house yet.

By 10 a.m. Kip was walking to the hiding place of his motorcycle. He pulled the camouflage netting off and swung his leg over it. Then using his feet to back it around and turn it towards the road, he inserted the key and stood on the starter. It roared to life and he turned toward Trout Creek Road. Once there, he swung to the right and picked up Sawtell towards town.

He cruised through Molalla and along Highyway 213 to Oregon City. At the library, he pulled off his helmet and unzipped his jacket, pulling the CD out of his inside pocket.

In the library, he sat down at one of the computers. He clicked into the Internet and then entered a series of nine-digit IPs until he reached a site far distant from where he was sitting. Inserting the CD, he activated it and swiftly copied a small bit of information to the website he was working through. Then he sent it to the bank of computers in the back of Red's office. Instantly he clicked off and pulled the CD out. "See I remember, Mike. Never bluff if you haven't got the goods. And lots of luck finding me in Libya."

As he walked back out into sunshine, he felt a weight lift off his chest. He had truly closed the door on his previous life. And he felt purged.

Chapter 26

Lacey sat across the table from Alyson in the staff room once more. After Tuesday's disastrous events, there was absolutely no question of them drawing anywhere but within the safety of the ranch house. She had brought a small polished jade dragon for Alyson to draw. Its intricate Oriental carvings would be good practice in light and shadow.

Alyson was working diligently, looking up from the paper every few pencil strokes to study the piece. Lacey had started another sketch of Alyson but her pencil took on its own mind and she found she was recreating the face of the man from the mountain.

"He's nice. I like him," Alyson said softly.

"Yes. I like him, too. I call him Ching-Ling. A friend brought him back from San Francisco's Chinatown."

"No, not the dragon. He's nice, too. I meant the man who helped us. The one who came here. Joe. I'm sorry he got hurt. Do you think he's okay?" Alyson's blue eyes were now looking directly at Lacey.

"Well, Aimee and I did our best medicine woman stuff on him. I think he'll be all right."

"Maybe he'll come see us again," Alyson said as she bent her head back to her work.

Lacey was inwardly startled by Alyson's admissions. It was the first time she had ever heard her openly express feelings towards someone. Lacey knew the girl was emotionally reliant on Boomer whether or not she was aware of it. She had seen her look towards the man many times, seeking assurance and security in the touchstone of his presence. But by Boomer's own statements, Alyson was still like a little mouse scurrying around behind the protective walls she had built during her years of surviving. She would peek out now and again but any sudden movement and she was back in hiding.

Lacey looked down at the face she had drawn. "I like him, too," she thought.

When she had seen Alyson off to Chayote's history class, Lacey went in search of Boomer. She found him and Harley building a chicken pen off the side of the barn.

"Quit complaining, Harley. It's only until the garden is far enough along to withstand the chickens," he was saying as she approached.

"But my girls won't like being cooped up. It's liable to affect them psychologically. Depressed chickens do not lay eggs, you know."

"Dead chickens don't lay either and Aimee has described to me in grisly detail at least twenty two ways to separate a chicken from its head."

Boomer stepped away from the post Harley was holding. "Maybe you'll need to hire a chicken psychologist," Lacey suggested as she stopped.

"It's not in the budget," Boomer said as he swung the sledge hammer at the top of the metal post.

"How about an animal man?"

Boomer swung two more times and it was set. He dropped the sledge and leaned the handle against the post he had just driven. He used the back of his hand to wipe sweat off his forehead.

"Are you talking about the mountain man?"

Lacey nodded. "Alyson likes him."

Harley looked up from where he was pulling the chicken wire into place. "She told you that?"

"Yes she did. She was worried about his injuries and 'hopes he'll come see us again' I believe were her exact words."

"Breakthrough?" Boomer speculated.

Lacey shrugged. "I don't know but since she brought him up out of the blue, it's pretty obvious she has been thinking about him. Maybe she feels a connection because he knew her father."

"She doesn't know that though, does she?" Harley said as he hooked a clip in the wire and around the post.

"No, she doesn't," Boomer said

Lacey hefted her bag up and over her shoulder. "Well, I just thought you should know. I've never heard her state a desire to see anyone ever before. See you next Tuesday." She turned and headed to her car.

Although he was looking in the direction she was going, Boomer wasn't watching her depart. He was thinking about Meri's comment to him, "Alyson is where she's supposed to be."

He turned around and looked at the ridge behind them. There was a deep thrum in him as he felt events were in motion on levels that he could barely sense let alone understand. Somehow their mysterious mountain man was part of it.

"You gonna go get him?" Harley asked as he unrolled more chicken wire.

Boomer didn't say anything for a moment; then shook his head. "Nope." He bent down and picked up another steel post and the sledge hammer.

Chapter 27

It was just past dusk when Kip rolled his motorcycle out and headed back to the road. He made the turn onto Sawtell and then onto the roller coaster of Leabo Road and wound his way down to Wilhoit. Turning left, he rode to where an old cattle gate was nearly consumed by wild blackberries. Here he switched off his engine and glided in to a place hidden from traffic on the road.

Getting off, he opened one of the saddlebags and pulled out clean clothes and his shaving bag. He followed a deer trail leading to the back of Mrs. Krevitski's property. She and her husband had been mainstays at the Lutheran church his family had attended during his growing up. He always had a sense of guilt as he approached the back door and, using a pick he had created with a magnet salvaged from a hard drive, turned the deadbolt so he could enter. But he never did more than grab a quick, thorough shower and occasionally wash a load of bloody towels and bandage material; items that might draw attention to himself at the local laundromat. He assuaged his guilt by making sure a crisp $100 bill showed up each month at the assisted living center Mrs. Krevitski was in. He hoped it bought her whatever pleasure might be left to her.

He was in and out in 20 minutes. As he started back to his bike, he heard the approach of a car. He pressed back behind a laurel bush and waited for it to pass. When the headlights lit up the sale sign in the yard, he caught something he hadn't noticed before. Hanging below the company sign was a name board. It said Lacey Emery, along with a phone number.

A strong woman…she was the antithesis of Steffi's needy dependence. As other images of the two women began to rise in comparison, he shook them out of his head. He was interested in only one female now. Any distractions, mental or otherwise, could cause him a moment of carelessness he would regret the rest of his life.

It was almost 10 p.m. when he made his way up the ridge to his self-imposed guard duty. He settled on the log and used all his senses to establish a baseline of information. It was a trick he had learned from a boyhood summer of observing spiders. They knew their web and could instantly recognize whether the vibrations going through it were from wind, raindrops or dinner. He was spreading his web so he would recognize a change should danger approach.

By 11:15 p.m. the big house was dark. There was a faint glow from the window of the Indian's lodge house until just before midnight. The halogens in the front and the back offered pools of light with shadows flickering on their peripheries.

At 1 a.m. Kip stood and stretched. A sturdy rain had started to fall and he was feeling chilled and drowsy. A sleeping watchman was of no use, so he decided to move farther down the side of the ridge to stir up his blood. He had just reached the huge old Douglas fir that had been his starting point for his forays into the herb gardens when the entire upper floor of the house lit up. He recognized something had triggered the house alarm.

He didn't see her come out. The shadows of the porch hid her until she was poised on the top step. She wasn't looking with her eyes, but was tilting her head as though she were listening or sensing. She reminded him of a small animal testing the air to determine which direction held safety. Suddenly she ran down the stairs and turned in his direction. She was running swiftly through the rain as though oblivious to it. He moved quickly to the faint trail the humans had begun to trample out in the last few days.

Boomer was now on the porch scanning the area. The girl had moved into the shadows and made rapid progress to the place where the land began to rise. Kip kept his eyes on her as he climbed down the path to a point of interception. They reached the start of the trail at the same time. He knelt on one knee so he could catch her in his arms. Although she stopped, she didn't seem to be cognizant of what was happening. Behind her he could see Boomer and two other men spread out in a search pattern.

He stripped off his jacket and wrapped it around the wet girl. As he did she suddenly drew in a breath and went limp. He lifted her in his arms.

"Boomer?" she said in an almost inaudible voice.

"No, Alyson. It's Joe," he whispered back. He felt her nod her head slightly as though she was not surprised.

She was unresisting as he carried her back toward the house. He stopped when a flashlight caught him full in the face, temporarily blinding him.

He heard Boomer growl from behind the light, "What the hell?"

The other two flashlights began to converge on them.

Kip's response was quietly urgent. "She's soaked. We need to get her inside."

"Go."

It wasn't a comfortable feeling for Kip as the three men closely followed him to the house but Alyson's needs far outweighed his own concerns.

The heavyset Hispanic woman was waiting at the door as Kip climbed the steps. Kip stopped in the entry while Boomer handed off his flashlight to the black man. He held out his arms and Kip transferred Alyson to him. Boomer looked at the other men, "He's doesn't move till I get back." They nodded grimly.

Boomer and the woman disappeared through the doorway at the foot of the steps.

The tableau of the three men was unchanged when Boomer came out a few minutes later. He was carrying Kip's jacket which he tossed at him unceremoniously. His words were hard when he spoke. "Harley, coffee. Everyone else to the staff room."

Boomer turned on his heel and headed towards the dining room while the two other men formed a wall driving Kip along behind him. At the kitchen, the red-headed man peeled away but Kip felt just as compelled to keep moving.

Inside the staff room, Boomer flicked on the fluorescents. All three winced at the sharpness of bright light in their eyes. Boomer gestured Kip towards a chair. It was a silent command.

Kip slung his coat over the back of the chair and sat. He fixed his eyes on the wall opposite and remained absolutely still, his face giving away nothing.

Boomer used the waiting time to study the man closely. The bruise along his eye had moved to the dirty grey melting into chartreuse stage and there was no trace of swelling around the mouth. The man's face was still haggard though as if he were sleep deprived. Oddly enough, despite the circumstances, he found he did not feel mistrust or hostility toward the man. What he found himself thinking was this man could either be a very strong ally or a very cold enemy. Boomer knew the man would let him make the choice.

The only response Kip gave as Harley came through the door with a tray full of coffee cups and a carafe was a barely perceptible tightening of his muscles. He still neither spoke nor looked at anyone.

When Harley had placed a cup in front of everyone and settled into a chair to view the man with icy blue eyes, Boomer spoke.

"Do you have an explanation for what just happened?"

"Yes and no," Kip said.

Harley moved impatiently in his chair. He leaned on the table and stared into Kip's face aggressively as he laid his unsheathed Bowie knife on the table.

Kip stared at the knife while anger began to boil in his belly. He loathed testosterone driven games. He hadn't liked it when he had first learned of Mike's perfidy while some casino-employed thug kept a 9mm Glock pressed against the back of his head and he didn't like it now. He lifted his eyes from the knife and looked at Harley.

He abruptly stood up, shoving the chair back. He turned and pulled his jacket off the back of the chair. He did not look back as he left the room.

Harley rose to go after him when Boomer put his hand out to catch his arm and shook his head.

Anger drove Kip up the side of the ridge but as he began the descent to his trailer, he was stunned when a sob tore out of his throat. Somewhere inside a huge canker of grief ruptured and the anguish would no longer be denied. He stumbled to his trailer in a maelstrom of agony.

Out poured the pain of a three year old boy who had been essentially abandoned by his mother after his baby sister was born. He had grown up overshadowed by his sister. Their whole world had revolved around her wants, her issues, her demands. Kip had spent years vainly trying to gather what few crumbs of maternal feelings that escaped his sister's attention. He would have starved to death emotionally had it not been for his father. The two of them created their own world in the mountains, spending as little time at the house as possible. They were not missed.

Even as an adult he had evaded his needs by making his work his life…until Steffi. The beautiful woman-child had been so sweet, so naïve, so vulnerable, she had broken through his defenses. In the passionate release of his pent-up feelings, he had entrusted her with everything.

When Mike's betrayal had placed brother and lover in opposite corners, Steffi had also deserted him as he had sold off his company bit by bit to rectify the damage Mike had done. She had never grasped that his company was him and it was like parting out his soul. She been too busy trying to protect her thug brother to notice he was bleeding to death right in front of her. The day he put Vegas to his back, he vowed to never open the chamber of his heart again.

And then he and a child named Alyson crossed paths. When she ran so blindly into his arms tonight, he had felt her dark fears and desperate needs pour through him. In an instant his heart had responded and he had wanted nothing more than to take her to a place of safety; to wrap her in protection; to bring healing balm to the frightened, lonely child.

But they had formed a solid wall against him, their actions plainly stating he was not needed or wanted; indeed, he was perhaps perceived as a threat.

He had pleaded for guidance. The message was unmistakable. To stay this close might tempt him to rash actions benefiting no one. He would leave. She could not be hurt by what she did not know. It would be up to him to pay the price for both of them.

His decision made, he slipped into a cold, exhausted sleep; there to fall into a black dream.

He saw them when he came into the clearing around his trailer; a cloud of butterflies dancing over his tiny herb garden. Their wings flashed lavender, yellow and pink as they floated gently in the air.

Entranced he moved closer and saw the slender bodies were curved like females. The delicate creatures fled his approach but when he stopped, they returned to circle him. He raised a hand as one hovered in front of him. Settling on his finger, it turned its sweet feminine face up to look at him and opened its mouth. Tiny razor teeth were visible for a moment before it swung its head, driving them into his finger. Blood spurted as he tried to shake the beast off. With shrill shrieks, the rest dove at him. They sank their mandibles into his neck, chest and belly. Feeding voraciously, they grew bloated; their weight pushing him down and down until he began to fall through the dream.

For a moment he saw himself sleeping on his narrow bed before slamming back into his body. Kip jerked awake.

Chapter 28

The change in Alyson was noticeable as she came to breakfast. She seldom spoke much but she was always an appreciative audience for the rest of the kids. This morning she seemed to have withdrawn into a small place deep within herself. She took very little food and spent her time pushing it around her plate instead of actually eating it.

Domingo watched her with worry in his dark eyes. He finally reached out and touched her hand. "Hey, Al, don't you feel good?"

She shrugged. "I'm okay," she said, but she gave up any pretense of eating and slipped off the bench to carry her dishes to the trolley. She pushed the food off in the can used to feed the wild animals and put her plate and silverware in the brown tub.

She automatically sought sanctuary in the library window seat. She sat curled against the wall behind the curtain as she looked unseeingly through the rain-splattered window. Her heart felt almost too heavy to carry in her chest.

Harley came out of the kitchen with a cup of Aimee's special rose hip tea for Alyson. It was a good preventative against any chill she might have caught last night. He was startled to see her absent. "Where's Alyson," he asked Domingo.

Domingo nodded his head in the direction of the library. "Something is not good with her today," he said.

Harley crossed to the library and located Alyson behind the curtain. "I made you some of Aimee's rose tea with an extra special spoon of honey," he said as he held the cup out to her.

The Alyson who had always been so painfully grateful for anything given to her now looked at it as though she couldn't comprehend what he was doing. She didn't respond at all, just laid her head back against the wall and turned her face to the window again.

"Right," Harley said as he looked at the cup and then at her. He felt the distance between them and the enormity of it frightened him. He stood up and left slowly, picking up speed as he entered the dining room.

"Boomer been down yet?" he asked generally to the kids still eating. They looked at each other as if they had never heard of the name.

Harley tried again. "You know. Big guy. Lives here. Boomer?" This time most of them shook their heads no.

He sat the cup on the table and headed for the stairs. He had one foot on the bottom step when he heard Boomer's door close. He waited.

Boomer spotted Harley's distress and speeded his descent. "What's wrong?" he asked as he got to the main floor.

"Alyson. It's like she's here but she's not."

"Where?"

"Library. Her hidey-hole. I'll get you coffee."

Harley swiftly moved to the kitchen and met Boomer at the end of the tables. He handed over the cup and Boomer carried it into the library. He took a couple of quick swallows before setting it on the bookshelf closest to the window seat as he sat down.

"Alyson?"

Her chest was rising and falling rapidly. It didn't appear to be one of her attacks but like she was sobbing inside. "He won't come back," she said in a pain-drenched whisper.

"Who won't come back, baby?"

"Joe."

"How do you know he won't be back?"

"Because I think he died last night."

Boomer reached out and turned her face towards him. "Tell me about it," he said. He carefully blocked his memories of the night before.

She gulped in air and then hiccupped like she was holding back tears. "I had a dream or maybe I went to my 'other place'. I don't know. But I saw that he hurt; hurt so very bad. I needed to go help him but when I tried I got lost and ended up back in our room."

"It was a dream, baby. A bad dream, that's all. I am quite sure the mountain man is fine."

"But I can't feel him this morning. It's like he's gone."

"Would it make you feel better if I went over there and made sure he was okay?"

"You'll tell me the truth, no matter what?" she asked.

Boomer nodded. "Yes, Alyson. I will tell you the truth, no matter what." They sat quietly for a couple of minutes and then he asked, "Have you ever dreamed of the mountain man before?"

She nodded. "Once when I first came, I dreamed someone was calling my name. I didn't know it was him then, I just heard it and I knew I was supposed to find him."

"Did you know Joe before? Was he someone who came to your mother's house?"

Alyson shook her head. "No. I never saw anyone except at school and sometimes the people who worked for her. Will you go now?" There was desperation in her question.

He nodded. "Yes. Tell you what. I'm going to excuse you from classes this morning. Why don't you get your drawing stuff and stay here. Maybe I can get Harley to make you some cocoa."

"And cinnamon toast?"

"And cinnamon toast."

Harley was pacing like a cougar in a cage when Boomer came out of the library.

"I need one order of cocoa and cinnamon toast in the library. I'm going to find the mountain man."

Harley raised a questioning eyebrow. "I don't get it."

Boomer shook his head. "Neither do I. But Alyson needs him and she's going to get him."

Chapter 29

The storm that had moved in during the night hadn't dissipated, just settled into a steady light drizzle as Boomer made his way back over the ridge. The areas under the thickly limbed Douglas firs were dry but it was still a soggy journey.

When he came to the clearing, he had to agree with Alyson. Something was different. It felt almost like no one was here anymore. He crossed to the trailer and lightly tapped on the door. There was no response. He opened the door and, stepping up on the metal tread, he looked inside. It appeared everything in the trailer was now neatly folded and stacked for moving. The trailer was too small to hide a man and Boomer backed out. He went around to the back and saw the door to the animal shelter was unlatched.

He pulled the door open and stepped into the gloomy atmosphere. Kip was at his table placing books in boxes and covering them with plastic garbage bags. The animals were moving agitatedly as they watched him.

"Joe?" Boomer said.

Kip stopped, letting his hands rest on the bench but not turning around. "Look, by dark tonight, I will be long gone. Then we can both forget the last couple of days ever happened, okay."

"Can't do that. You're needed here."

Kip turned slowly around from the bench and then leaned back against it wearily. If his face was haggard last night, today it was absolutely ravaged as though the man had taken a shortcut through hell on his way home.

"Last night, the tune was different. More like "The Executioner's Song" if I remember right."

"Nothing wrong with your memory. I tend to come on like the village heavy when something hits too close to the heart. Don't much like that part of me. Any threat to Alyson makes me really ugly."

"Alyson," Kip looked away as he breathed her name but there was something in his tone that pierced Boomer.

"Look, I don't understand but she seems to have developed some kind of connection with you. She ran out of the house last night trying to find you." There was a rough note in Boomer's voice now. "Today she's shutting down because she couldn't 'feel' you. If she loses you without an explanation, we may lose her to that dark little cell she's hidden in most of her life. I am asking, would you come back to the ranch with me now? Would you do that for her?"

Kip stared at the ground. He knew if he crossed the ridge again, he would not be able to walk away no matter what the consequences.

"Please," Boomer said quietly.

Kip expelled his breath like a man who had just been forced into an unwilling surrender. He pushed away from the bench. "I'll get my jacket."

It was a silent walk back to the ranch. On the porch, Kip carefully wiped his feet and slipped out of his jacket to shake the rain off.

Boomer waited in the doorway. "If you could teach that to the wild bunch in this place, you could have anything you wanted including my job," he observed.

The house was quiet as they entered. "Kids are in class," Boomer said when he saw Kip looking around.

He led the way to the library. The toes of Alyson's tennis shoes were all that showed from behind the curtain.

"Alyson, I've brought Joe," Boomer said.

There was a flurry of papers being shoved aside and then the curtain moved back as she peeked out around it. Kip took a step forward.

Alyson slipped off the bench and scurried to stand in front of him. Although Boomer saw it for only a split second, Alyson's eyes had absolutely sparkled. Too quickly, she caught hold of her feelings and the eyes were once again guarded.

Kip looked down on her. He put his hand on his chest. "You breathing okay?"

She nodded without speaking.

"That's good. Were you drawing?"

She again nodded without speaking.

"Would you show me?"

This time, as she nodded, she reached for his hand but gave it only the barest of touches before she snatched her hand back. She turned towards the window seat and Kip stepped up beside her, very lightly placing his hand on her back as they went to the window seat.

While Alyson showed her work, Kip was studying her face. A face he hadn't even known existed three days ago was now engraving itself on his heart. The conversation was difficult. Alyson would start to speak and just as fast lurch away from her words as though she feared them. Using the same techniques he used with the wild and badly injured domestic animals, Kip was quiet and slow in his movements. He took every opportunity to lightly touch her hands, arms and back to quell the fear the feel of a hand could bring to the brutalized.

He was surprised when noise suddenly filled the house. Boomer came into the library. "Lunch."

Alyson quickly began to gather up her drawings and art box. Kip picked up his jacket.

"Thank you for showing me your work, Alyson. You have a wonderful talent. I predict great things will be in store for you in the future," Kip said as he slid his arm into the sleeve. Alyson immediately looked at Boomer, panic in her eyes.

"You're welcome to join us for lunch. In fact, I think Alyson would like you to meet her friend, Domingo. Domingo is an animal communicator. He can hear what they are thinking and is able to speak back so they understand him. I think you two may have something in common."

The plea in Alyson's face was plain.

Kip slid his jacket off and dropped it back in the window seat. "I would very much like to meet your friends."

As they approached the dining room, Boomer leaned close to Kip. "Have you ever eaten with a bunch of jackels? Let me give you some advice, if they start grazing on your plate, feel free to use your fork."

At the door, Boomer gave a sharp whistle. "People, we have a guest today. This is Joe. Some of you might remember him from the other night. He's a friend of Alyson's."

The kids all stopped and took a look. There were scattered, "Hi"s, "Hello"s and one "Yo, Joe" from the group.

Perhaps it was the presence of a strange adult, but it seemed the noise level diminished and the kids were more orderly in filling their plates with soft shell tacos, tortilla chips, guacamole, salsa, and a corn with red pepper and black bean vegetable dish.

A Hispanic boy who looked to be about the same age of Alyson immediately separated himself from the line of kids and came up to Joe.

"Dom, why don't you and Alyson show Joe where the food is."

The two kids led Joe to the buffet-style line and Alyson handed him a plate. They went through and filled their plates, then sat at the table.

Domingo showed the unique kid ability to pack away a mountain of food while still carrying on a conversation.

"Do you really know how to take care of wild animals that are sick or hurt?"

His own mouth full of food, Kip nodded.

"How do you know what's wrong with them?"

"I can feel it. I feel exactly where their pain is and how the pain feels. That helps me figure out what is wrong with them."

"Doesn't it hurt you?"

"Yes, except now I know just how much to feel and then I shut it off. It took me a long time to learn to do that."

Dom was steadily shoveling food in his mouth but his eyes begged for more information.

"When I was a kid, I would feel their pain and think it was my own. I was hauled to the doctor many times only to find out nothing was wrong; I was just picking up information from an animal close by. It embarrassed me so I stopped telling anyone when I felt pain because I wasn't sure if it was me or something else. I got so good at not telling, I ended up with a burst appendix because I thought I was feeling our old dog. It took a long time to recognize which was which."

"You're an empath," Aimee said as she set her plate down and swung her leg over the bench next to Domingo.

"Empath?" Domingo said, looking at her.

"Yes. It's a person who has the ability to so identify with people or animals they can actually feel precisely what the other is feeling."

Kip smiled. "I'm glad to know it has a name, I always thought I was just weird."

"That's the great thing about this place," Domingo said. "Everybody's weird so here you're really kinda normal."

The kids were getting up one by one and putting their dishes in the tub. Kip looked around and saw the tall boy from the computer room gesticulating madly as he talked to Boomer. Boomer's expression was somber as he listened. Finally, he nodded and then waved his hand in the direction of Kip.

The kid came over, grinning broadly. "Hi, Joe. I'm Jesse. Remember me?"

Kip nodded. "The computer man."

"Look, I just got Boomer to agree to let me skip English if you would be willing to take a look at some equipment I've been trying to modify so I can get some Kirilian photos."

The eagerness in the boy's face was so obvious to say no would be akin to kicking an excited puppy.

"Sure, I'd love to see what you are working on."

Domingo's tone was pouty. "That's not fair, Jess. I wanted Joe to take a look at Bandito and see if he knows what would make him feel better."

"You've got class," Aimee said as she got up.

"But Jess gets to cut."

"How about I stick around till your class is over and then we can take a look at Bandito. By the way what is Bandito?"

Harley came out of the kitchen. "One ugly-tempered raccoon," he said as he held out his finger with the red scar from Bandito's bite.

Kip lurched up from the table. There were still some issues that needed settling. No one threatened him without understanding exactly what they were going up against.

He looked at Harley with unmistakable chilliness. "And you are?"

"That's Harley," Aimee said. There was a wicked glint in her eyes as she recognized the male dance of dominance.

Kip kept his voice mild and inoffensive. "I was admiring your Bowie knife last night. Might I take a closer look at it?"

Harley was unsettled by the request. He glanced past Kip's shoulder to Boomer. Boomer gave a small nod of his head.

Keeping his eyes fixed on Kip, Harley slid the thong off the top of the knife and carefully pulled it out of its sheath. He handed it handle first to Kip.

Taking it, Kip examined it carefully and hefted it to get a feel for the weight. Then in a sixty second display of brilliant dexterity, he made the knife literally blaze a dance in the air as he moved it from hand to hand, around his hands, even around his back.

He politely handed it handle first back to Harley. "It's an excellent knife," Kip said quietly to a room stunned to absolute silence.

Harley looked at the knife and then at the man. Abruptly a huge grin split his dour face as he slung his hand out in age old recognition of a soul mate. "Damn, you are a mountain man," he said. "I'm mighty glad to know you, Joe." The room erupted in cheers.

The buzzer sounded for the start of the afternoon classes.

"Come on, Alyson. We got geography," Domingo said with a sigh.

Kip reached out and tugged her hair. "Since I promised Domingo I'd look at Bandito, I'll see you afterwards."

The time passed quickly as Kip hunkered down with Jesse in the computer room. Jesse explained his attempts to get pictures of Helga and Canute. This led to a discussion of the length of energy waves and how to speed or slow the shutter speed of a digital camera by utilizing the computer's program instead of the camera's.

Boomer wandered by the room occasionally. He heard Joe gently but firmly lead Jesse's thoughts through the logic and then help launch him into a different level with questions. The disappointment when the buzzer rang was sharp on Jesse's face. Kip took a tablet and quickly scribbled down several points.

"Follow this flowchart. It will take you where you want to go," he said as he handed the paper to Jesse.

Domingo was already at the door, bouncing from foot to foot. "Okay, Jess, my turn," he said.

Kip stepped out of the room and Domingo immediately grabbed his wrist. "This way, Joe, we can take a shortcut through the kitchen."

They met up with Alyson who was coming from the library with Joe's coat in her hands. Boomer stepped around the arch to the classrooms as Kip was putting his coat on.

"When you're done with Bandito, I'd sure appreciate it if you would stop back at the house before heading home," he said.

With the kids standing there, Kip felt compelled to say yes.

On the way to the outbuilding that was home to the raccoon, they were joined by Aimee. They made a strange little parade with Dom dancing backwards most of the way. Alyson stayed close to Joe. Aimee admired the way he was able to lightly place his hand on her shoulder or on her back without eliciting the skittishness the rest of them did. It was a gentling technique she had once seen at a horse workshop.

The building had two floors. The first floor was half covered in wood with the rest still dirt. Bandito's cage was sitting on the dirt side. It was large with a big branch and a small hollow log for the raccoon. There was a wide heavy dish full of water and several smaller dishes with dog food.

At the cage, Kip squatted and studied the animal. The raccoon was blind. Its dark button eyes were hazed over with grey.

"We found him as a baby. We think he was accidentally sprayed with ag chemicals when he was still in the nest and that's how he lost his sight," Aimee said.

"Too little to survive by himself and too spoiled by the time he was of age," Kip said.

"Okay, Domingo, tell me what he's thinking."

Domingo leaned close to the cage and silently stared at the raccoon for several seconds. "He's hoping he gets sardines for supper. He loves sardines." He concentrated some more. "He wishes the sun was shining and we'd put him out in it like we did the other day. The heat makes him feel better."

"Ask him about his pain."

Domingo concentrated. "It starts just above his tail and goes into his left leg. It just aches all the time and he's tired of hurting."

"Very good. My turn."

Domingo stepped back and Kip closed his eyes and bent his head slightly as he concentrated. As the others watched, they saw the pain flash across Kip's face. He instantly opened his eyes.

"He needs more room to move…not up but out, like a run. Do you happen to have heavy gloves; leather if possible?"

"Over in my potting shed, Dom. Look in the old green chest. Top drawer," Aimee directed.

Kip spoke softly to the raccoon as he waited for Dom to return with the gloves. Once he had put the gloves on, he opened the cage door and reached in. He took a firm hold of the raccoon at the scruff of his neck and placed his hand on his bottom to keep him from twisting away. He worked his hand over the spine and hip. He began to massage the hip area, gently, then more firmly. Then positioning his hand, he let go of the scruff and quickly twisted the raccoon's pelvis. There was an audible pop. Grabbing the raccoon again, he went back to massaging. Finally he drew his hands out of the cage.

"He could use two tablespoons of an infusion of celery seed with either dandelion root or devil's claw morning and evening for the next week. That should pull any toxins out of the hip area and allow the inflammation to dissipate," Kip said to Aimee as he stood up and pulled off the gloves. "How's he feeling now, Dom?"

The raccoon stretched his leg and then reached his front paws up the branch and stretched his spine. "He says it still hurts but better. He says you have nice hands; they don't scare him."

Kip handed the gloves off to Domingo. "Remember what I said about building him a run. He'll stove up again if he doesn't get more exercise."

When they returned to the house, Kip squatted down in front of Alyson. "After I've talked to Boomer, I have to go back. The baby bobcat missed her noon meal and the others need their medications. But I will come whenever you want me, okay?"

Although she nodded, Alyson's downcast eyes were fearful, like someone who knew to hope was to be disappointed.

Kip put his finger under her chin and lifted her head so she could look him in the eye. "Trust me. I will be here for you."

The longing to believe was strong in her expression but the tautness of her body showed the war going on within her. It reminded him of another child who had felt betrayed, abandoned and left out of love's circle. Nature had placed so much dependence on a mother's love and nurturing that when it was absent, the repercussions would echo a lifetime. His own heart told him that.

Harley came out of the kitchen with a large cup of fresh coffee. "Thought you might like something to warm you up," he said as he handed the cup to Kip. "Take anything in it?" Kip shook his head.

"Boomer's in his office. Said he was expecting you. And you," Harley said as he pointed to Alyson, "you owe me some kitchen time. We have about a hundred cupcakes that need expert frosting and somebody has to decide whether it's vanilla or chocolate."

Kip made his way to the office. Aimee was standing in the doorway holding a couple of magazines in her hand. "It's not rocket science, you know, Boomer. You take something out, you put it back. If it's junk, you trash it. If it's for staff, it goes in their cubby." She looked at Kip who had stopped a respectful distance from the conversation. "I just hope you understand the concept of organization," she said as she left. "King Clutter is on his throne, go on in."

Kip peered around the door. He pursed his lips in a silent 'whooo'. Boomer nodded. "That's why her gardens always look so great. The weeds are terrified to grow in them."

He motioned Kip to the overstuffed chair. Whatever Kip thought he was going to hear when he sat, he was totally unprepared for Boomer's question.

"What would you say to coming to live on the ranch? Maybe sign on as one of the staff?"

The unexpected questions left Kip with an incredulous look on his face.

Boomer leaned forward and rested his clasped hand on the mountain of debris covering the desk. "You've got abilities that could fill in some big holes around here. As you know now, Jesse's got a computer chip where a brain should be. We're failing him because none of us understand the technical points he's always trying to accomplish. Domingo has dreams of using his gifts to more appropriately align human/animal relationships. He's got the gift but not the guidance. And Alyson…," he paused to reach for his coffee cup.

"Alyson needs someone who can lead her into the light of living. You're the only adult she's reached out for since she's been here. Whether you know it or not, you possess some kind a key to the girl's soul prison. Maybe if you were around to edge the door open, the combined efforts of all of us could bring her out enough to heal her."

Boomer stopped and looked at Kip. His watchful expression was giving nothing away. Boomer decided to push ahead.

"Here's the way it works at Spirit Wind. You get your room and board including three squares a day. The ranch purchases all your instructional needs and supplies for your particular area or areas of expertise. You get a monthly stipend, use of the ranch vehicles, health and dental insurance, and a couple of months in the summer for downtime."

"I'm not saying it's a cakewalk around here. You're dealing with kids, teenage ones for the most part. They can figure out 99 ways to aggravate you before they get to breakfast. They all have gifts they are learning to focus and control that puts a whole other spin on life. Things can and do get hairy occasionally. Hell, the truth is if things go smooth for more than 30 minutes, I start looking to see if they have all been murdered." He paused, "More coffee?"

Boomer got up from behind his desk and took Kip's cup along with his own to get refills. It would give the man time to think.

He came back, handed Kip his cup and returned to his chair behind the desk. He didn't say anything further.

Kip knew it was his turn. He was walking on the edge of a mental razor. The last thing he wanted was anyone to start snooping into his past. There were things he wasn't ready for anyone to know or piece together yet. And he knew any place dealing with kids always required extensive background checks. He couldn't risk that. But he realized he couldn't abandon Alyson either. Boomer was right. There was a connection to Chris' daughter and her needs were pulling him in deeper each time he was with her.

He was so consumed by his own thoughts, he jumped when Boomer spoke. "You know, Joe, Spirit Wind is a different sort of place. What we look for can't be found in a background check or by running fingerprints through an agency. Good people sometimes get caught up in bad things. It sours them on life for a while. Been there myself. If you choose to come to Spirit Wind, you're Joe until you tell us otherwise. You come, we don't ask questions; you go, we don't ask why and we leave you alone."

A few more minutes of silence passed as Kip processed the information. "Where would I stay if I were to come?" he asked.

Boomer led the way out of the door by the classrooms and back to the building housing Bandito. This time Kip paid attention to the building. It was a nice size, 20x30 square feet. Boomer led him to the second floor. "It's needs some work and cleaning up. And we would need to get some furniture. But I think we could make it com…." Boomer broke off mid-word as the top half of him disappeared in the upper area. "Well, that explains a lot of doings around here," he said more to himself than to Kip as he stepped up into the room.

As Kip's head cleared the flooring, Boomer reached out to the wall at the top of the steps and flipped a couple of switches. The room lit up.

The two men looked around together. At the far end of the room, windows overlooked the gardens. Fitted neatly around and running the length of the wall under them were bookshelves. A reproduction pot-bellied stove sat on a small platform of old bricks, flanked by a kindling filled bucket and a wood crate stacked with small logs. Two older overstuffed chairs with ottomans were arranged in front of it. A metal bedstead was already made up with a thick quilt while a couple of more quilts sat on top of an old trunk at the foot. A reading light arched over the pillows.

The end they were standing at had been divided into a tiny kitchen with a dorm size refrigerator and small microwave. There was a sink not much bigger than the one at the trailer with cupboards above and below it. A closet had been built into the wall dividing off the bathroom.

A small gate leg table made from plywood sat just outside the kitchen area together with two mismatched wooden chairs. On the table was a tent folded sign. Written in neat calligraphy were the words, "Welcome, Joe!" In front of it sat the little knife he had lost here weeks ago.

Kip realized Boomer was just as surprised by everything as he was. "You didn't know all this was going on?"

Boomer looked at him with a certain resignation in his face. "I am just the director at Spirit Wind. Why would anyone tell me anything?"

The two men became aware of a rising noise level at the foot of the stairs as a growing number of people kept shushing each other. Boomer motioned for Kip to lead the way down.

The moment his head cleared the floor, a great cheer went up. Voices clamored from all sides. "Surprise!" "Do you like it?" "Will you come live with us like Chayote said?" "We all helped." "We painted the table and chairs."

Kip was reeling from the barrage. He had had more human contact in the last few days than he had had in nearly a year. His nervous system was approaching overload. The noise was cut short by a sharp whistle from Boomer.

"First of all, people. I want to thank everyone for keeping me informed of this project."

The staff standing behind the kids looked at each other abashedly.

"Second, Joe hasn't exactly said he was coming. And although, I'm sure he appreciates all you've done and your enthusiasm, it still is his decision."

Kip saw disappointment sweep over the kids' faces generally but it was Alyson's face he sought. The little glow in it snapped off. She burrowed her way back among the other kids, using them to shield her.

This was the moment the universe had somehow contrived to bring him to. Walking away was no longer an option. He took a deep breath. "Yeah, I'm in."

Domingo jumped out in front of the group. "Can we go get your stuff now? And the animals? I want to see the bobcat baby."

Kip reached out and lightly cuffed him on the chin with his fist. "Might as well. I'm pretty much packed up."

In less than two hours of controlled chaos, it was done. They had brought the van and the truck around to the back way close to the little trailer's location. Aimee and Chayote supervised the kids carrying his personal belongings, books and medical supplies to the van and loading it.

Domingo and Jesse volunteered to help Kip move the animal cages to the truck. Once in the shed, Domingo had moved from cage to cage demanding the story behind each animal. "There was an owl living in your room but we made her move. We told her she would find more mice if she took up living in the part of the barn where we kept the livestock feed. I can't hear what happened to this one. Her thoughts are all fuzzy."

"She ran into something. She's what's called 'stargazey'. She has a concussion. She just needs time to heal and for her brain to clear then she'll be ready to go back to the woods," Kip said as he settled a tarp over the owl's cage.

At the hawk's cage, Kip put a tiny leather helmet made from the finger of a glove over the hawk's head. "This is a Cooper's hawk. It looked like he had a toenail ripped out and it got infected. His foot was so swollen he couldn't grab his prey. He was a very sick bird when I found him."

Jess was kneeling on the ground by the dog's cage. "What about him?" he asked as he reached into stroke the dog's head.

"Her. Somebody condemned her to a long slow death by starvation when they dragged her out into the woods and left her chained to a tree. At some point she got her back leg wrapped up in the chain and she was too weak to get it off. When I found her, it was embedded in what was left of her flesh."

Jesse's face grew dark with anger. "You know, Joe, human beings suck sometimes."

When all was loaded, Kip went to his motorcycle and uncovered it. He guided it out to where the other two vehicles were waiting. Although the kids oohed and ahhed over it, Aimee was the one who stroked it and walked around it commenting on its power and performance abilities.

"You ride?" Kip asked.

She nodded, never taking her eyes off the bike.

He pulled the keys out of his pocket. "Would you like to take it over? I think I would really like to walk back, if you don't mind."

Aimee lifted the helmet off the sissy bar and put it on. Pulling the chin strap up, she took the keys and turned on the ignition. It was an experienced foot that kicked the starter and revved the engine. Then she smoothly roared out towards the road.

Kip waited as, first the van, and then the truck pulled out. He walked back to the trailer. He spent time setting it in perfect order as he thanked it and the area it sat on for sustaining him during the dark months of his return.

He stood in the small circle that had been his home and felt the shift in the response of the land. His time was finished here. He turned towards the ridge and began the walk into his new life.

By the time he had made his way down the other side, he saw the truck and van were already unloaded and parked back on the gravel. He guessed he was home now.

He slept hard that night. When he awoke in the morning, he sat up temporarily disoriented by the strange surroundings. He pushed the quilt back and swung his bare legs out of bed. The still chill air made him reach for his jeans quickly. He appreciatively went to the tiny bathroom. No more sneaking showers.

He was just finishing buttoning a flannel shirt over his tee-shirt when he heard someone talking below. He moved silently in his stocking feet to the stairs and listened. The voice was too quiet to catch the words. He carefully made his way down until he could duck his head and see who it was. It was Alyson. She was sitting with her back to him. She had the door to the dog's cage open and was stroking the animal as she talked. He sat down on the stair and listened.

"I'm sorry someone was so horrible to you. Domingo told me what they did. I know how awful it is. Sometimes I didn't get food either. And sometimes I got hit a lot. She used to tell me all the time that I was a monster and I was only getting what I deserved. Maybe someone thought you were a monster, too. Maybe there's something wrong with us so nobody wants us. But I'll like you so you're not alone and you don't even have to like me back if you don't want to, okay?" The dog thumped her tail. "Domingo says we should call you Milagro. He says it means miracle. Would you like that?" The dog's tail thumped again.

Kip felt an almost uncontrollable urge to race down the stairs and grab Alyson up his arms when she backed away to shut the door on the cage. Instead, he silently moved back up the stairs before she saw him.

He stood at the windows watching her cross back towards the ranch house. There was so much he could tell her about her daddy, her grandparents, her past but how much could she absorb? He felt instinctively she would not be able to take in more than small doses. For like a starving animal, it had to feed tiny amounts many times a day until its body readjusted to receiving food, otherwise the big meal given to save it would kill instead. Patience, he told himself. The opportune moment will come when she will be ready. Now, just build her trust in you. He hoped the advice he was giving himself was right.

By the second week, the routine at Spirit Wind had reshaped itself to fully absorb Kip. It was too late in the school year to teach regular classes in computers or animal husbandry but he worked with the kids on an extracurricular basis. Chayote and he joined skills to build a bench, bookshelves and a locking supply cabinet in the lower part of the building. Chayote expertly wired in lighting to suit his every purpose; from a strong examination light to a soft light for providing night care.

When he commented on the Indian's skills, Chayote just shrugged. "I paid for my college by working in construction. When there was a drought in teaching jobs, I went back and got my electrician's license."

Although no one else had ever seemed to question the foreknowledge of his coming, he asked Chayote about it during one of their hammering sessions. "You showed up in my medicine fire one night."

When Kip had looked at him strangely, Chayote explained. "I use the medicine fire to clear myself and to talk to the mountain spirits. They showed me a tall man surrounded by many animals coming. You see that has been on our wish list for a long time."

"Wish list?"

"Yeah. When we need something or someone, we put it on a list in the staff room. We all focus on it and envision it coming to us. Then we wait and keep ourselves open to possibilities. Sooner or later, like you, it shows up. So when I saw you in the fire, I figured I better get some place ready for you. The kids had a ball keeping it secret from Boomer."

The next opportunity Kip had to go to the staff room, he looked around until he spotted a small index card thumbtacked to the bulletin board. He was amazed to see just how closely he paralleled the information on the card.

He was working Thursday morning on the raccoon's run. Chayote had left him with the finishing work to go teach his class. Kip was adding strips of half round over the top edges of the wire to protect from anyone snagging themselves on the sharp points. He had already opened the door to the cage and Bandito was carefully patting his way down the length of the run. Its ten foot length by four foot width and three foot height would give the animal plenty of room to keep his joints moving.

"Mind if we join you?" a woman's voice asked.

He turned and shielded his eyes from the sun. It was Lacey with Alyson in tow.

"We're going to draw Bandito," Alyson said.

He held out his hand to Alyson. Lacey was mildly surprised but tremendously pleased to see Alyson reach out and take his hand. "Pull up a piece of the grass, girls," he said, "I got just a couple more nails to put in and then you three can share some quality time."

Chapter 30

It was one of those feel good days, Boomer decided as he steered the van up the mountain. The sun was shining, the trees were fluffy with their brand new leaves and there was money in the bank. Although the ranch operated as frugally as possible, it would have been a stretch to get Joe on the payroll until the new grants and tuitions rolled in. But the man refused to accept any money.

"I'm not teaching yet, just helping out here and there. I don't need the money. Still got some put back from before. Room and board will do it for me for a while."

Joe was a good fit. He was very patient with the kids. He was heading Jesse down avenues that Boomer hadn't even known existed. Domingo and Alyson were shadows to him whenever they were free. He had instructed the staff on how to physically contact Alyson without raising fears by recognizing she was an abused animal in human form and needed the same consistent treatment as an animal would. He had pointed out the most healing thing in the world was another person's touch. They were all practicing his techniques and Boomer swore he was seeing a tiny bit more of her every day since Joe came.

The only thing he had still to accomplish was getting the other girls over their crushes. He kept hearing words like "fox", "hunk", and "stud-muffin". He was amazed Joe didn't trip over their tongues whenever he walked by. Carlita and Aimee had taken to doing morning clothing checks to make sure the appropriate things had been placed on the appropriate parts of the anatomy and more clothes than skin was in evidence.

He hoped this phase burned out quickly. Nothing made him more nervous than a female's hormones. That part of the world traversed by women easily reduced the strongest, most macho men to quivering jelly.

The steepness of the mountain leveled out slightly as he approached the Leabo Road junction and he shifted back into fourth gear. He caught sight of a motorcycle swinging around the curve on Leabo leading to the stop sign but it showed no signs of slowing. Instead, it accelerated, pulling out in front of the van. Boomer hit the brakes and swung the wheel hard to the left.

***

The junior high kids were bent over their test papers. Dao was sitting cross-legged on the floor at the front of the classroom as he monitored the anatomy test. Domingo looked up from his papers, "Dylan's copying my answers," he said from his desk at the front of the room.

Dao looked severely down the row to Dylan seated in the last desk. "Dylan, stay in your own head or I'm going to make you take the test alone while everyone else is outside."

Dylan stuck his tongue out at Domingo and went back to his paper. Dao closed his eyes and breathed.

As Dylan tried to remember the name of the bones in the toes, he suddenly felt like metal and glass were shattering around him and a great pain sliced through his shoulder. He came up out his chair with a shriek.

Simultaneously, Dao heard a scream come from the Spanish class. He leaped to his feet. Dylan was out of his chair and running to him.

Carlita flung the door open. "Brandy, she has felt an accident."

"Dylan," Dao said as he grabbed the shaking boy by his shoulders. "Dylan, what did you feel?"

"An ac..cid...ent," the boy said through chattering teeth. "I could hear the crashing."

Harley loped to the room. The kids from Carlita's class had already pushed into the room. Chayote was outside the door with his class pressed close to his back. Harley managed to get into the room only to be pushed aside by Carlita as she headed to the sobbing Brandy. "Brandy, did what you hear sound like a car accident?"

Brandy was crying too hard to do more than nod her head.

"Boomer. Boomer went into town this morning," Harley said. He turned to a white-faced Scott. "Scott, can you see where?"

Scott scrunched up his eyes but he was obviously too rattled to focus. Dao came over and sat in one of the desks. He turned Scott towards him. He put his hands on either side of the boy's face. His voice became the quiet monotone they were used to hearing in meditation. "Scott, Breathe. Follow my voice. Breathe in. Breathe out. With each breath the fog is clearing and you can see. Breathe in. Breathe out. It's getting clearer. Breathe in. Breathe out."

Scott jumped. "I see. It's square like our van."

Dao held on. "Where is it?"

The boy scrunched his eyes tight as he concentrated. "It's by the big arena."

Harley shot out of the room. "I'm going. Call the ambulance." Chayote followed him. The two men leapt from the front porch and sprinted towards the truck. Lacey and Alyson got to their feet in confusion as they watched the truck rev up and in a crash of gears back around and roar towards the gate.

The sight of the van up against the tree with the driver's side crushed chilled Harley's and Chayote's blood.

"Grab the fire extinguisher," Harley said through tightly clenched jaws as he pulled off the road in front of the van. Harley went to the passenger door. He hesitated a second to steel himself for what he might see before he pulled it open.

The air bag had deployed and was now draped over Boomer's lap. Boomer's head was leaning back, eyes closed. Harley could see an abrasion on his chin and one cheek bone where the airbag had struck him. There was blood coming from the side he couldn't see. It was oozing down Boomer's neck and spreading across the front of his tee-shirt. It was hard to tell if it was the angle he was looking from but Boomer's left shoulder seemed distorted.

There was shattered glass from the windshield and side window scattered across the seats. Harley leaned across carefully and managed to get his fingers on Boomer's wrist. He felt for a pulse. It was there and it was strong. That was the good news. The bad was Boomer hadn't responded to his touch.

"Hang in there, Boom, old man. The ambulance is coming." He pulled back out of the door and looked down the mountain. Like anyone who waits for an ambulance during a crisis, it felt like they were going by way of Walla Walla to get there.

Chayote was at Harley's back peering. "His pulse looks good," Chayote said as he watched the carotid pump.

"Hurry, hurry," Harley was muttering through clenched teeth.

"Listen," Chayote said as he grabbed Harley's arm. They could hear dogs begin to howl from below them to above them. "The ambulance will be here soon." In a matter of two more minutes, the ambulance crested the hill and pulled in behind the van. A second siren was heard as well. A country sheriff's car pulled alongside the van and stopped, its lights flashing. Garner got out.

He moved between the two men, clasping their upper arms and pulling them away. "Give them room to work," he said.

He pulled his notebook out of his pocket. Harley noticed his pen wasn't quite steady, as he asked, "Any idea of what happened here?"

Harley and Chayote shook their heads. "Two of the kids, Brandy and Dylan picked up the accident telepathically. They felt Boomer have it. Scott helped us find him."

One of the EMTs came up. "Has he been conscious since you got here?" he asked as he held a clipboard. The two men shook their heads. "Can you give us any information about him?"

Harley assisted by Chayote was able to answer most of the questions. The other two emergency personnel were now maneuvering a backboard with Boomer firmly strapped into place out of the van and onto the gurney. They moved it to the back of the ambulance and loaded it. "Either of you want to ride with him?" the driver asked as he made ready to get in front. Chayote pushed Harley. "You go. I'll follow."

They were nearing the bottom of the mountain when Harley heard a weak but familiar voice speak. "Damn, people, that hurts."

He turned in the seat and peered back. One of the emergency personnel looked up and gave him a quick smile of reassurance. Something inside him let go and he had the most inappropriate of mountain man responses. He wanted to cry.

***

After witnessing the abrupt departure of Harley and Chayote, Lacey and Alyson hurriedly collected their supplies and ran back to the house. The kids were all gathered in the living room. Several of the girls were openly crying; the rest, white-faced, moved in random patterns as though they didn't know what to do.

Carlita had her arm around Brandy and Dylan. Dao had a tight grip on Scott who was still shaking.

Lacey stopped and looked around in confusion. "What happened?'" she asked generally.

Carlita looked up as she pulled still another tissue out of her pocket and gave it to Brandy. "There has been an accident. Boomer…the van he is driving, it hit a tree. The niños, Brandy and Dylan, they felt it as it happened. Scott, he is able to find it. Chayote, he called and said they were on their way to the hospital. He does not say but there is much fear and worry in his voice."

Aimee came out of the kitchen with a stack of paper cups and a large pitcher. "Valerian tea. It will help calm nerves." She handed the cups to Lacey and poured as Lacey held each one out then handed it to one of the kids. The only one who refused was Jesse. "Nah, I'm good," he said in a voice that squeaked with tension.

As soon as the tea had been downed, Dao moved to the center of the room. "We cannot help Boomer by falling apart. Now is the time to put your gifts to real purpose. I want everyone to sit in a circle on the floor and join hands. Carlita, Lacey, Aimee and myself will sit at the four points." He pointed Aimee to the north position, Carlita to the south position, Lacey to the west and he took the east. He then called the kids, three at a time to sit between the adults. When everyone was positioned, he sat down and motioned for everyone to hold hands.

"Now, I want everyone to close your eyes and listen. We will breathe, calm our fears and gather our strength." He spoke the cadence drawing everyone into the same breathing pattern. An aura of quiet and strength began to settle over the group. The only sound was 16 people breathing as one.

"Now, beginning with you, Katy, I want you to think of Boomer as well and strong as he was when you last saw him. Picture it clearly and then picture yourself handing the image to the person next you. As you hand it off, squeeze that person's hand so they know they are receiving your gift of wholeness to Boomer. Take as much time as you need. When Scott delivers it to me, we will ask that it be delivered it to Boomer."

It was nearly 30 minutes later when Dao released Scott's and Katy's hands and lifted his own. "Carlita, a prayer for delivery, please."

The prayer emerged in Spanish but Lacey felt the message in her innermost being and she swore she heard a rustling in the air above them. Dao brought his hands down.

No one moved. The sense of unity and love they had created seemed to hold each person to their spot. The cell phone sitting on the coffee table began to ring. Aimee reached out and grabbed it.

The kids barely breathed as she mouthed Harley's name and then listened. Finally she said, "Thanks. Keep us posted." She clicked off.

"Boomer has a dislocated shoulder, a mild concussion, bruised ribs and a couple of minor cuts. They are taking him to surgery to anesthetize his shoulder and put it back in place. They haven't decided whether or not to keep him overnight just to make sure nothing else shows up. If they do it will be strictly precautionary. Harley will call us when he's out of surgery."

No one said anything or made a move. Aimee clarified it for them. "Boomer's going to be alright, guys. He won't be up for volleyball for a few days but he will be all right."

In the way of young people who have come through a tremendous emotional storm, the room erupted in goofiness.

Lacey looked around to see how Alyson was handling it and realized for the first time, she wasn't there.

A wave of fear rose in her as she stood up and slowly checked the room one more time to make sure she hadn't overlooked her.

She crossed to the girl's dorm room. There was no sign of Alyson.

She ran out of the house and down the steps, looking around her wildly. She spotted Kip coming out of the barn. She ran across the yard to him.

"Joe! Joe, have you seen Alyson?" Her voice was as frantic as her eyes moved back and forth over the area.

Kip shifted the used syringes to one hand and put his other on Lacey's shoulder. "Steady. What's going on?"

Briefly Lacey recapped Boomer's accident. "I lost track of her when we were calming the kids down and I guess I didn't realize she wasn't there during the healing session until it was over. I thought she might have come for you."

Kip shook his head. "I was in the pasture worming the cows. She wouldn't have found me unless she had gone down the drive."

Lacey twisted towards the drive. "I should go look."

"First go check the library. Alyson's favorite security place is the window seat behind the curtains. If she's not there, check the drive. I'll check the outbuildings."

Lacey turned and sped back towards the house.

Kip sprinted to his building. He stepped inside to ditch the syringes in the trash can. Although he couldn't see while his eyes were adjusting to the shadowy interior, he heard a whimper coming from somewhere inside. He moved slowly in the direction of the sound allowing his eyes time to adjust. He found her half in Millie's pen, sobbing into the dog's neck. Millie was licking the side of her face, stopping when she saw Kip approach. Her dog eyes were dark with worry as to how to help the distressed human.

Kip put his hand on Alyson's back. The girl was shaking violently. "Hey, hey Aly." Alyson went rigid under his hand. Kip reached in and scruffled the dog's ears. "Thanks, Millie, I'll take it from here."

He placed his hands on Alyson's shoulders, firmly pressing her out of the pen. He put his hand under her chin and tried to turn her face up to look at him when she pushed it away violently. "No, no, don't. You'll get hurt like Boomer and die, too." Great sobs began to fight their way through her body, challenging her already struggling lungs.

"Alyson, you didn't have anything to do with Boomer's accident. I don't know exactly what happened but I know you didn't cause it."

Alyson turned away from him and wrapped her arms around her stomach, doubling over as she fought the pain and tears for air. "But I did, I did! It's me. If someone likes me they have to die. She told me. I'm a monster and people die when they like monsters. That's why Daddy and Grandma Meri had to die. They liked me. And now Boomer's going to die, too." She dissolved into convulsive sobbing.

Kip grabbed Alyson up and sat her on the stairs with enough force to startle her. He needed to break the mounting hysteria. She looked up at him in surprise. He caught her face in his hands and held it tightly.

"No, Alyson, no. Those were lies. There were horrible, terrible lies told to you by the real monster. I know. I knew your Daddy and your Grandmother. Your Daddy was a friend of mine from college, for a while my best friend."

The shock of his words stopped her cold. She searched his face. "You knew Daddy and Grandma?" she whispered.

"Yes. I did. I am going to tell you the truth about them. And I want you to listen with your heart. Your heart will know if I'm lying or not, won't it."

She nodded.

"Your daddy died in an auto accident. An accident caused by a man who was mentally unbalanced. The last words the man said were "tell her I did it for her." He was saying he killed your father and himself for your mother, not you. She was the reason behind the accident, not you."

Alyson's eyes were wide as she absorbed the information but a shadow passed over them as she asked, "Grandma?"

"Your Grandma Meri died of leukemia. Do you know what that is? It's cancer of the blood. She got sick with it long before you were born when your Daddy and I were still in college. They weren't sure she would live then. But she got better and she did live. But leukemia often comes back especially if there is a lot of stress. It was the stress of your Daddy's death that probably triggered your Grandma's relapse and death. In fact, I believe it might have happened sooner than it did if it wasn't for you. Your Grandma loved you very much. I know she did because I knew her. Far from killing her, you are the reason she lived as long as she did. You gave her life not death."

He loosened the grip on her face now and brushed at the tears with his thumbs. "Alyson, you are a very brave, wonderful girl who had to live in the monster's house. But living with a monster doesn't make you a monster. And maybe, just maybe, your mother did what she did to you because you weren't a monster and she was scared of you."

"Scared of me?"

"Baby, you're an artist. What happens when you put light by the shadows?"

"They get darker."

"You were the light that kept showing her just how dark she was."

Tears began to well up in Alyson's eyes again.

"And, Aly, Boomer's not going to die. He's banged up but he's not going to die. He cares for you. He cares very much. They all do. They wish they could take an eraser and make every bad, painful, horrible thing that happened to you go away from your memory so you would know it is safe to love someone."

Her heart cried out its need from its deep, dark chamber. "Please keep me safe. Please love me."

Kip felt it cut through him. But he did not shut off the cry. He held onto it as if he could pull the pain out of her into his own body.

Sweeping her up in his arm, he sat on the stairs. She wrapped her arms around his neck and all the tears she had never shed, never been allow to shed poured out of her. Kip kept his arms tight around her and rocked her, stroking her hair and whispering her name over and over.

A shadow appeared in the door way to the building and he looked up to see Lacey standing quietly, tears streaming down her face. Keeping one arm tight around Alyson, he reached out his hand. Together, they might neutralize the poison infecting Alyson.

Lacey went to them. She put her arms on Alyson's shoulders and laid her head on top of the girl's head. Kip pulled her around until she was wrapped in his embrace as she wrapped Alyson with hers.

In time, Alyson cried herself into emotional exhaustion. She turned her face from the tee-shirt she had soaked with her tears and nuzzled her forehead under Kip's chin. She went limp as her body sought cessation from the tempest.

Lacey pulled back slightly from the place where her head had rested on Kip's chest while she held onto Alyson.

"She's asleep," she whispered.

He moved slightly and Lacey pushed away from him. He got his feet under him and stood up with Alyson still in his arms. Lacey took a step in the direction of the house, but Kip jerked his head in the direction of his apartment. He turned and carried Alyson up stairs. Lacey followed. He looked to the bed and Lacey hurried to pull the quilt back. He laid Alyson on the bed and covered her up.

He pulled one of the ottomans close to the bed. Sitting on it, he reached for Alyson's hand. As he enclosed it in his own, he leaned close to Alyson and spoke softly, so softly that only by holding her breath could Lacey hear his words.

"I'm so sorry, baby, so sorry you were left alone with her. She is a black shadow sucking the love and light out of every life she comes in contact with. She is a soul monster. But monsters can be slain. Together we will do it. Together, my little Alyson, we can create a place of light that her black soul cannot survive."

Lacey was spooked by the words. There was more going on here than she could divine. She understood Joe's anger being directed to a woman whose merciless actions had nearly destroyed a child. She herself had felt a similar consuming anger. In fact, she had more than once fantasized about bringing retribution to Rhonda Maguire. But her thoughts had traveled in the direction of seeing the woman behind bars, shuffling her youth and beauty away in endless days of prison. But Joe's words spoke of familiarity with places she shied away from even acknowledging existed.

As she looked down on the man's face, she wondered, "Who are you, Joe Meek? And what has drawn Alyson to you? Is the danger greater or lesser because you have strayed into her life?"

Lacey suddenly wished Boomer was anywhere but the hospital. She felt a great need to try to understand what was going on at Spirit Wind; to understand why they brought this man onto the ranch without even knowing his real name; to understand why his presence was alarming her.

Seeking a reasonable escape, she took refuge in the banal. "How about I get some coffee for us from the house?"

He gave her a quick look. "Thanks. That would be appreciated."

At the top of the stairs, Lacey looked across at the man as he sat quietly watching over the sleeping girl. Despite her fears, it was a sweet picture; one she might try to put on paper.

Lunch was underway at the house. The staff had resorted to the great American standard of a quick meal. There were platters of hot dogs, bowls of potato chips, and a huge pan of pork and beans.

As Lacey came into the kitchen, Carlita looked at her questioningly. "Sorry about disappearing but Alyson took the accident pretty hard. You know how much she relies on Boomer's presence."

"She is okay?"

"She's with Joe," Lacey said wondering if that was okay.

Carlita nodded as she scooped more hot dogs out of a pan of boiling water. "Then she is to be okay." She handed the plate to Lacey. Lacey carried it into the dining area and sat it on the table. A phone began to ring. Instantly the noisy room quieted. From the living room, Aimee's voice answered.

Nobody moved or spoke until Aimee came around into the dining room. "That was Harley. Boomer's out of surgery. They've put his shoulder back and taped it into place. The doctor wants to keep him overnight. They can keep him more comfortable at the hospital. They'll release him in the morning. Harley and Chayote will be home as soon as Boomer gets settled in a room. Boomer says thanks, he got our message."

Lacey took the time to load a tray with plates of food. Carlita poured coffee into one of the thermos jugs and added a soda pop to the tray.

Lacey carried it back to Joe's room. Alyson was still sleeping as she came through the opening in the floor. She crossed to the small table and set the tray down, swinging the jug up beside it.

She poured coffee into one of the mugs sitting on his counter and carried it with one of the plates to Kip. Although he released his hold of Alyson's hand to take the food, he did not move from his place.

"I don't want her to wake up and not see someone," he said quietly. He nodded towards the other ottoman. "Join me?"

Lacey pulled it over and went to get her own plate and coffee.

They ate without speaking as they sat guard over the girl. Lacey had just taken the empty plates and gone to the table to refill the coffee cups when Alyson stirred. For a moment her hands flailed in the air as she came up from the depths of sleep. Kip instantly caught them and called her name.

"Aly, it's okay, we're here."

Her eyes fluttered opened and sought him. She almost immediately closed them against the light streaming through the windows. "My head hurts," she said hoarsely.

Kip pulled the quilt back and slipped his arm under her shoulders lifting her to a sitting position. "I'm not surprised, baby. But Lacey here may know what to do."

Lacey looked at him in consternation. Do? Other than getting a couple of aspirin, she didn't know what to do. But suddenly, her hands tingled and she realized she might know what to do.

She went to the bed, moved the pillow and sat down. She placed her hands on Alyson's forehead and began to stroke. It was almost like looking at the pictures in a how-to book inside her head. She could see where to put her hands each time and how to move them. She worked her way from Alyson's forehead to her neck, shoulders and back. She felt things with her hands which she didn't understand but she sensed what she was to do about them.

At last she dropped her hands into her lap. She felt enervated, as if something had passed from her into Alyson.

Kip reached out to stroke Alyson's cheek. 'How do you feel now?"

"It's gone. I'm..I'm," Alyson hesitated. "I'm hungry."

"That I can take care of," he said smiling. He looked at Lacey and saw her drained expression. He reached out and took her hands in his own. He turned them up and lightly ran his thumbs over them as he studied them. "You have healing hands."

Chapter 31

She could still feel his touch hours later as she sat curled up on the end of her own couch. She reached for the glass of wine sitting on the coffee table and took a swallow. Its dark dryness bit her tongue pleasantly. She pulled her drawing pencil out from behind her ear and bent to the sketch she was working on.

It was a slightly altered version of the scene from this morning. She had changed the perspective so she could capture both Alyson's sleeping face and a three-quarter profile of Joe.

Several of her early art instructors would have chided her for it. She could hear words like "maudlin", "mawkish", "sentimental" echo in her brain. In their esteemed opinions, the only work worth producing was edgy, provocative, even perverted. Anything reflecting the more tender emotions was to be scoffed at.

Years later, when she had raged to another instructor about her inability to take her art to higher, more marketable levels, he had told her she was creating from her mind. "Art must call to people, speak to them. The only art that does that is created out of the blood of the heart," he had said to her. "To find your art, you must find your heart."

She paused to reach for her glass again. Looking over the rim at her drawing as she sipped, something caught her eye. She moved the glass and looked more carefully at the drawing. She used the pencil to lightly flick imaginary lines in the air as she retraced the outlines of eyebrows and mouths. She had drawn Alyson's and Joe's so similarly as to be nearly identical. Why had she done that? She strained her memory to see the two faces again but the images fuzzed and faded out as she chased them. Their elusiveness pissed her off.

She pitched the tablet at the other end of the couch, slammed her pencil onto the table and drained the last of the wine in her glass. She was going to be bed. Maybe tomorrow the world would be once again the sane place she had lived in before she wandered in the wonderland known as Spirit Wind Ranch.

Chapter 32

Rhonda sat at her desk, phone still in hand. She could not believe Simon had turned her down even though she had reminded him it was his people who had failed to get Alyson.

"Too true, Mrs. Maguire. But in any nefarious operation, there are always factors which cannot be anticipated. In this case, two factors. The woman who accompanied your daughter up on the ridge was well versed in the art of self defense. And the unexpected arrival of the man who appeared to have been spat up by the mountain itself was an additional complication."

"Then get people who can do the job properly. After all it's not like you are stealing gold from Fort Knox. It's one lousy brat."

"I appreciate your need to reacquire your daughter, Mrs. Maguire, but unfortunately someone has taken an interest in her welfare and the word is out through the places I usually secure assistance that she is not to be touched."

"Who would care what happens to her?"

"I don't have the name but apparently it carries a great deal of weight in certain circles."

"Then look elsewhere. I don't care what it costs."

"I'm afraid our relationship is at an end, Mrs. Maguire. My own sources have let me know you are shortly to be scratched from the list of serious players. I do wish you well in whatever the future holds. Goodbye."

A trickle of cold sweat slid down Rhonda's back. Somehow Simon's words made the letter she had read and wadded up in anger seem more real.

She didn't have to unball it to see the words again. They were emblazoned in her brain. Couched in the politest of legalese was the notice that she was to vacate the house within ten days from the date of the letter; all credit cards, open accounts and checking accounts once formerly funded by the Maguire Trust were being closed. The Trust would not be responsible for any further debts. Though they were stripping her of her jewelry and furs, they were generously going to allow her to retain her clothing. Once she vacated the house, they would return with their inventory lists and verify every item was still in extant. The removal of any furniture, furnishings or household items would be treated as theft and they would prosecute accordingly.

The kicker paragraph was at the end. They put her on notice they were planning to appear before the Clackamas County Court and request a revocation of the bond they had put up the security for. They suggested she might wish to contact family or friends for assistance in reinstating the bond if she desired to remain out of jail during the pendency of her case.

What family, she thought bitterly. She had cut them off the minute she walked back down the aisle with Chris' ring on her finger. So drearily middle-class, they were not going to bask in the rarified atmosphere of her new life and they certainly weren't going to be permitted to exploit her connection to the Maguire family. For all she knew, they could all be as dead as the Maguires.

A thought electrified her nerves. If any of her family was alive, they could step in on Alyson's behalf as her lawful flesh and blood. And if they were appointed her guardian, they would have access to the money. The thought of her family being able to touch it made her skin crawl.

God, if only they had been able to break Meri's Will. It had been a black day when Virginia informed her there was no chance of challenging it. As long as Alyson was to inherit, a court would not overturn it. The only chance would be if Alyson died before her.

Virginia had caught the thought that ran through her mind and instantly pointed out the paragraph stating Alyson's death while in Rhonda's care, regardless of the cause, would permanently ban any claim she might want to make.

Virginia...something Virginia said was niggling at her. She turned and studied the room trying to remember what it was. Then she caught it. "You may not have broken her but you can bet you did plenty of damage." Buzzing behind the thought were statistics...all those long boring child-related statistics she had sat through at the Maguire Foundation meetings. That was where she had first gotten the idea of turning her abuse of Alyson from just a random release of her own pent-up feelings to something more methodical...ritualized...purposeful.

A constellation of ideas lit up Rhonda's mind. Alyson wasn't in her care anymore. If something happened to her now, it would be the fault of Spirit Wind Ranch. She would be free to challenge the Will. And if the Maguire Trust failed a second time in their charge to protect Alyson, they might be much more amenable in settling a suitable amount of money on her.

It was so simple. All she needed was a few minutes with Alyson. Just long enough for Alyson to do one more thing for Mommy.

Chapter 33

The early May morning was proving to be unseasonably warm with the temperatures already approaching 75 degrees by the time Lacey swung her car through the gate at Spirit Wind. As she pulled around in front of the house, she could see the staff was conducting classes outside.

Dao and the freshman group were sitting under the big maple tree at the far end of the porch. Boomer sat in the rocker on the front porch, his arm strapped to his chest by the shoulder immobilizer, while the older students perched on the steps in front of him. Chayote was seated in the shade of the lodge house with three of the younger students.

She could see Aimee and Joe working in the herb bed. As she let her eyes pass over them, she felt the sting of jealousy. It startled her and she applied the brakes with more force than necessary, raising a small cloud of dust that drifted over the students on the porch.

"Sorry," she called as she got out of the car while the kids went into exaggerated coughing and choking.

Boomer's deep voice called them to order. 'Okay, people, we still have not satisfactorily come up with identifying traits exhibited by warriors throughout the epic literature we have read this spring. Teresa, give me one."

Alyson had been sitting on the porch rail with her art tablet and box. She slipped off and made her way carefully around Boomer's class to scamper down the steps.

As she approached, Lacey held out her canvas drawing bag. "I thought today we would paint in the botanical tradition using something from Aimee's gardens. Why don't you take my bag over there while I get some water from the kitchen?"

As Alyson dutifully grabbed her bag and turned towards the beds, Lacey gagged internally. She had had no intention of doing botanicals today. She had thought of it on the spur of the moment as an excuse to be in the vicinity of Joe and Aimee. Why? So she could see if there was some sort of attraction between the two as if it was any of her business or she cared?

Lacey came back out of the house with a pint jar of water and saw Aimee heading towards her potting shed with a handful of cuttings. Joe continued to work the spading shovel along the edge of the bed.

She and Alyson had just decided to do a study of the clove pinks when they heard the rumble of the old pickup coming up the drive. Harley swung the vehicle off the drive and across the grass. He pulled up in front of the potting shed; then backed around so they could off load the pile of bark dust in its bed.

Watching the truck maneuver through the yard, everyone failed to see the little forest green BMW sports coupe arrive hidden in the truck's dust until it pulled to a stop behind Lacey's car.

A woman got out of the car and looked around her with barely concealed distaste. Boomer eased himself to a standing position. The kids were looking at the woman with open curiosity as she approached.

"What a charming, bucolic picture this makes, Mr. Evanrud…or do you prefer to be called Boomer?"

Boomer gave a curt nod. "I suggest you get yourself back in that car and leave, Mrs. Maguire…it is Mrs. Maguire isn't it?"

"I've come to see my daughter."

"Over my dead body."

"What a terribly noble sentiment. But there I see no reason to go so far. I just want to talk to her for a moment."

"Mrs. Maguire, I'm sure you are aware you are in violation of the court order put down at the time Alyson was placed with us. Get in your car and leave or we will remove you."

Rhonda ignored him as she shaded her eyes and examined each of the groupings of kids. A movement out of the corner of her eye caught her attention. She turned towards the place where Alyson and Lacey were sitting.

She started walking towards Alyson in the deliberately languid gait she had always used just prior to administering her punishments. Only she and Alyson knew the mental torture the child went through as she watched each slow step bring pain closer.

Kip had dropped the shovel and squatted low by the bed. He reached out to grab Lacey's arm. "Go."

Lacey's eyes were ablaze and her face flushed with anger as she watched Rhonda's approach. "Right after I tear the bitch's face off," she said through clenched teeth.

Kip's grip tightened on her arm until it was painful. "No, this is not your fight. Trust me and do as I ask."

Lacey looked at Joe. Coldness burned in his eyes. She stood up and headed towards the house. She kept watching as she hurried across the yard. Rhonda paid no attention to her.

Alyson stumbled to her feet. She was shaking so hard she could barely make her body function; the wheezing of her breath becoming audible.

As Lacey reached the house, she noticed something odd. Despite the silent motions of the staff pointing the kids into the house, they were quietly collecting along the end of the porch.

Rhonda stopped a scant four feet from Alyson. Her lips pulled back from her teeth in a mockery of a smile. "Well, look at you. Eating does agree with you after all. Now Mommy is just going to talk to you a few minutes and then I'll go away. I promise."

A shadow loomed behind Alyson and hands settled on the girl's shoulders, pulling her back against something solid. "I don't think you have anything Alyson needs to hear, Rhonda."

Rhonda stared at the man for a few moments; then her eyes opened wide. "Kip?"

"Hello, little sister. We missed you at Mom's funeral." He felt Alyson start under his hands.

"So, it is you. Always turning up where you aren't wanted. And just look at you. What's it been…almost twenty years and you've worked yourself all the way up to yard man. Mom would have been proud of you." She enjoyed the flash of pain on his face.

"No, Rhonda, Mom wasn't proud of me. Mom scarcely remembered I existed. Even at the end when Dad and I were holding her hands, her last words were for you."

"Oh, and they were?"

"Guess you're going to have to find them, if you can." Kip watched Rhonda's eyes. They were the signal she was going to root through the dark closets of someone's mind in search of exploitable skeletons. As she narrowed her eyes, he opened himself to the feelings and memories rushing through Alyson. His mind filled with pain and terror. He saw through her a woman's face twisted into a malevolent gargoyle's mask.

He released the images when he heard a sharp intake of air. He looked at Rhonda as her angry face contorted into an image not unlike the one he had seen through Alyson.

"Interesting how we look to other people, isn't it," he said quietly.

Rhonda's eyes were literally bulging as she stared at her brother. He looked back at her evenly. Then she remembered. He could also feel his way into people's minds. Kip had channeled Alyson's thoughts into his own head and he had unwittingly given her the knowledge she needed. She still held Alyson's mind hostage.

Ignoring Kip, she looked deep into Alyson's eyes, and began to spew hissing words over the child. "So, you think you found someone who's going to care about you now, huh. You were always such a stupid little monster. Always dreaming that someday someone was going to come along and love you. But you know the truth, don't you, Alyson. Monsters can't be loved. Death comes for anyone who loves a monster. You killed your Daddy. You killed your Grandmother. If you love him so he'll have to die too, won't he. But you could save him. You could save them all, Alyson. Take their place. Die, Alyson, die."

Kip felt Alyson's mind begin to splinter in the wash of her mother's words. She was decompensating under the weight of returning shadows. Her body started sucking for air she couldn't take in. Even as he held her he was losing her.

He spun her around and kneeling down on one knee grabbed her face in his hands. Her eyes were unfocused as she followed the words toward the abyss. "Alyson, don't listen to her. Remember what I told you about monsters. Alyson, come back to me."

Watching from the porch, Dylan suddenly spoke up. "Hey, guys, Alyson is in trouble."

Domingo grabbed the porch railing and leaned on it as if he were going to vault over it. "What's wrong?"

"She is getting lost in the darkness. She's falling to a place where there is no love," Brandy gasped.

Domingo grabbed Scott's hand next to him. "Come on, we have to go get her. We have to make the dark go away. We have to get love to her…lots and lots of love."

Quickly the kids grabbed one another's hands. Jesse spoke the cadence for them. "Breathe in love, breathe it out to Alyson. Breathe in, breathe out."

Tumbling through black hole gaping in her center, the world began to slip away from Alyson. Kip's face blurred and melted. The words he spoke were swallowed by the growing void. Just as she reached the point where she would vanish, something billowed up through the hollow place in her. Warm and sweet, it began to lift her. Waft after waft came, each one pushing her up…up until she could see light glimmering around her. Up until she broke the surface of life and found Kip staring into her eyes. She collapsed into his arms.

As he held and rocked her, she felt his heart pounding against her own. He stroked her cheek. "Look at me, baby, what do you see?" She lifted her head to look in his eyes and as she did something touched her back. It was a spot of warmth that gradually spread around her. Perfume, she could smell perfume. She knew that fragrance. It was her grandmother's. Mixed in it was another scent; she had smelled it long ago in her daddy's shirt. Then a wave of emotion engulfed her. It was pure love. As it washed over and through her, the paralyzing fear holding her heart and soul captive for so long shattered. In its place was knowledge, the knowledge she possessed what her mother never could. Only humans can love and be loved. Monsters never knew love.

Even as Rhonda watched, the girl's face literally changed. The truth burrowed into the very essence of Alyson's being and exploded. She had been loved! Truly, really and honestly loved! It was as if a huge magnificent light had been turned on within her. She glowed.

On the porch, the kids were squealing, giggling and bouncing with excitement. They had brought Alyson back. Suddenly, Brandy caught the thought erupting in Rhonda's mind. She leaned over the railing and screamed, "Joe, watch out."

Rhonda grabbed the shovel Kip had dropped. She swung it back over her shoulder and took aim at Alyson. Kip slung Alyson around and pushed her down in the shelter of the garden bed timbers as the shovel whistled through the air. It connected with Kip's thigh, the edge tearing through his jeans and into his leg.

Although it dropped him temporarily, he pushed himself up and staggered to his feet. Rhonda swung the shovel back again but something grabbed it and it tried to jerk out of her hands. She struggled to maintain her grip but it pulled free and flew behind her. Turning to grab for it, the shovel slithered just beyond her reach. Each time she stepped after it, Ralph and Katy lifted their joined hands and the shovel continued its journey towards the porch.

Rhonda swung back on Kip, her fingers curving into claws. She lunged at him but stumbled and sprawled on the ground as though she had been tackled.

Kip dropped onto the timbers of the herb bed as Alyson crawled around to him and he pulled her up into the protective circle of his arm. A voice spoke between them. "I don't think that's allowed on this side. I may have just earned a time out."

"Meri?" Kip said.

"Grandma?" Alyson whispered.

Each felt a loving arm wrapping around their neck, then the softest sensation as though a kiss had been given. The voice came again. "Call me when you need me. I love you both."

Then she was gone and, in her place, an unseen hand clamped onto Kip's shoulder. He heard another voice. "Long time no see, bud. Missed you...missed you a lot. Give her the safety and love I wasn't able to. Let my daughter know what she meant to me. Will you do that?"

"My promise, Chris," Kip whispered.

A county sheriff's car pulled into the parking area, its lights strobing across the front of the house. Garner bailed out of the car and looked around bewildered. Boomer eased his way down the stairs towards him.

"I got your call. It was pretty garbled. Didn't get much other than there was trouble here." He said as he watched his sister cross to where Rhonda was pushing herself to her knees. Lacey assisted by grabbing a handful of blonde hair to haul her to her feet.

"Nobody called that I'm aware of ...," Boomer said.

Dylan hopped up on the porch railing. "I called Garner, Boomer. It works both ways you know."

"What's he talking about and what the hell is going on?"

"First, I believe Mrs. Maguire needs a ride to the county lockup. Secondly, you have possibilities, Garner, real possibilities."

After delivering Rhonda into her brother's waiting cuffs, Lacey hurried across to the herb bed.

Alyson had her arm around Kip's neck and was touching his cheek with wonderment. "Are you really my uncle?"

"Yes, I'm really your uncle, baby. And I'll be right here to take care of you."

"Ah, but who's going to take care of you?" Lacey said as she knelt beside them and began to carefully examine the bleeding gash on his thigh.

"With a diversified twist on the paranormal and characters overcoming their heartbreaking past, *Blood Will Tell* is a mesmeric tale. Good read for fans of paranormal romance."

Armchair Interviews
www.armchairinterviews.com

Blood Will Tell...

by L. Lee Shaw

ISBN: 978-0-9814709-1-7   Price: $10.95

Two cousins find their future stalked by the past…

Daphne meets the man who breathes life into her long dormant heart, but others, dead and living, don't foresee a happy ending.

Edmund traded his soul in a quest to illuminate the long ago darkness that destroyed his family. The time has come to pay and the only one who can ransom it back isn't in the mood.

About the Author

L. Lee Shaw is also the author of *Blood Will Tell*.... She has had her work appear in such diverse publications as *The Oregonian* and *Quilting Magazine*. She has taught fiction writing, formed a long running writers' group and had several of her plays and playlets produced. She produces *Mo' Allie*, a journal of writings, and co-coordinates a regional writer's faire.

www.bohobooks.com

Printed in the United States
138372LV00003B/4/P